R

About The Author

FRANK PALMOS is one of Australia's most experienced foreign correspondents. He has worked the majority of his thirty-five years in journalism in Asia, where he began as Australia's youngest foreign correspondent at twenty-one. Through the *Sydney Morning Herald-Melbourne Herald* groups of newspapers and magazines Australian audiences knew him as their Jakarta correspondent in Indonesia's Years of Living Dangerously before he went on to cover the Vietnam War. In the UK, Europe and the United States and Japan he was known through the *Sunday Times* and the *Economist*, the *Niew Amsterdammer*, Radio NHK Japan, the *New York Times*, the *Washington Post/Los Angeles Times* network and as First Person Prizewinner in the *Readers Digest*. Frank now commutes to Asia on writing and film assignments from Perth where he lives with his wife Alison and their daughter Anna and son Lachlan. Frank's first son Jay studies aerospace engineering in Idaho and daughter Sirie is at high school in Los Angeles heading for a media career.

RIDDING THE DEVILS

Frank Palmos

ARROW BOOKS

Arrow Books Limited
20 Vauxhall Bridge Road, London SW1V 2SA

An imprint of the Random Century Group

London Melbourne Sydney Auckland Johannesburg
and agencies throughout the world

First published in Bantam 1990
Arrow edition 1991

Printed and bound in Great Britain by
The Guernsey Press Co. Ltd
Guernsey, C.I.

ISBN 0 09 987790 2

SAIGON, May 5 (AP).

Frank Palmos, 28, an Australian journalist, was one of five newsmen riding in a small vehicle Sunday morning to cover the Viet Cong attack on Saigon. They were shot by the Viet Cong and only Mr Palmos survived by playing dead. Here is his account:

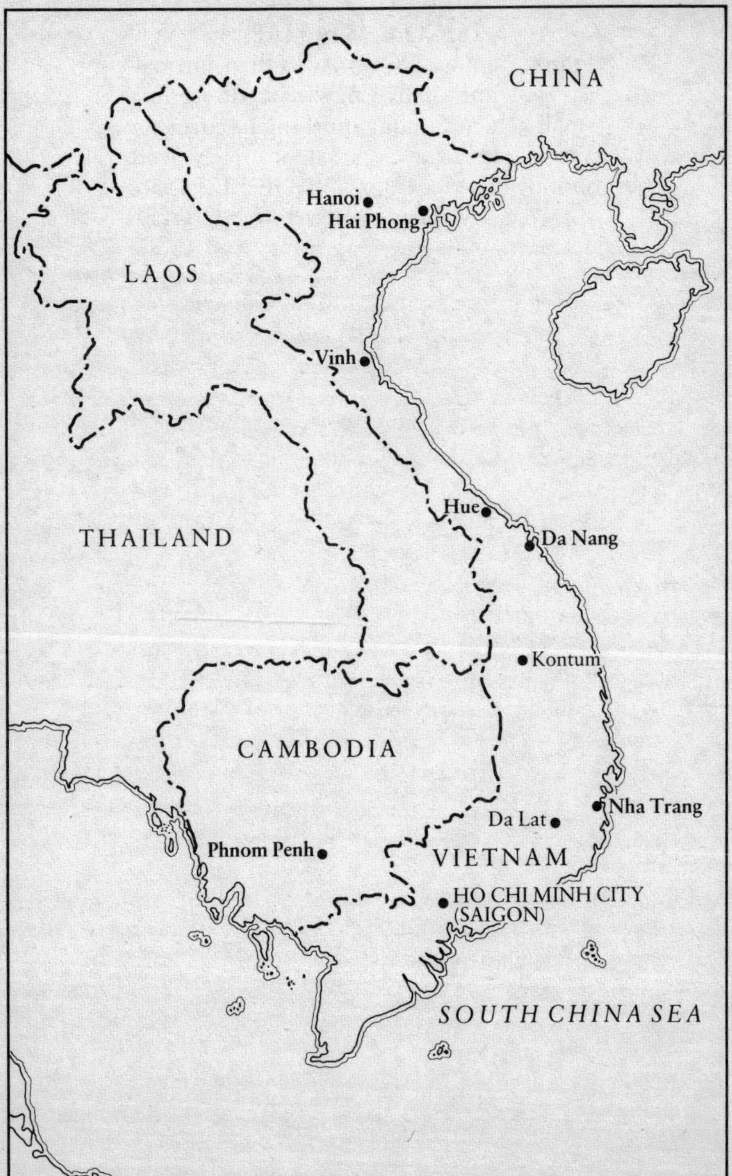
CHINA
Hanoi
Hai Phong
LAOS
Vinh
THAILAND
Hue
Da Nang
Kontum
CAMBODIA
Nha Trang
Da Lat
Phnom Penh
VIETNAM
HO CHI MINH CITY
(SAIGON)
SOUTH CHINA SEA

Prologue

The man is five feet seven or eight inches tall. For a Vietnamese he is very well built; well muscled, weighing about 145 pounds. Handsome. An oval, smooth-skinned unblemished pale face with almond eyes. He has a cap over black hair.

A professional soldier. He is decisive and cautious at the same time. Maybe well-born, he is uniformed and properly shod. His own men have a tougher, rougher appearance, look more like me than him in some ways.

They are trying to shoot me. I am trying to stay alive.

My mind is cryogenically speeding up the input of audio and visual information, and I watch as though a detached observer. You won't kill me, you bastards.

He has already killed two of us and now points his automatic at the other two wounded and dying men. For him all five are dead. For me, four dead and the dice still rolling.

But he makes a mistake. He thinks I am dead. If I was armed I could shoot him through the head at close range, for he stands before me full front and relaxed as he starts to reload his .45 automatic.

I am not armed. Otherwise his life would end. My life too would end soon after.

I escape. I put the man between me and his squad; for them to kill me as I run would mean shooting through him. He runs after me, his boots slopping on the wet unpaved Cholon road as he empties his new magazine at me.

His footsteps have chased me down the dark lanes of my nightmares for many, many years. I went to Vietnam to find him. A man who had ignored pleas of innocence from my friends, but who had killed them in hatred. A man who had no need other than the need to perform according to an indoctrination that told him he had to kill Westerners.

I was certain he understood us to be saying we were press, not soldiers. I believe he knew we had no weapons and that we had no intention to harm anyone.

But this man went ahead anyway, in a simple ambush, on his home territory, killed two unarmed journalists outright and wounded two others. This same man then came forward and after killing my two wounded colleagues prepared to finish me off, too. I was lying there, pretending I was dead in a Cholon street, some metres behind the civilian jeep he and his men had fired on as we came into their ambush.

I had watched as he ignored pleas from one journalist who called to him in acceptable Vietnamese that we were press. He shot the boy/man who was wounded and unable to move, twice through the chest with his handgun. He moved forward deliberately. He noted two more were dead.

That made three certain dead.

He would have seen there were no guns. No grenades. No military insignia. He moved deliberately to the back of the jeep where the driver lay wounded. The driver, John Cantwell, lay there badly wounded, trying to follow me to some safety. The man shot and missed, then shot again and again, hitting.

He seemed to enjoy his work. Not only did he ignore all pleas of innocence, killing Westerners seemed to appeal to him. Some honour for him. No possible response from us. He had, in his mind, killed five Western enemies.

It didn't quite work out that way.

I was still alive, and as cold as ice. Watching and waiting my chance. Some blood ran from my left elbow. Nothing more.

"I will survive," I said to myself.

I watched as he made another mistake. He had spent so many bullets he needed to reload. He pointed at me then decided to reload, considering me dead anyway. He got to the point of no return, when one has to pull the gun back, dispense with the finished magazine and load a new one.

I jumped up, stared him in the face for a moment, then ran. I knew where to run. I ran to the point of the triangle he had made with his own men at the other two rear points. I ran straight at first. To shoot me they would have to shoot through him. And they could not, and did not.

Only when I turned the corner I had to turn did they shoot at me. And shoot at me they did. They emptied an AK47 and a Burp gun at me in wildfire to his left as I turned left. They hit a sign above me. I knew I could keep running unless they hit me in the head, spine or legs.

After that burst of automatic fire he began running too, after me. He trudged after me at half my pace. I turned to see where he was. He was thirty metres behind me, firing his newly loaded handgun. I was between him and a large group of civilian refugees whom he dared not approach. After two or three shots at me he stopped running and stopped firing. He would not fire into civilians. I knew his face. I knew his body actions. I knew his eyes, his grimaces. Age would not change those things.

He knew that I knew the final killings were plain murder. I knew he knew he had killed two innocent men after an ambush on a civilian jeep. He knew that I knew he wanted to finish everyone off so there would be no one to tell the story. History is on the winning side.

I had this man in mind in 1987 when I asked the new Prime Minister of Vietnam to allow me in to make a documentary film. Of course I had a documentary film I wanted to make. Of course I would make the documentary, and I would send the film out. Then I would deal with a personal problem, the problem of this man.

Dedication

to
Bruce Pigott
and
John Cantwell
Michael Birch
Ronald Laramy
killed
in Cholon
5 May, 1968

1

WHEN I STARTED SCHOOL just after the Second World War, Vietnam was part of Indo-China and Indonesia was the Netherlands Indies. In our tiny timber town of Noojee in the heart of the mountain country of Victoria, southern Australia, the news from the war and then the dramatic years that followed came to us in two forms: the *Argus* newspaper, which arrived on the afternoon bus from the nearest big town, Warragul, forty-two kilometres away, and by the 6 p.m. news, which required us to hook a car battery to our radio set until our two-hour ration of power was used.

By the age of eight, my mother was reading to me such news as I could understand. By ten, I had started high school and we were both reading the "Behind the News" columns by a remarkable Australian Asian commentator, Dr Peter Russo, who annoyed the Conservative government and puzzled others by claiming both Indonesia and Indo-China would be independent soon, and the French and the Dutch would depart.

If I was going to be a journalist — and this slowly became a more conscious plan — I thought I would like to be in those countries when the French and the Dutch departed. This simplistic view stayed with me as a sort of self-generated purpose or compass direction, although I had no idea how I would achieve my goals.

On graduation from high school, I discovered that people who wanted to do these sorts of interesting things were expected to also graduate from university, which was a complication. No one from our region had ever been to university, and all I could learn on the matter was that it was expensive and only children from wealthy families who could support students for four or five years would ever be allowed in.

In 1954, a couple of months before my fifteenth birthday, I left the timber town. There were no jobs, I could go no further at high school, and there was no money to support me unless I worked in a sawmill.

I went to Melbourne, and with the help of an older cousin, Jim Kruse, got a job as a copyboy and messenger with the *Argus,* a stroke of inordinate luck. My salary was £3 9s a week, my board in a dirty East Melbourne rooming house was £4 15s, paid in advance, thank you. To make up the difference and to eat, I worked nights in the newspaper cafeteria. I used the same clothing which included two shirts, a thin jacket, a football jumper for weekends, and a pair of very worn boots, which I re-soled from the inside using cardboard to plug the holes.

On my first day I chose the worst "delivery floor" in the building to bring around mail and packages and run errands because on that first and mezzanine floor was Dr Peter Russo. From the start he was puzzled, sometimes irritated, but always slightly incredulous that his fifteen-year-old messenger boy would do anything he wished, ran errands, asked for discarded Indonesian and Japanese newspapers and who appeared far more often than necessary in his elegant wood-panelled room and stared in wonder at his bookcase.

I once heard him say he could hardly interest any senior politicians or academics in South-East Asia, so I asked him to let me borrow a book or two "for my mother". This lie persisted for several months while I slowly read the material, stopping at simple words such as "epoch" or "conflagration".

One day I found him in his office with two senior executives, the three of them standing before an impressive wall map with all placenames in Chinese. There had been some tension. They had apparently challenged him on his assertion that China would not only remain independent but that the French and the Dutch were forever gone, in reality, from the region. Russo looked over at me and asked me to approach the map.

"Show me the Yellow River," he said. "Show me some other rivers or places, son."

As it happened, I had in the previous two weeks laboured over two of Russo's books, ten or fifteen pages at most at night, another ten or fifteen in the *Argus* library where there were good dictionaries, and my knowledge was fresh. So still holding my messenger boy's basket I stepped forward and began with the

Yellow River, then to the Mekong. Back up to Peking, Tiensin, Vladivostok, Tsingtao, Nanking, Hanoi, Saigon, Phnom Penh, Cheng-Mai, Bangkok, Kuala Lumpur, Penang, Singapore, Jakarta, Jogjakarta.

Russo stared at me with some pride. One of the men said, "Good. But Jogjakarta is the same as Jakarta."

I said, "No, Jakarta used to be Batavia. Jogjakarta was the ancient capital."

Russo ignored me and spoke to them. "We need four young men, as I said." I was dismissed. Russo seemed slightly annoyed with me.

A couple of hours later I cringed into his office on my delivery round. He accused me, "Those books were not for your mother. Hal Jones [the personnel officer] tells me your mother lives a hundred miles away in a timber town down in Gippsland." I agreed. I told him the books were for me. I was half waiting for him to say how well I'd done on the maps, but he simply said: "We'll have to get you to university." Many years later he told me how he'd felt very proud at my performance. He had been trying to convince the two executives, who were friends, not opponents, to send four young journalists to Asia and have them trained in Indonesian, Japanese, Hindi and Mandarin. They had argued that only senior reporters should go, Russo said they had to start with very young people. The idea never did get off the ground. Of all the journalists he tried to influence to learn to speak, read and write at least one Asian language and stay on as a foreign correspondent, only one finally went. Me. And I did that work by financing myself from gambling, not financed by the publishers.

Russo was about to dismiss me when he asked me what section of the newspaper I wanted to concentrate on.

"Turf. Horse racing," I replied.

He was horrified. Speechless.

But he continued to loan me books, and continued to test me. On my behalf, he even rang Melbourne University to set up an appointment.

"See Hume Dow," he said. "Professor Dow will tell you what you must do to start at university."

I did that. But I stayed in the horse racing section for three days a week, the other days doing general work.

Russo finally condescended to discuss horse racing, which he abhorred. "Why the horse racing?" he asked.

"I get paid more and I can gamble on the horses. I have to win enough money to go to Asia."

Russo, a wealthy man, whose own Melbourne University years had all been spent studying in style in a lavishly appointed college within the grounds, had never considered finance a problem. He half-offered to help, but decided wisely that it might take some of the fight out of me. The truth was that I would have welcomed any help.

I lived a miserable life, cold, wet and often hungry. Riding a bicycle to work, working nineteenth-century hours for children . . . at fifteen and sixteen I was working midnight to 7 a.m. and often returning to start at 2 p.m. to finish at midnight on tiring and bewildering shifts.

With a name like Palmos in an Anglo-Saxon dominated conservative Melbourne, I got all the tough work. Had my mother been the Palmos and my father been the Fitzpatrick, matters might have been different. But with a Greek-born father — no matter he had come to Australia in 1922, no matter his wonderful record as a forester — I was the son of a migrant and therefore barely considered for advancement, although needed for my energy.

Still, I was on my way. The *Argus* was closed down in 1957 by a competitor, so I became a fulltime horse racing writer on another newspaper and went quickly through the ranks.

In the meantime, Russo continued in puzzlement supplying me with both books and advice, for I had chosen Indonesia to concentrate on; he must have thought he was wasting his time with a teenage gambler. He was finally appeased when I started at the University of Melbourne, and was stunned when I went to him a couple of weeks after my twenty-first birthday to say that I had won £1500 and would be leaving for Indonesia the following month.

I was well-ranked in journalism by then. My weekly salary of £25 was then quite high. A thrifty person could have saved £10 weekly from such an income. I said to Russo that even at that rate, without gambling, I would have needed a further three years hard saving to get abroad. But I was not prepared to do that or wait that long.

My first Indonesian visit in 1961 extended to a two-year stay. I won a United Nations Fellowship, the Indonesians welcomed and aided me, and I emerged speaking, reading and writing the

Indonesian language to an upper high school level. By the time I returned as the accredited foreign correspondent in Jakarta, the first post for any independent newspaper group (The Melbourne *Herald-Sun* group, now owned by Rupert Murdoch) my Indonesian was at university level.

While my colleagues in Australia had been winning their way through City Hall and Police Rounds and Supreme Court work, hoping that by the time they were thirty-three years old, they might be considered for an overseas post, I had been investing in myself and my new Asia.

In those days correspondents went to the country in question, talked to their embassy people, and anyone in the government who spoke English, but lived almost entirely apart from society. They sent back reports with or without political meaning. They certainly could never write about the people or have an inside knowledge of what was happening. Even though I was only twenty-four and fifteen others wanted the job, the publisher took a chance and appointed me as the paper's foreign correspondent in Jakarta. Things were tense in Indonesia and the paper wanted no mistakes. They considered someone who had lived in villages, studied in two Indonesian universities and who could write modestly well and take photographs would be their best bet.

I arrived in Jakarta in December 1964. Within a few days I was asked, as the only Westerner who knew the language (except for a few US and Australian academics) to help with translations of the rampaging President Sukarno's speeches to diplomats and press. By late December I became convinced Sukarno was going to do something that would send shudders through the world: he would take his country out of the United Nations. There would be echoes of Germany's withdrawal from the League of Nations in 1933; a move that signalled the Nazification of that country and a coming war.

I didn't test my theory on anyone, especially not diplomats. I sent the story and the report fell into the hands of two of Australia's finest newspapermen, Cecil Wallace, then news editor, and John Kiely, then chief sub-editor of the Herald and Weekly Times group. No one else had confidence in my report, but Wallace and Kiely went with it.

The report was picked up by agencies and went round the world, while Wallace and Kiely no doubt wondered whether they had done the right thing.

In early January 1965, Indonesia announced its withdrawal from the UN, citing the newly-formed Malaysia's inclusion in the UN Security Council as its reason. Indonesia was then on a "Crush Malaysia" campaign, backed by the Chinese, whose policy of "exporting revolution" was then rampant. Sukarno had given me all the hints I needed. In his 1964 Independence Day speech, he had called the time the "Year of Living Dangerously" ("Tahun Vivere Pericoloso", a mixture of what he thought was correct Latin and Indonesian).

It was, indeed, a year of living dangerously. In 1964 the Chinese pushed Indonesia toward their own Long March, towards ridding the foreign devils, the British Embassy and the United States Information Service in Jakarta were burned to the ground, and India (holding out against Chinese incursions in the Himalayas) had its embassy ransacked. It was also a year of extreme violence, burnings, demonstrations, mob-attacks on any opposition, 10,000 per cent inflation, almost total collapse of the economy, and extreme harassment against Westerners.

By steady steps the correspondents from Western nations were also expelled; first Europeans, then those from the United States. So also, of course, were Malaysians, or representatives of any other firmly non-Communist nation. Neverless, during that year I was able to file 365 articles on Indonesia and the civil war and 1000 photographs, something which I still find hard to believe.

Of course the civil war had to come. The Indonesian Communist Party, pushed hard by China, attacked and took power for forty-eight hours. I had written that a coup attempt would come and the Communists would lose. That was all very well, but there was the possibility I might be wrong, so I had organised an escape route through west Java down to a small port in south central Java. The idea was to travel not as a Westerner, but as a night-trader, wearing Indonesian clothing, carrying only food and a hidden radio. I had two staging-points already well established, though not a third, but there were friends in the southern port who would take me on a salt boat to the islands closest to Australia.

The escape route was not needed. Fortunately I was right that the Communists were not wanted in Indonesia except in certain parts of Java, and the strike force led by General Suharto (now President Suharto) on the edge of Jakarta eventually dispersed the frail Communist Party leadership. Then followed four months of civil war, including killing by night. "Consolidation" was the polite word, but it was really the removal of the Communists by brutal, revengeful killing.

I saw pieces of bodies in canals and streams, the emptied houses of Communist Party (PKI) leaders, families gone. Perhaps one million people were removed in the reprisals against the Communists. I considered that the Communists themselves would have killed even greater numbers as they "straightened out" society and sent the country into a downward spiral, ruling by terror and taking the people even further into poverty.

By March, 1966, I had done my job and was ready to leave. My newspaper had sent me on one assignment outside Indonesia, to the Philippines, to cover the election in which Ferdinand Marcos came to power.

I accepted because at that stage seven days was not too important in Jakarta, and because the assignment would take me through Saigon twice. For while the newspaper considered the Philippines the next story, I considered what was happening in Vietnam to be of even greater international significance. Three men influenced my thinking at that stage. The first was the cameraman Neil Davis, who had come to Asia much later than I, but who had been in Cambodia and Vietnam. He gave me the general, unpublished news of the area. The second was the Communist journalist Wilfred Burchett, for whom I had done translations from Indonesian to English during one of his visits in 1963.

He had agreed with me that the Communist Party in Indonesia was noisy but underneath very weak, whereas the other Western journalists and especially academics claimed it would take over. I remembered him saying, "The boy's right. The PKI are weak. If you want to see some really well trained men, come back with me to Vietnam."

The third was the most important. Neil Sheehan had come from United Press International in Vietnam to join the *New York Times,* for which I worked as a special writer in the absence of a permanent correspondent. In 1965, Neil unfolded for me what he thought would be an horrific scenario in Vietnam over the next few years.

I went into Vietnam first in September 1965. The buildup had begun. The jet fighters were lining the Saigon airport runway, the US advisers were there in growing numbers. On my return in

October 1965, I knew that the Vietnam business would be bigger than the Indonesian war. I calculated I had a year to prepare myself for Vietnam.

In early 1966, with the new Suharto Army in power and the PKI now out of the way, I left Indonesia for France. My plan was to learn French before going to Vietnam. I went first to the Sorbonne, where I worked for a month, then transferred to Besançon University's Foreign Languages Institute. While in France I also joined Agence France-Presse as a translator for some months.

During two short vacations from Besançon, I drove to London to visit Bruce Pigott, one of the young journalists I had encouraged to go abroad. Bruce had been a cadet journalist when I was a "senior". He wrote very well indeed – certainly better than I did. I rated myself as a good reporter rather than a great stylist, while he was a pretty good reporter, but a very good writer, despite his youth (in 1963 he was only nineteen). I had pushed him to move from Melbourne to Sydney, then from Sydney to London. When I told him I was going to Vietnam, the next thing I learned was that he had volunteered to join Reuter's bureau there.

In London I married Pat Price, a girl whom I had met in Jakarta. Pat had gone there on an invitation from President Sukarno, whom she had met in Cairo when completing field work on emerging nations for Sarah Lawrence University, New York. Pat joined the student protest movement at the University of Indonesia, from which she was expelled shortly afterwards.

When the Indonesian coup was over, and having become firm friends, I met her again in Singapore. She returned to New York to complete her degree, while I went to the Sorbonne, then to Besançon. It took great courage for her to marry somebody who was going into the Vietnam war.

Before Vietnam, however, I was to work on the *Washington Post's* foreign news desk for a month — and before that happened, Pat and I went to Holland. There, I lectured at the University of Amsterdam, held a photographic exhibition on Indonesia, and wrote for the Amsterdam press, activities generated more by the fact that I seemed to be in demand than anything else.

My nightmares had already begun — that is, nightmares in the accepted sense; horrible dreams at night that caused me to wake in a sweat. They began so gradually that I never realised that normal people did not suffer from them except very occasionally; I was getting them two and three times a week, because of what I had seen in Indonesia; twenty months exposure to violent social conflict, while I was still quite young, was having its toll.

I kept dreaming that men with rifles were shooting at ordinary people from hip level, and people were all falling forward, the wrong way. The soldiers looked at each other with nervous smiles, speaking with the victims. Everybody seemed in terrible danger. Sometimes there were huge holes in the thin terracotta tiled roofs; we would often try and help the dying people stand up, and then I would recognise them as family friends. In my dreams, I recognised the soldiers shooting as my friends, too.

Then everybody sat around, mostly on our heels, our knees high and forward, eating grilled corncobs, while my closest Indonesian student friend Kusumo sat next to me. I was always, in these dreams as in real life, helpless to hold off some dark terror that surrounded us all.

There were two middle-aged Indonesians in Besançon who had missed the civil war. Together we would cook Indonesian meals with spices from Amsterdam and talk into the night. Nightmares followed every one of those meals. I made the connection and restricted my evenings with them.

Marriage and the escape from the rule-bound French into a more freedom-conscious US society eased matters for me. Soon, I was physically fit and, I thought, prepared for Vietnam. I left Washington for Saigon, via Melbourne, where my American wife would wait for me while I went to war. In Australia I was, according to my editor, "a household name" on Indonesia. (The real household names were Peter Russo, my mentor, and Denis Warner, two men who strangely had little time for each other, but who both had time for me. Denis had often helped me when I was a young man in Jakarta.) In any case, at twenty-seven, I had been writing for the *Washington Post*, the *Los Angeles Times*, the *St Louis Despatch*, the *Sunday Times* and the *Economist* of London, NHK Radio in Japan, the Singapore *Straits Times* and fifty other publications, including *Time* and *Newsweek*, as well as the *World Book Encyclopaedia* (on the coup in Indonesia, Islam in Asia and linguistics). I was certainly building up some form.

There seemed a window of opportunity, from the university work I had done in Oxford, Amsterdam, Cornell, the Sorbonne and in Australia, for me to turn away from journalism and take a long deep breath and rest peacefully in academia. Publisher Andre Deutsch in London had commissioned a book on Indonesia and a US publisher wanted the definitive reporter's report on the Indonesian coup. I started on both, but went to Vietnam instead.

I am willing to admit that every one of my personal problems has been brought on by my intense curiosity. I have never liked the thought that the world might change in some profound moment or crisis without my being there to witness it. Though I have never felt the need to be present when the next little colonel overturns a small African nation, or some religious fanatic is made ruler of a Caribbean island, when world powers clash I have always wanted to be there, in the arena of battle. It is there, rather than at the conference tables, that the shape and direction of the world are determined; and it is there I would rather be.

So I went to Vietnam, where the new world was unfolding. The Communist powers were putting everything into Vietnam and the Vietnamese saw the "Communist system" as their only salvation. The US saw the defence of the relatively democratic system in the south of Vietnam as a test case. The Chinese and the USSR, the main suppliers to Vietnam's Communist Party and army, saw it as a test, too.

All this was in my mind when I went back to Vietnam for the third time in March 1968. The False Tet Offensive, the first of the major drives to take over Saigon, had been launched in January 1968. That Tet was a psychological victory in so far as the Viet Cong had occupied the US embassy for some hours using a suicide squad, and had done some other damage. The real Tet Offensive was, in my view, yet to come. Today the Vietnamese call the 5-9 May attack by the same name as Western military historians: The Battle for Saigon.

My first program was to go on land, air and sea missions and to stay clear of Saigon. Saigon I considered to be my last reporting defence line. And that, I figured, would come in June or July of 1968.

The first day back in Saigon the Visnews cameraman Neil Davis, with whom I had travelled to West New Guinea and shared many evenings in Jakarta, gave me a briefing on reporting the Vietnam war as he saw it. In summary he said, "Do what you did in Indonesia. Stay solo. Learn everything you can about sights and sounds. Travel light, stay clear of buddyism and get the job done." He followed this with some comments on the differences, as he saw them, on reporting the civil war in Indonesia and the open, armed warfare in Vietnam.

That was the road from Indonesia to Vietnam, via France and Washington. Until I knew the sounds of the most used automatic rifles and explosives from both sides I hadn't truly started in Vietnam. By the third day there I could recognise every common weapon or explosive used. On that day I was setting out for Kontum where there was heavy fighting. A newsagency reporter I had met in Singapore took me for a drink. I told him about these new sounds. "Beats me. They all sound bad to me," he said.

The road from the bush tracks I had walked to school in Noojee, the roads I had travelled in the school bus to and from Warragul, eighty-six kilometres every day through my high school years, the thousands of kilometres I ran around Melbourne's Caulfield racecourse training for my athletic events in the Melbourne University track team, all led to Asia as far as I was concerned. For I was on a single-minded, perhaps simplistic, mission to be a professional reporter of events which would change the world.

In Australia in those days the "soft" left had a quite intense dislike of the United States; this was even more pronounced among those who had never visited the US or studied its history. My attitude was that if one lived in Carthage in the days of the Roman Empire, one was obliged to visit the capital at least once. For Rome was the engine, the source of the power and inspiration. The alternative would be to die wondering how your world had come about.

That's how I viewed the United States: like it or not, that was where the changes postwar had originated, and where ideas of personal and social freedom had expanded. Elsewhere the doors were closing. But in Vietnam the US was straying into a conflict with the odds heavily stacked against them, and the impassable wall they faced was a widespread belief throughout developing nations that only the totalitarian systems under the red flag and based on an inappropriate hundred-year-old set of Western writings could free them and push them into the modern world.

The results were never in doubt. How they unfolded was going to be very interesting, and dangerous, to any observer. The excitement and pain that followed for me were self-inflicted. Strangely,

I was never in doubt there would be a personal cost, just as I was certain both Vietnam and the United States would pay a high price for their wars. The plural is deliberate — I always saw the Vietnamese fighting one war and the United States fighting another.

2

For me there was no specific moment for the onset of war-related-problems. I had chosen to go into these places and I chose to keep going in. My feeling — shared by friends who did the same sort of work — was that nightmares were part of the job. When I got to France after the civil war in Indonesia I regarded them as something I had brought upon myself. In all the years from then until now, I have heard few correspondents with similar problems complain about them.

After the Tet Offensive in Vietnam in 1968 I returned to Indonesia, and was not troubled during the daytime. However, because my house was a meeting place and a stopover for scores of correspondents passing through — some going into Vietnam for the first time, most on their way to other assignments — the late nights over my dining table, or more rarely at restaurants, had their repercussions.

The famous Indonesian-Chinese dish of *kepiting-chingkong* (crabs' claws with spicy sauce) brought on vivid, technicolor dreams of the war. We would order the dish, then drink to some more moving pictures later that night. It seems absurd now, and perhaps it was. But we were confident such problems would pass as the war wound down.

Compared with the loss of life and the tens of thousands maimed, forty or fifty nights of unpleasantness was minor. One's mind would heal over a couple of years, but life and limbs could never be brought back.

I kept myself busy in Indonesia with regular reporting and in free hours I brought all my work diaries from 1965 to 1969 up to date. They were in fifteen A4-size 300-page lecture notebooks, which included every possible detail of the coup in Indonesia and the Tet Offensive. From them I was preparing my doctorate on the Indonesian press from 1928 to 1965 and working on the book for Andre Deutsch on the fall of the Communist Party (PKI).

It was wonderful therapy (although I was unaware of it then) for it brought realism and reinforced understanding of both the period of the Indonesian coup and the Vietnam war, a much faster-moving event.

On the righthand pages I used to write my daily work schedule, the flights, the thoughts on the action and predictions. On the lefthand pages I pasted in photographs, airline vouchers, ferry tickets, restaurant bills, small notes of the money I'd been using, stamps in current use in the country I was in, carbon copies of my official press reports, notes on books I'd read and frequently letters from officials or colleagues. The notebooks were excellent source material. In the back of my mind, always, they would form a running, illustrated story of those years, something my children and their children could read for a personal glimpse of the times.

From Indonesia I sent all the diaries back to Australia for storage, where a few months later they were destroyed in a suspiciously convenient warehouse fire. Not only did I lose the diaries, but all my other personal possessions as well as all furniture, clothing and household equipment. Among the more precious things I lost were my doctoral research library on Indonesia and the writing and photography from almost a decade spent in that country. For nearly a week I was unable to come to terms with what had happened, and I often found myself sitting and staring ahead for hours on end. As bad as this reaction was, I did not take it for the sign it really was — that mentally I was far more fragile than I realised.

My wife, Pat, tried to come to the rescue: we would forget journalism. Forget Indonesia and Vietnam. I would change direction entirely. No more perilous assignments. Back in Australia we would buy elegant, old rundown houses and renovate them. Pat imported some capital from St Louis and bought a big house in the heart of Melbourne; I sold a small house to finance the renovations. We were very successful, even though it meant working long hours, seven days a week. With one small child, Jay, and another one, Sirie, on the way, there was little time for reflection. Practically the only person who questioned the way I was leading my life at that stage was my own doctor. I remember him saying "You think you're over those psychological problems but you're in for a surprise. All you've done is work so hard you've exhausted yourself and pushed them aside". But after two years I wanted to return to writing so when I was asked to apply for a Churchill Fellowship, I did. I chose aerospace reporting as my subject and was assigned to NASA to cover the Apollo missions. In those relatively peaceful years I watched almost detachedly as Vietnam wound down and began to close up. Nothing that was happening in South-East Asia could compare with the moon missions. The nightmares seemed a thing of the past. False hope.

But I was not free of it. Four years after my return in 1980 to the US I went to a Brooklyn movie house to see *Apocalypse Now*, and the balance was finally tipped over. I thought I'd be able to handle Vietnam after all that time. Before too long, I had broken into tears of disgust and walked out to the foyer. Real Vietnam had been bad enough; to watch the parable, shot in a land that looked nothing like Vietnam, with incidents nothing like reality, while hearing people who had never been there gasp in wonder at it all, was just too much.

There was one other man in the foyer; tall, black, about my age, and about as tearful as I was.

"Da Nang," I said, taking a good guess.

"Da Nang. Right," he said. "Have you ever seen such crap?"

We took a coffee together. He had been in Kontum when I'd been there, although none of our missions seemed to overlap. We talked and talked. He'd lost his way, several jobs and several friends. Even his black friends had given him a hard time, and he was now separated from his wife. He now worked in a fruit and vegetable shop owned by a Korean refugee from Communism.

We spent a lot of time together over the next week. He was the first of many very bad cases I encountered in the year to come. Whatever was coming for me would be horrendous, that much I knew; after the meeting with my Da Nang friend Jerry, my nights were screaming hells, and working my way out of it seemed best.

At that time I was boarding in a darkly lit brownstone in Brooklyn, while my wife and kids were in Los Angeles. But it began to close in on me. I needed some space and light. I did a deal with the owner, a girlfriend of mine from university days in France. She had a house in a small holiday community on Long Island, facing east to the Atlantic. The deal was I would renovate the house in return for free use of it.

I got a bicycle, got the paint, got the job into gear and started working as hard as I could. Soon I became a fixture on the island, riding thirty-five or forty-five kilometres a day, in and back to Sag Harbour for supplies, crossing on ferries, riding to local shops, and when there was a break in painting, building floating docks for the local pleasure-boat dock-owner.

There were a dozen Vietnam veterans rotting away out there and we congregated in the Black Buoy bar, Sag Harbour, where I was welcomed as the Aussie Alien. They got me small jobs; I needed at least $10 a day for food and booze. I worked in various teams reblocking John Steinbeck's widow's house and painting Kurt Vonnegut's fence, or perhaps it was the other way round. We wore tracksuits and overalls, and when I wasn't riding my bicycle I was squeezed in the front of a pickup truck with the bike in the back.

We went to an East Hampton bar one night after a local job and the author Irwin Shaw joined us after sending over some drinks. He had heard the word "Vietnam" over our table and caught my accent. As the others drifted away, we talked and talked long into the night about Vietnam and reporting and mental hideaways. By two in the morning we were both drunk. He fitted my bike into the boot of his car, with a wheel sticking out, and drove me back to a house the team was working on — the ferry to Shelter Island had long closed — and I slept on the floor. He left a card with his private number on it, asking me to call him. But I lost the card and never did see him again.

I was soon having more and more encounters with men damaged by Vietnam. Bernard, from the mid-West, had been brought from South Vietnam to New York and had little idea of why he was heading east. He travelled with two brothers from Philadelphia who couldn't face their Italian family. They had been in terrible firefights and the younger one had become almost speechless by the time I first met him at the Black Buoy. The elder Carlo used to tell us the younger Vani had seen too many killed for someone so young, but in a rare breakout while Carlo was at the bar, Vani said Carlo had seen more action before he, Vani, had even arrived, than he saw in all his time.

There was one, a Canadian, who'd taken US citizenship and gone with the Marines to Da Nang. He was thirty-five and the most experienced soldier. His assessment was that the brothers had killed a lot of people and were now regretting it. Alien One, as he was more often called, used to warn us when he was going into a slide. He started the system of each of the group doing a morning check on one other Vet, so it was a surprise when he first said: "You check on me in the morning. Okay?"

Russell was one of the few who came from this strange but lovely area of Long Island whose eastern end opens like a crocodile jaw with Shelter Island in its bite. He came from Southold to Sag delivering hardware and that's where he met us all lined up in the Buoy one day. He was having a drink to his divorce. "Go to Vietnam, get a divorce. Don't have to go to courthouse or Vegas. Just go to Vietnam, get a divorce. Just like that!"

My divorce was well on the way. After the Apollo Missions had finished and the Asian work had begun again, Pat would look at me like I was someone she had never known. She had already settled in Los Angeles.

Alien One's divorce had been messy. Carlo's wife was "away". Vani hadn't married and as he curled more into his shell any form of relationship seemed unlikely. Not a single marriage in our group had survived Vietnam. Maestro, who played a guitar rather poorly, had had two women leave him since he had returned. Marriage carnage. Men in mental foxholes. Peeping out quietly at night.

The Vets from Southold, Greenport, Shelter, the Hamptons, gravitated to Sag Harbour by evening and I found myself taking jobs around Sag Harbour during the day, even though it meant a long bicycle ride carrying equipment. It meant I had less time on my own in that house, less time lying in bed. I was in the most terrible state and I was certain others in the group were worse off. My house was well apart from neighbours, surrounded by trees and shrubs which, although still in late winter, gave off a swirling, swaying sound at night, drowning any of my violent, loud nightmares.

Alien One and a mixture of the boys at one time had checked on me three successive mornings. They'd come in through the snow, turn off the radio that had been blaring all night, light the fire, pick up the bottles and make coffee and wait for me.

One morning the boys came across a long magazine article about me. "And we thought you were just a bad painter!", they said. But they were quietly proud of me, and had mentioned my background to a local Shelter Island reporter.

One evening soon after that the entire group went to the Upturned Canoe bar on Shelter where the owner, Carmel, gave us cheap drinks. The Brothers and Bernard had helped me on a boatshed job down the road. Carmel had warned me the journalist had a filthy tongue and was jealous of any younger reporters "from the mainland" because he'd never made it.

The journalist had been there drinking since lunchtime, when Bernard called over to him to join us. But the journalist was already into the whisky, and shaping for a fight.

He said to Vani: "Where's your fucking war reporter hero? You, nutcase, I'm asking you!" There was a terrible hush, but the drunken journalist was determined to go on. As he started talking again Carmel stepped in, pretending she'd not heard his comments.

"This is Frank. He's the journalist. He knows just about everyone on the Island so . . ."

"You mean he knows every fucking weirdo. HE'S weird. THEY'RE fucking weird. What is this place? First we have a lovely little island and now we have all these fucking arsehole heroes here . . . THAT ONE, he's a basket case . . . "

Vani was in turmoil, in real trouble. One moment I remember standing by, peacefully ignoring these insults. The next thing I was violently shaking and shaking this stupid idiot back and forth. I was strong from years of physical work, so this office softie shook like a wet rag. It took three or four people to drag me off him.

The barman shouted, "He's broken his neck!" Carmel was immobile with fear. Bernard gathered the group together in two vans and a pickup and we went back to Sag Harbour.

Carlo and Vani were absent from work the next morning so after lunch we checked on them at a little rented cottage not far from the fire station. The landlady said they'd gone. "I can't say I'm sorry," she said. "They looked a bit nuts. Liable to kill someone."

That bar scene and the landlady's assessment of the Brothers told us all a great deal. From being ignored and left to fret on our own in our little hideaways we were now actively scorned. No matter that the journalist was driven by his own private motives, the whisky gave him the strength to say what others were now thinking. What he said that evening I would soon hear again and again.

Although I wasn't quite ready to go, Shelter Island had lost its original appeal. With the Brothers gone, then Bernard going walkabout, I knew it was time.

The snow began to melt, the crocuses came out. The squirrels appeared in numbers in old trees I had pruned and with the unfolding of spring the trees and the shrubs I'd cared for sprouted anew. The sunshine came through a skylight every morning where before it had been iced up. My friend arrived from Brooklyn and I lost my job; she and her boyfriend needed the house now spring had arrived. But no matter — I had paid my way.

By then I had parted with everything I cared for in Australia and the US. My wife and I had gone our seperate ways. Most of our Australian property was sold. I thought I was hopelessly broke (having genuinely forgotten I half-owned a mansion in Melbourne, rented to Union Carbide). On average I had survived on $100 a week and was surprised when winding up my Sag Harbour bank account that I had a useful few hundred dollars from the Black Buoy team work.

I parked the bike with a neighbour, then packed up. Carmel drove me to the north ferry. She asked where my other bags were. There were no other bags. I had one small airline bag with bathroom kit and a couple of T-shirts and one sweater, and a pack of Sag Harbour and Shelter Island postcards signed by the Black Buoy gang, with lurid messages. That was all I had when I got off the ferry from Shelter Island to Greenport. I rode the bus back to Queens, then crossed to Manhattan where I attempted to rejoin the real world.

The press was awash with stories of what was called the Vietnam Veterans Syndrome. Counselling centres had been established in a dozen cities. If one read between the lines it meant: "Counselling for unfortunates." I didn't connect with them.

"Psychos", they called us, a term then being used for anyone active in the dirty Vietnam war, from Marines through to pilots, nurses and war correspondents.

By the time I got to LA I was feeling better. I had regained some humour and a lot of energy. The Sag Harbour money I used to buy an old station wagon to drive my two children, Jay and Sirie, around California, Nevada, Utah, New Mexico and Arizona. I used my Shelter Island knowhow to get daily work and we travelled as a team on less than $500 for a month. Once a week I would park the children for three or four hours while I did plumbing jobs, picked up from local small-town newspapers. My speciality was putting Insinkerators (waste disposal units) into kitchens at $50 a time. Each $50 bought for us $20 in gas and $30 in fruit from orchards and some canned goods.

Only once did I falter. Coming into Durango late at night the local radio station was relaying an eastern states interview with Vietnam veterans, complete with recalls of shooting and mortar bombs from old tapes. It was a truly unlucky coincidence for I had been in one of these recorded firefights and knew that two of the men doing "live" interviews were long dead. I pulled off the road into a Greyhound bus station and sat quite still. Jay and Sirie, who had been saving their quarters for a candy treat, got out unprompted. A man in Greyhound uniform walked over and handed me a beer.

Six hours later, with Jay and Sirie sleeping on the mattress I'd placed in the wagon, we at last got to the LA home. They were to stay, I was to return to Australia that evening. I was barely awake when Pat unloaded the children and the wagon. She was ecstatic. All the maths and geography and history lessons we'd done in the wagon as we drove they repeated to her within the first hour of arrival. I went straight to sleep.

Around 2 p.m. I awakened and started to sort out departure plans. A limp-legged man from the film industry arrived. He had just finished treating some stars to lunch and he made a point of saying the bill had come to more than $500. As I came into the room he shouted: "So, here's our whacky Vietnam hero!"

He and his Hollywood friends had been scathing of what they called "Vietnam people" when I'd been with them over skimpy salad lunches in Westwood on my way over to New York. Now, with the emergence of the Vietnam Veteran Syndrome, there was a new tag for us: Whackos. Little wonder that Oliver Stone knocked on doors for two years before getting the money to make *Platoon*. People just did not want to know about Vietnam. The war had wasted their time and money. The lives lost were a lesser consideration.

Despite that inauspicious start the next weeks were wonderful, and I was coming out of the Sag Harbour troubles so quickly I started to feel that they'd be done forever. After the children returned to school another friend arrived, Alison Puchy, a journalist I'd worked with on a travel magazine who now worked in the metropolitan press. She had never been to the US so we travelled California, Arizona and Mexico, all on a shoestring during her holidays. The romance of it all, the travel, the rest, and the sunshine all helped. I might have been carrying some mental time bombs but for the moment I was in very good shape.

When I arrived in Australia it was like stepping back two or three years in time. The first glimmers of hope for suffering Vietnam veterans were in the Letters to the Editor columns of newspapers. At that time I still considered war correspondents as people who had brought problems on themselves and who therefore didn't qualify for help.

I returned to my mansion, the five-storey house I had hardly given a thought to during my time in the US. Union Carbide had taken the top four floors and only used the basement for laundry or checking the heating or accessing the garden. I had forgotten there was a vast basement otherwise unoccupied, with a separate entrance, and the company was not at all worried that I took back this unused area to live in. I had my small bag from Shelter Island, I found I had $3300 from rent in the bank, some leftover furniture, an old Datsun which I had lent to a young journalist, and some bedding. This was enought to start over again.

I decided I should get back to Asia. What I had done in the US seemed to reinforce the feeling that my scars were permanent and probably shared by hundreds and thousands of others, so I might just as well return to Asia — although the prospect of general daily writing held few attractions.

Vietnam was then closed and in deep turmoil. Few reports were filtering out, just a few images of a poor country, undergoing massive changes. We could anticipate the typical results associated with a Communist party takeover. What with the inadequacies of a group of indoctrinated, elderly party men untrained in management, and the hefty international financial sanctions then being imposed, poverty and more suffering were inevitable.

There were some encouraging signs. The party had been tough on the southerners who had fought against them, but there was no bloodbath. That was to follow later through China's increasing support of Pol Pot and her determination to contain the plucky Vietnamese. The party men might not have been good at peacetime administration but they had had an unparalleled record in directing military strategies. Even from the outside those of us even modestly skilled in reading the situation saw that Hanoi would defeat the Chinese.

Strangely, it was a time when the US was not reading the situation at all well. Perhaps they were doing better in the intelligence sections, but not in the political domain, and they backed China.

The inevitable followed. Vietnamese troops removed Pol Pot and his Chinese backers, then turned on the Chinese within their nation, The leadership considered this had the potential to be a double fifth column danger. First, there were those Chinese within Vietnam, particularly the south, who, no matter they were "Communist" preferred to follow Mao; second, there was a financial threat from their thriving businesses and their entrenched wealth. Their "shadow government" in finance made a mockery of the pitiful attempts at financial reconstruction by a totalitarian government. One week's turnover in the Cholon business centre would have exceeded the yearly non-military budget up north. Such comparisons and inequities would have to be removed before the new government could ever hope to convince the people the new Socialist system was working.

The dark episode of the exodus of Chinese-Vietnamese, who were to be known as the Boat People, began at this time. Indonesia, too, was under military rule, but ironically safer and sounder than it had ever been. The expected stories of a corrupt ruling elite began to surface; but certainly there was nothing happening in that country that would change the way of the world.

After a brief tour of South-East Asia, calling in on my colleagues and the usual meeting places like Singapore, Bangkok and Jakarta, I came to the decision not to re-establish in Asia. The best of the old correspondents had settled in Hong Kong and Bangkok, earning very good money, enjoying a fabulous and enviable nightlife and awaiting the great stories that would surely come from Indo-China. This was not for me. With some relief I decided to give Asia away for a few more years and abandon the possibility of whatever great stories might emerge.

A new life also began to present itself. Having got on so well with Alison over the preceding months, we started planning seriously. A second family seemed likely. Now faced with an alternative to a stop-and-start career of waiting in Asia, there was no choice. I discussed the new family with the old family, now firmly settled in the US. It should work well, we agreed.

Had Alison known what she was getting into, she might not have gone into marriage. The disturbed nights on Shelter Island were just a prelude to the real thing. Alison was still living at home with her parents and understood little of it except to note than on some days in the office of the magazine where we worked I was barely able to maintain my concentration.

Selfishly, I thought this new life would eliminate most of the nightly harassment I was suffering, dreams in which men, most likely long dead, continued trooping through and firing or threatening or fleeing.

I had another period of attempting to rid myself of these mental movie shows. I went to Perth on assignment to redesign a newspaper for the talented businessman Robert Holmes a'Court in 1981. He had started a new weekend newspaper. He was later to cut a strong figure in world business, but at the time I had never heard of him. I liked him immediately, and I liked the work, underpaid but very absorbing.

When Alison joined me for a long weekend I was convinced the devils had all been melted away by the excitement of the new job and the prospect of marriage. We planned to marry and return to Perth after our Melbourne obligations were completed, which would take two years.

Two years, it was, but two of the strangest in my life. In the lead-up to the marriage and after my return from Perth there were no real problems. But a few months later, in total peace, the moving pictures returned at night and I could no longer hide the facts. I dismissed the nightmares as "occasional events" to Alison, but as the months went by I knew I had to do something quickly before I hurt more people.

I then did a strange thing. Instead of seeking help I thought I would work my way out of it while keeping a fairly conservative face to the outside world. I had never let go of the idea that time-consuming and distracting activities could help in some way. In this mood I leased a New Zealand thoroughbred named Snow Feather.

Although I had made my name as an Indonesian expert, then as a linguistically competent foreign correspondent, few were aware I also knew something about thoroughbreds. Yet it was writing about and gambling on thoroughbred racing that bankrolled me into Asia in the first place. I was a bit rusty, but such skills are never lost. I seemed to be going the way of so many modestly successful Australians. Instead of looking outwards, we return to our favourite escapes: property, sport, some comfortable domesticity, with a win in the daytimes and polished dining habits at night. For me however, it was a way of dealing with a problem.

It worked. Snowy never won a race for me, but he was in the money, meaning he was second or third or fourth, in every race he ran. He was a wonderful horse. And we certainly had a wonderful trainer. In Yarra Glen, a little riverside village east of Melbourne, John Nichols looked after Snowy, and placed him in races for me. Nichols was a man with a strong work ethic, never used drugs on his horses, and was untainted in any sense. He was the perfect partner for me in this exercise.

We got another two horses in training, both very good lookers but slow. It was Snowy who helped me through. The exercise cost me very little, brought me great friendship with John and his wife, Jillian, and allowed me and my family to travel the State. I took Alison and my children, to all his races in the bush. We would have a barbecue, help with Snowy, put a small bet on him, talk to the apprentice jockey Neil Perryman, and sit down in a state of muted excitement in the wooden grandstands to watch the race. Snowy and Perryman never let us down. They brought in some money every time, usually coming from near last to run second or third.

Tuesdays and Thursdays I would get up at 4.30 a.m., drive an hour to the little Yarra Glen racetrack and watch Snowy training. The atmosphere was very comforting. Before arriving I would stop at the village newsagent's shop and get a bacon and egg toasted sandwich. Then I would join the trainers for a coffee in their little room near the track, from where you could watch the horses go through their training gallops. John Nichols knew everyone and I became known as the eccentric journalist who had entered an unraced horse in the Melbourne Cup (akin to sending your untrained fifteen-year-old son to the Olympics). They took that to be typical of my eccentricity, as well as a waste of $50, but made no more of it.

Snowy got better and better under John Nichols' care and was heading for a nice handicap win in the city when I got a call that changed everything.

It went like this:

"I have some bad news, Frank." said John.

"Tell it straight," I replied.

"Your mate Snowy is in trouble."

"What sort of trouble?"

"They've operated on him, to remove a piece of floating bone."

"Why is he in trouble?"

"Well, they've operated."

"He's dead."

"Not yet. He's in trouble."

The place Snowy had been sent for the operation tipped Snowy over the wrong way and he landed on his disabled leg, breaking it completely.

I rang the veterinarian at his surgery.

"We'd like to put him down," the vet told me.

"Shoot him dead?"

"Bluntly put, yes."

"What if we save him?"

"He'll be in agony with arthritis until he dies."

"It's that bad?"

"Yes."

"How could you let that happen?"

"I was called away when the assistants were unloading him from the operating table," he replied. "My wife called to say my five-year-old daughter had fifty per cent burns from her waist down in a home accident. My little girl's legs are all swollen and peeling away."

I hung up, and the pictures began.

I am sitting in a newspaper office overlooking the Yarra River. A little girl with burnt legs is running towards me over the little ripples of the river.

Employees are saying goodnight and leaving me in a gradually darkening office. Their voices are competing with radio calls of Snowy running in some country race. He is closing in the straight.

When Neil brings him back through the gate from the track to the saddling enclosure Snowy is being led by a soldier screaming and shouting that this horse was typical of the filth that must be removed from society and he unslings his automatic rifle and shoots Snowy in the legs. Snowy buckles over, throwing off my jockey friend Neil Perryman, whose hands are tied. Perryman rolls over and over like a jockey falling from a stumbling steeplechaser but the soldier follows him and hits him with the rifle then shoots him anyway, then looks up for others to shoot.

The soldier leads half a dozen others around the grandstand and I hear more shooting and more calls. I am left frozen, holding the reins which my eyes followed down to his halter. Snowy is lifting his head time and time again, his eyes ablaze in death throes.

John Nichols is dead, in the saddling area. Neil Perryman is dead, handcuffed, still wearing race silks in my colours. Snowy is dead. I notice then his reins are wrapped around my wrists and sealed like a plaster cast, and I am held firmly there.

The shooting slows down. They are coming back to get me. The lead soldier stops, having decided to shoot me from across the small parade ring. They are crouching now, aiming at me, creeping around the parade ring fence, shooting, but missing. All the missed bullets enter into Snowy's body, and he kicks every time they hit him.

They keep firing and firing and making knocking noises. Finally one of them decides to come close.

He unlocked a gate and approached, then spoke kindly to me. "Are you ready?" asked Alex Sandy. Chief sub-editor Alex Sandy and co-editor James Crown were standing in my doorway, watching me. Whatever they'd seen and heard made them thoughtful. It was past edition time, the paper was on the streets. Time for our regular weekly drink at the terrace bar.

"You look as if you need one or two," said Alex.

Getting home took some time. As the evening progressed I began to doubt that I had even had a telephone conversation. Had the trigger been a telephone call, or was it someone I heard on the radio that had led me to jumbling Vietnam and my plans for Snow Feather's next race into one daytime picture?

The next morning I called John Nichols to ask if Snowy was dead.

He certainly was.

I called Alistair the veterinarian to ask how his daughter was.

"It could have been much, much worse. We thank our lucky stars." He continued, "Look, Snowy was a beautiful horse. I'm terribly sorry about this. Thank you for understanding about my little girl."

Triggers like this now began to come frequently. It was impossible for me, in the news business, to avoid the films and references to Vietnam. Furthermore, the stream of suicides, criminal violence, mental breakdowns and divorces being reported weekly had brought the issue into the open. There were debates in all forms of media and it was from one of those newspaper reports that I first learned of Ruth Perkins and her work.

3

Sometimes it was 1969, sometimes 1975, sometimes 1981, and then it would slip back to some intermediate year. What we thought could only awaken us in fright at night would creep slowly into the daylight hours, into everyday life, where it was accepted, and harnessed or smothered by the need to work and behave in a certain manner during daylight hours.

We could go to hell at nights, but that was our business. We were not to bring these problems into the light, for it was embarrassing to us and those around us. Like countless other survivors of Vietnam, for a long time I too had managed to get through life by suppressing bad feelings, putting a can on guilt, anxiety, anger. But I couldn't do it forever.

In 1984, only days after Snowy had been shot, I read an interview in the Melbourne *Age* with Ruth Perkins, the head of the Vietnam Veterans' Counselling Services in South Melbourne. Something she said led me into finally going for a talk. Even then I used subterfuge to get in. This was related to war, and when dealing with war, where people are out to kill others, I had learned to tread very carefully.

Once inside the door, having been introduced as a journalist, I had to face the difficulty of speaking, telling her why I was there. Ruth sat quietly. The interview went like this:

"I need help."

"I know you need help."

"How do you know I need help?"

"You're here."

"Perhaps I don't need help. I may be around the bend."

"Perhaps."

"Should I come back?"

"If you like."

"Will you be here?"

"You know I will be."

I stayed. I remember very little of the first talk except that it was peaceful, and a kind of protection from the greying afternoon outside. It was a small comfortable room, where I talked with someone who didn't sneer or laugh.

It felt selfish to be doing this after discovering that my own problems were not unique, but paled in comparison to others. As I came across US and Australian veterans, then Viet Cong and civilians north and south in Vietnam, I saw the war as a cavalcade of deaths and half-deaths. My seven uncles had been killed in Gallipoli, men who were younger than I had been in Vietnam, transported by ship to the Dardanelles to land at a cliff base and hope to live through eight months of shooting from above.

There were the strange outcasts from the Second World War who filtered slowly into my bush town to live on handouts and drink themselves into a stupor every night. One walked stiffly upright, as we thought gentlemen should do. He had a steel brace in his back. He could not bend, he could not sleep except in this strange, arched position, but few knew that.

It wasn't my first attempt to get help. My own doctor had three years earlier recommended me to a very well known psychiatrist who was often photographed at cocktail parties and was "seen" at special functions with elegant hostesses. I wrote to him, telling him of a growing absent-mindedness and a strange increase in nightmares, and I described one of them, as he asked. I got a reply on richly embossed notepaper, setting an appointment for me. "My fee is $200 per hour payable from the first appointment," it added.

I left the South Melbourne Vets' counselling office. Driving home in heavy traffic, I thought how dangerous it was. It was storming over Melbourne and I turned the lights on to see the peak-hour traffic. The radio was on the ABC where someone was talking to someone on a drive-home show. Tonight's upcoming program on ABC-TV is on Vietnam, and we mustn't miss it, the announcer interrupted.

A bridge ahead, over the Yarra River. On Vietnam. My curtains come down. The entire street is black. I work mechanically to take the iron tank to the safety of the roadside. I telephone someone. The telephone is out of order. Everything is out of order. Out of order.

Beeps and honks. Then the soldier comes. Grey uniform, grey cap. He draws his notebook.

"Can't stay here. It's a clearway."

Silence.

"You're from the Vets?"

Nod. Yes.

"I'll close the door for you. Take a breather. Drive down that little street." He indicates a small lane. He stands guard on the corner.

He pulls out his rifle and places it at the ready, helmet lowered. As the sky darkens more he flattens himself against a wall and pulls out a small transceiver and starts reporting, quietly, in coded Vietnamese. The first snipers for the evening start firing, an unsettling random fire. He turns to me and shrugs. There is no way we can tell the origin of the fire as the bullets and the following sounds bounce from wall to wall, like a vandal plucking a fine violin and breaking each string.

He helps me home by pointing out a safe way, but he stays. He has slept the day long, he is on night duty.

I share the apartment with an American reporter whose newspaper is on strike. He has filed again. I envy him. He filed, but was told No Paper Tomorrow. The Foreign editor says Stay, well done, valuable copy. This is Day 23 of the strike, 1968. Others have smiled at his dedication. I realise he is here now not on his original mission, but on his own mission.

We sleep on the floor, beds apart, on flat mats on the tiled floor. We have no shared things of living. No paintings, no saucepans, no knowledge of where things are.

He creeps back as the firing outside continues, carrying two small glasses of filtered water and a Red Cross pack of bandages, tiny bottles of tinctures and pads and tweezers, and places them between us. He holds up into dim light a small plastic hose. For kisses of life. Sucking out bits in guts. We sleep with our boots on, our flak jackets covering our chests.

In the dark he says: "I took this place six months ago from my predecessor. In 1967 it looked great. I was with the people, away from the centre. Now its not a great idea. Can't get a place in there now."

Tet has put a line between him in the suburbs and the city centre. The fire is heavy all night.

In self-consolation he says, "At least I'm close to the airport." I slumber, but he speaks. His wife is in despair. He longs for his children. I am warned on pain of death to visit him in Chicago, next time I go there. He has no irony in his voice as he says this. An expression, slipping out. On crossing my heart and pain of death, I will visit him. He needs to believe he will be alive in 1970.

The traffic clears. The curtain lifts. The previously desperate drive from South Melbourne to Clifton Hill is now not so perilous. It is just a normal fifteen-minute drive.

Alison is waiting for me. I am to light a big log fire and look at the baby girl in a sheepskin wrap on the floor. She has showed a shadow of a smile and I am to watch, for it may be repeated. Just for me. The fire burns nicely, the baby refuses to smile, but looks good. We have no TV. The Vietnam program goes on without me.

Ruth sits quietly as I talk. Why doesn't she take notes?

"There is no need," she says.

I was not in Vietnam. Somehow the talk ran into a bloody gutter. I was in the sunny Javanese mountain area visiting a family whose father was a member of the Communist Party. The mayor of the town was a friend of his, but sadly, he said, not a party man. His children sit on my knee and we talk about foreign countries, and he teaches me more of another regional language, Sundanese. They laugh when I mispronounce some special word.

Months later I am with Don North from Canada's CBC News, looking over the ashes of my communist friends' home. We hear the story of how they were jailed for safety as the Moslem mob burned their house down, then the story of the mob turning on the mayor and the jailers: You or Them. The "infected" communist parents and three little children were taken from the jail and cut to pieces. They had been my friends.

"Could you have helped them?" Ruth asks.

No.

I loved her so much, yet I can hardly remember what she looked like. Big blue eyes and older than I could ever be, she sat listening and helping.

We went to a small pub one night, the Clare Castle, on one side of the Flagstaff Gardens. A big log fire, but not many people. We continued to talk.

When it came time to drive out in our separate cars I hugged her, aware that it was a transgression of trust.

A long time and many hours later Ruth set some chairs up in a new room. Not our cosy room, a bigger one, with dimmer lights.

She sat with an array of large plastic toy rifles, out front. There were two chairs just before her. Jeep driver and front passenger. There were two chairs behind them, Bruce and Ron Laramy. My small chair was the rear left mudguard — I sat in that small chair.

"Why are you sitting there?"

"It was safer," I said.

"It *is* safer," she said.

"Yes, I have just moved. It is safer. I expect an ambush."

In the dim light she re-created a drive down a small lane in Cholon on 5 May 1968. The people were running from the firing.

"But Bruce Pigott says you should go on. Why?"

"He is uncertain. But he wants to show me he has grown up now. He is in control in Saigon. He knows I don't know Saigon as he does."

"Does this worry you?"

"I am proud of him. But I worry that it's a wrong decision. I argue against all of them. It is not just Bruce's decision. The others could have disagreed but they overrule me. I move to this seat."

"Why not just jump out?"

"Into what? The middle of a VC area?"

"It is a VC area?"

"I know it, from the start of the street."

Ruth waves the plastic guns. Say what you like, she tells me. I am silent.

"Were you silent?"

"Always."

"You are angry that they've brought you into this."

Silence.

"You are angry," she repeats.

"Yes."

"Yes, you are. But now you feel responsible for their deaths."

Silence.

"Could you have done any more than you did?"

"No."

"What did you do?"

"I saved myself."

"Could you help the others?"

"No."

"What's so wrong about saving yourself?"

Silence.

"What were you telling yourself?"

"You won't get me, no matter that you have the guns."

It was the turning point. From then on there was no more play-acting and no more vague sessions. I was to have just two more meetings with Ruth before the counselling was over and before I left Melbourne.

In one of our last encounters I was able to explain to her that I had always, I thought, managed to contain the general experience of Vietnam, as well as the ambush in particular, reasonably well — except for those instances such as in Sag Harbour when it all became too much. But there was another thorn that would smart from time to time, one that really had little to do with the night terrors I had tried to cope with over the years.

As if it wasn't enough to have lived through that ambush itself, I had also to deal with a vicious story circulated in Australia that I had never even been on the jeep in the first place. Trying to stop the gossip, spread in particular by a Melbourne tabloid photographer, got me nowhere. Although I complained to the Australian Journalists' Association, the gossip was still around as late as 1982 and it was still distressing. No one challenged me in print or conversation, for the claims that I had not been there could be easily dismissed. Nevertheless, this too was something I would have to deal with if the catharsis was ever to be complete.

As I came to see the psychological importance of once again returning to Vietnam, I also saw there would be another purpose to tracking down the man who had shot us and chased me — by finding the man or men involved I would not only be able to ask that fundamental 'why?', I would also be able to finally put to rest some very hurtful innuendo.

In January 1988, I rang Ruth to tell her I was going back to Vietnam and would look for the man.

"Be careful," she said. "Tread carefully."

4

In 1985, with counselling almost complete, I moved to Perth with Alison and baby Anna. I began doing radio work, then turned to television and documentary film making. Life had begun to regain some semblance of normality. Counselling had led me to recognise I had a problem and encouraged me to do something about it; it also brought home to me how many Australian men were, like their American counterparts, experiencing Vietnam-related torments.

As I slowly became able to be objective about my own ordeal, I also began to take an interest in the welfare of local, and until that time largely ignored, Vietnam veterans. When they finally won recognition and were to be accorded a welcome home march, I was more than pleased — this seemed the least that could be done. In early 1987 I became involved in a projected film of this march, which was to be held in October of that year. As a tail-end to it there was to be a section for non-combatants like Red Cross and medical staff and journalists, should they wish to join in. As well as marching myself, my brief included locating some of the many "hidden" Vietnam Vets with the idea of encouraging them to also take part.

With six months' preparation there was sufficient time for searches in the larger States where it was known hundreds of veterans had hidden away in minor jobs for a decade or more. I had met many of them when making gold mining films where the only access was by light plane.

I came across one of them in Wiluna, in the centre of Western Australia, a man who worked as a surveyor's assistant. He'd been on the usual twelve-hour shift and returned to camp with us in a four-wheel drive through flooded roads.

The driver had called out something like: "Hey Kel, not like

Vietnam is it? No trees for miles, just water and sand."

The cameraman, just twenty years old, joined in: "You blokes might have met?" He meant me and Kel.

Kel just said: "Doubt it."

I invited him to a few games of pool back in camp, which was a group of sixty air-conditioned, self-contained mobile units placed in semi-circular arrangement around a large kitchen mess and games room. In these camps men live for six to nine months at a time. The food is excellent, the medical care, rest facilities all one could ask, and the money good. Outside, there is nothing for hundreds of miles in either direction.

The film crew had started by filming that clichéd, but still useful, establishing shot — a signpost showing Darwin, Perth, Sydney, Bali, and so on, thousands of kilometres away. The main road out was little more than a worn dirt track.

He wiped me at pool in the first two games but wanted me to keep playing. So he devised a handicap for me wherein he would have to sink nine balls to my five before we got to the black, and that evened it out, and made it easier for him to talk.

We were left alone at the pool table. Kel was clearly a leader of men there, and must have signalled to them he wanted some peace. Another table lay empty for most of the evening so we weren't concerned we were blocking anyone. Behind us men in football sweaters, shorts and sneakers, showered and with hair and beards brushed wet — this was Sunday best for them — lined up their Emu beers and laughed uproariously at each other's jokes.

They cared for Kel, and small cans of Emu arrived at the chalk table every thirty minutes or so.

Now that Kel had handicapped himself heavily the games were close and I won one or two of them, which pleased him, for he was not a man to throw a game. There is similarity in sighting a rifle and shooting good pool. One first spreads the body weight evenly, spreads arm weight evenly, then sights. This was a game like that, but with an eerie difference, which took me a game or two before I adjusted: Kel would only speak while sighting.

When I got into harmony with this I began to do the same, and asked him a few questions as I sighted. He was easy about it, and often interrupted me to tell me to put a backspin, or a certain "side" to the ball, to make it more difficult for him to play the following shot.

During one of these quiet talks he said: "It's only when I talk about Vietnam that I do this."

I asked how often he had spoken about Vietnam.

"About three times," was the response.

He had been in the distant goldfields for eleven years.

I told him I was going to the march, in Sydney, and then going back to Vietnam. He surprised me by saying he was returning there as soon as he felt happy about leaving the goldfields.

It was a difficult conversation. Had I tried to prolong any one game by shooting even less well than my modest game, he would have cleaned me up just that much quicker. He couldn't tolerate anything other than a close game.

"I like the Vietnamese people. 'Course, I didn't like the dirty tricks, but I saw what they were fighting for."

Sight. Shoot. "I like people on the land. Don't like cities."

Sight. Shoot. "Don't like asphalt, light poles, traffic lights."

There were no heroic stories, just accounts of step by careful step through minefields, step by careful step on patrols. He disliked Saigon and its noise and its brightly lit bars and he was frustrated at being penned up on the rare visits there, for he wanted to get into the suburbs or the peripheral villages.

"Impossible," he said. "That's why I'd like to go back and walk through and talk to them. I get by with a few words and a smile. I'm a country boy. Start at four, do the milking, breakfast, go to state school on a bus, play footy at lunch, back on the bus, meet Mum with the ute who'd bring little Donna (his little sister) and I'd give her a musk stick and they'd drop me out in the paddocks and Dad'n'I would finish the afternoon out together."

When he spoke of his father he said "Daddeneye".

When he spoke of his mother he said "MumenDonna".

When he spoke of being called up for Vietnam, of the departure, of the arrival in Asia, or the war, he said: "No drama".

The drama was all at home, when he got back. Politics he didn't understand. A bank foreclosing on first some machinery, then some land, leaving them very little to work and commercial debts they could not comprehend. His father had to share-farm.

Sight. "Know what my idea of share farmin' is?"

Shoot. "Where the cows and dogs don't have their own names."

He saw his family shrink from broad acres to permanent town life. From their own land to another's. From milk pickups by tankers, and feed drops, from the enjoyable monthly trips, to having to live in a big town. The town had only existed for fencing wire, or things for the kitchen, or something for Donna, or Mum, and a beer with Dad and grown men in big sweat-stained hats, a talk with the old cop. Where the Dalgety agent could leave their order in front of the closed shop in the dark street for them to pick up on their way out on the road home.

The idiots shouting at him when he arrived back for his short stop in the city, disgusted him. When he called to tell them at home he was on his way, he found no home. The new number was in the big town of Midland. A house in a street with sixty others. The old pickup truck there for daily commuting to a farm owned by a big company. No yellow ribbons around trees. No farm dog Bluey jumping to meet him. No stars, just dull street lights on dead tree poles. No quacking, no clucking, no birds, no need to check the cow bales, no need to check the feed, no need to bring in an armful of wood for the old slow-combustion stove.

Sight. "So, after a while I took off. Little Donna was big. Her teachers told her Vietnam soldiers were the pits. Disgusting. She stuck by me, but soon she went. Got married. Early. Went east."

Shoot. "I decided to get them a small farm. That's why I'm here. Well, that's why I was here. We've got a place now. Much smaller. But they're independent, sort of. I send a fair amount down home."

Vietnam became a bit of a problem later, he admitted. Over there he'd seen the war beginning to wind down and followed it back home through the newspapers as it had fallen into a heap of confusion, then withdrawal. He wasn't wanted in the towns. He had no farm and no farm family to return to, so he went bush, into the goldfields.

Sight: "That's about it."

I asked if he would join me in going to Sydney for the march.

Shoot: "I won't say no. It's about time, I'd say."

Extraordinary efforts were made to get the few Vietnam veterans from the goldfields to Sydney. In some towns they placed a digger's army hat on the bars, where it stayed until it collected the $150 needed for the subsidised trip. Australian Airlines would pay the rest of the money. The vets came out of their goldfields hideaways, where they'd hidden for many years. The years had slipped by them and they felt increasingly useless, but this march, and the publicity, encouraged their friends to help them make the big trip to the big smoke, Sydney.

Kel came down from Wiluna, arriving at the last minute. He stayed close but was somehow pleased I had a job to do, which would mean he did not have to speak. How could he speak without a pool table? No bend, no sight, no shoot, no background noise — But he was always close by.

On our return from Sydney I wrote a quick summary of the event. Aware that I had kept a record, Kel sent me a letter a year later, asking for a copy — to be forwarded to a coastal mining town. It turned out he had finished with the goldfields, had married a Filipina and was now settled into iron ore mining. It was a surprise. I had not imagined him as a letter writer.

I imagined him to be saying to me as he took his stance at the pool table, "Needed a change".

This is what I wrote:

7 a.m., September 30. On a plane for the first time since the war. 8 a.m., daring to look around. Friendly faces. A closer look . . . mates from the same company, the same year. Meet. Talk. Shared apprehension. A thin aluminium dart at 30,000 feet, encapsulating and isolating a group who'd long thought sharing a relationship was now impossible.

Below them a convoy of fifty cars and minibuses for those who would not fly. Those who needed time to think. Five days to cross the great Nullarbor Plain, five hundred kilometres of straight road, a slight bend, then three hundred kilometres of more straight road and a million kangaroos and parrots, a gas station every four hours. Where other Diggers waited. An ex-vet squadron of taxi drivers, bus drivers, an aged general in a posh auto bringing four much younger less well-heeled vets. Time to talk and slowly recall.

Timing the convoy to arrive on September 30. To bunk with eastern States vets in barracks around town. And a reunion. More of an adjustment to the city of Sydney, hosting the march. Shave. Change clothes. Call home. Count remaining dollars.

Most had never seen Sydney. Awed. Twice as big as San Francisco. Punks and chains and crime and skyscrapers and wealth beyond country town imagination. Suddenly their Sunday suits and Best for occasions felt like shrouds, setting them apart from real people. People who don't go to war. People who don't seem bothered at all. Who keep hold of families or don't even need families but are *free to drink from the stream. Noble, wealthy, smooth. Polished autos, not pickup trucks. Fine leather, not steel-capped work boots. Unstained shirts. Flick for a cab without checking the back pocket where the last notes and coins are. Candlelit tables with $40 main courses that belittle a man who carries a plastic box of sandwiches, an apple, a celery stalk, like C rations to his mindless daily labour. This is a mistake, coming to the big town.*

Until: A crowded barracks hall. A familiar uniform. A soldier we know stands on a chair. Older. Proudly he welcomes: "Words can't describe how happy we are in our battalion to see you here tonight. We have waited so long. You blokes from Queensland (waves an arm, cheers), South Australia (group cheers), bloody Victoria (whistles) and Western Australia (Yeah!) . . ."

Tonight we settle in. A meal, a quick drink. The morning bugle is for 3 a.m. Does anyone sleep? Did anyone really sleep for the last eighteen years? The women are pals. Nurses. Red Cross. Familiar faces, friendly faces, all sisters. They seemed made of sterner stuff. But they too are now part of the team to face the October 1 march. All together.

The hours went by as in a movie. Colourful scenes, faces, flags, medals, music, the characters moving on and off camera regrouping at 4 a.m., herding into buses in the dark, driving off into the heart of a city, to the Cenotaph.

In Martin Place, the heart of the city, there stood before them in the otherwise dark skyscraper-lined streets and malls five hundred young children and teenagers. Grandfathers and grandmothers and brothers and wives and husbands of the Vietnam dead. Each with a bright, high-burning candle. And row upon row of today's soldiers in beautiful uniforms and a Highland band with metal on their drums and bagpipes glinting. An amber-lit Cenotaph stone.

The candle-holders break into song and a bugler plays and an otherwise silent line of men and women begins heaping wreaths at the base of the Cenotaph as they slowly file past.

A man said "Damn and Damn and Be Damned those who turned us aside — but recognise this — that today we are a new Australia and we are welcomed home as we should be, and what we fought for was lost, and is forever lost for those we fought for." And as he said it Vietnamese soldiers walked by the Cenotaph and placed their wreaths and embraced their new country. And were embraced, and their children followed, carrying candles alight, held high.

And I stood among them. A colleague placed a wreath for five war correspondents killed and I read my words of farewell for them. My final goodbye. My only goodbye to my best friend and the others I knew less well. Was there a city so silent but for the strains of the Last Post? No one moved for minutes and candles burned slowly down. To dawn. We stared, unseeing.

Morning. The atmosphere of comradeship held us together as we in thousands assembled under banners, our wartime entertainers, now a bit out of tune, played for us from a sound shell in the green gardens, and we recognised amongst us a large US gathering, some in 1968 uniforms, some with special, homespun banners, a remake of their Da Nang or Cam Ranh units, and South Vietnamese soldiers, in stylish suits of their new country, in clear, ironed Sunday suits of shop people, their solemn Australian-born children handing them a drink before the march, bewildered by the scene of massed men and women who embraced their fathers as no other had. And in a band of proud South Koreans, fifteen behind a banner-carrying leader who stood solemnly awaiting orders to step off.

In this gathering of many thousands, our small group of war correspondents. Reunions after seventeen and twenty years. Many dead, since the war. Many fading quickly. And me, obscenely young and healthy. Semi-young. In wartime, nearly always up north, Quong Tri, Kontum, Da Nang. And now the sole Warco from the west, the brazen and brassy State.

The skyscrapers hide both the noise and the first mile of marchers from us. We see them two hundred metres below us, downhill, swinging around to the left and starting their run up the kilometre-and-a-half stretch where at the post, the Town Hall steps, we know there are cameras, politicians and soldiers of high rank to see us file past. But would there be people? Our own people?

A few hundred people quietly raise their hands to us as we walk on past, but the sidewalk crowd is pitifully thin. We're now on the turn. Swinging left. Suddenly we see a storm of tapes, flowers, streamers, ribbons lifting into the air, fluttering down on those ahead of us. Then on us. The crowds ten, fifteen, then thirty and forty deep, from kneeling children at kerbsides, through to masses on the sidewalk and children held aloft at the rear, and teenagers on ledges or lamp poles. Cheering. Running into the march, giving flowers, kissing. Crying. Wave after wave of cheering and thousands of hands clapping, clapping, and the showers of friendly human voices and sounds of flowers and streamers wash over us, like the friendly rain on the tin roofs that comforted us as children, washing away for us the years of filth and slime others poured on us when we returned from Vietnam.

The fears the crowd would turn on us, would produce some band of cretins to throw blood-red paint over us and chant lunatic praise for those who would soon turn on their own people, were groundless. The politicians who rode to synthetic prominence on a nation's anguish now absent, finding solace in new causes.

The home stretch was a street of blurred beauty. More help in five minutes than in hours of counselling.

Our lines began to lose form. I cannoned into my mate Jack Darmody, and he put his arm around my shoulders, as another linked arms with him on the other side, and hands from behind on our shoulders linked us all. Formations were lost as the march spilled into a wide parkland and fed us all into the waiting arms of family and friends.

The Australian-born Vietnamese children stood in happy awe as their fathers were embraced by Australians and Americans and Koreans and cameras flashed to record forever their acceptance as new Australians and the prints would be placed alongside the meagre possessions they carried as Boat People in their escape from Vietnam when the stinking war was over.

Amidst this I slowly recalled my film unit was somewhere close. I looked up to see them all staring at me, camera running. Regrouped, we started to walk clear. One in tears, the others deep in thought. Vietnam for them, so young, had been something far away, a school talk by teachers when they were just children. Now it was different.

From a no-sleep night, to 4 a.m. candlelit procession, and the march, to a regrouping in the barracks. The newspapers, passed around hand to hand, played the march all front page, all page two, all page three. And a vet who had hidden away for sixteen years was pictured with his wife, and the two children he had not seen since their infancy, since before we went to Vietnam. He had called the newspaper to find his family, to tell them, "I'm home!" After his arrival in Sydney, he had been abused, had taken to the bush where he survived as a menial on a plantation where he lived for three thousand days unable to cope with the shame they told him to feel.

After him a drove of men emerged to face the light of day. To pick up threads of their home life.

Sunday. Back to the west, 350 of us. To our desert towns. To our goldmines. To our opal mines. To our farms. To our desks. To our fishing boats. Our same chartered silver bullet at 30,000 feet.

A young man in starched uniform walked down the aisle and said: "The captain wishes you his deepest thanks, and would like you all to have a drink on him. Our tab, please. You are all wonderful people." The beers came around. The toasts were drunk, the refills arrived.

The young steward said, "The captain's brother was killed in Vietnam".

Nearly two years later I was the writer for a small film about gas wells on the Northwest Shelf of Australia; the operator had its base at Karratha, only an hour's drive from where Kel lived in the small iron ore town of Wickham. This presented a good opportunity to make contact once again.

The film crew flew back without me. I took a small Australian-made Holden Gemini down to Wickham to be inconspicuous. I could have driven a pink Cadillac for all it mattered. Wickham had no streets lit, no one was on the roads at evening, nor were there any sidewalks. Some lights from a small hotel/motel, some other lights where girls were playing netball to a crowd of thirty in what looked to me an oasis in a dark hot desert.

I had meant to surprise him. But not this much. There were no street signs, just a crisscross of roads with a few hundred cyclone-proofed houses, all with beautiful trees and gardens, but just walk tracks between blocks.

The addresses were phonies. Everyone got their mail at the post office. I went to the bar of the hotel and asked for Kel.

"No use in directions," said the barman. "We'll show you."

A bar assistant led the way, on his motorcycle. We drove in and out of ditches, his short cut, then he pointed the headlamps into a house, swung around, then left, with a wave. Back to his work at the pub. Lights were on, music was playing. I got out into the heat of night. I rang a string, not a bell. It was string of sea shells headed by coconut shells which clonked and tinkled for many seconds.

A girl I recognised as Mindanaon opened the door. *"Selamat malam"*, I said.

She was astonished, yet happy. *"Selamat malam"*, she replied.

There was Kel, surrounded by six or seven Australian workmates, and a mixture of Australian, Indonesian and Filipina wives. And there was his small baby, in an Australian rock-a-bye wire cot with a mosquito net folded around it. There were steaks on the barbecue, Emu beer in cans for the men, and a big pitcher of fruit punch for the women and children.

I felt I was intruding. It was all a big mistake, me trying to surprise him. Kel looked up as I came in, stared and stayed seated. A man in a football jumper beside him grinned a welcome. He had been at the bar during our pool-table discussions back in Wiluna. He arose from his seat and came to me, then escorted me back to what had been his own seat next to Kel.

Kel had no pool table to talk to, no goldmine to refer to. No farm to talk about. After a hesitation he overcame his shyness and stood and embraced me. He took me inside, and as his Filipina wife followed, he showed me who she was, and who he was. He had almost nothing to say except that he had gone to the south of the Philippines to Mindanao Island, where there were farmers and villagers he understood. He had met Sari in a farming village and had married her. "A real farm village, you understand?" I understood. Not a marriage by newspaper advertisements. Not a marriage through date-by-computer, by old photographs exchanged.

Sari said, "Frank speaks my language."

I used English: "You are Muslim."

She replied, "Yes, from five hundred years."

Nothing of that mattered any more. The show was in the dining room and the lounge, where Kel's photographs of Sari's villagers working in the fields were displayed, and in between, twenty or thirty photographs of Kel's old dairy farm were displayed.

Conical-hatted women plucking rice, Kel's father rounding up the cows, a tiny boy leading ducks, an old Holden pickup truck in the middle of a wide field, women threshing rice, MumenDonna picking up wood, a man in a Mindanao robe selling spices, Dad in wide hat smiling as he milked a cow, Sari as a tiny girl carrying a cane basket.

The photographs were intermixed as only country people like them, all over the walls, hung on top and beside each other.

Sight: "Sari knows more about farming than ninety per cent of Australians."

Sight: "Stay here, of course. Sari loves speaking the lingo."

Shoot: "Our own farm, we call it. A red farm in an iron ore desert."

5

In late 1987, an opportunity to return to Vietnam presented itself. For the twentieth anniversary of the Tet Offensives (known in Vietnam as the Spring Offensives) the Vietnamese were planning a round table conference to which they were inviting former war correspondents who had been in Saigon in 1968. Along with the score of fellow-travellers, necessary to swell the ranks, invitations went out to independent correspondents from the United States, France, the UK, Japan, Malaysia, Thailand, Australia and the Philippines.

Of those who had been in Saigon for the Spring Offensives, there were not so many to invite. Twenty years on, the most senior Vietnam war correspondents had died, some, like cameraman Neil Davis, killed while filming, others in the Middle East and other war zones. Correspondents already in their fifties in 1968 were long retired by 1988. Finally, only two of us attended: James Pringle, who headed the Reuters-AAP bureau in the first Tet, and myself. I had followed Tet One from the foreign desk of the *Washington Post* and returned to Vietnam for my fifth tour just twelve weeks before Tet Two, their second Spring Offensive, now called the Battle for Saigon (5–11 May), the turning point in the war.

In the intervening period, while I got myself organised to return, I busied myself with such routine matters as trying to raise finances for a film project, with the everyday business of making a living. I wondered, during quiet times, whether I would ever be able to go through with it, enact the scenario I had run through in my mind so many times, and at last confront the man who had intruded in my life for the last twenty years.

Air France brought me into old Saigon, now Ho Chi Minh City, early in January 1988. A businessman in Bangkok had told me to hide US dollars in my underpants, to hide any gold I was carrying in my back pockets, to put away any gold rings or my expensive watch in a little bag and wrap it into a sock. The Vietnamese Customs were ferocious, he said.

I had no gold. I had no expensive watch. The US dollars I had would just see me through. I had never smuggled anything into Australia so why should I bother with the Vietnamese Customs? I was the liability, not what I might have been carrying in my bags. I was bringing with me my partner; my eighteen-year-old son, Jay, heading for a US military career.

Bangkok's Vietnamese Consulate officials had been told about Jay. If they were happy that I was bringing someone who in later years might be the architect of another war on them, then I was too. If he could see Vietnam today, after those years of war, he might be the last to push a button. He was utterly calm. I was outwardly calm, but inwardly in fear. If I could get through the first hours I would be safe. An irritational but real fear.

The familiarity of the countryside I saw as we came in was calming. We circled in a holding pattern for ten minutes, which upset many of the others coming in for the first time, but not me. I was looking at familiar lands, with poor fishing villages on the edge of modest rivers, at tiny tile and bamboo factories with smoke drifting through the shafts of uneven clay tiles on the roofs. At handcarts, piled with freight. At tiny trucks pulling massive loads on narrow roads. At workers in the fields with backs bent, nearly doubled over. At docks, immobile. At an airfield, on our several passes, with the old concrete bunkers now grey and overgrown with weeds. At a city busy with motorcycles running between the same small buildings I knew well, along avenues I recognised, but that now took only domestic traffic. No troop trucks, no armoured personnel carriers. Streams of bicycles on small roads running to torrents along the boulevards.

That was at the conscious level. At another level I felt I would step into a concreted tarmac field where someone would have me in his gunsights, not to shoot, but to follow, until the right time. Someone who had caused them so much trouble in May, 1968, the start of their almost-successful Battle for Saigon. Again, irrational.

With me in those imaginary gunsights I stayed mid-group all

the way down the placid Air France steps, into the ordinary bus awaiting us. A woman, far more open in her fear than I, began distributing cigarettes to the bus driver, to the military-uniformed man standing on the bus steps, and on the bus's arrival, to anyone in uniform.

As we approached the terminal building I started to feel a little more at home. Apart from the name — big letters against the still unpainted and unchanged building — it was just the same Tan Son Nhut airbase. Jay was silent, in some appreciation of having arrived in Vietnam, the place he had heard so much about. As a child he had seen demonstrators marching in Melbourne and Los Angeles streets about this country, seen TV films on it long after the war had ended. Heard his father being interviewed about it, talking about it. Waited up for me when I went to my mysterious Vietnam veterans' counselling evenings. Had big colour picture books on Air Force aircraft used in Vietnam. Had been on the *HMAS Perth*, the US aircraft carriers and destroyers which had been in Vietnam waters, when they docked in Fremantle years later.

All I saw was the familiar building block where I had arrived thirty or more times between 1965 and 1968. I was riding a bus where there had before been no such bus. A long walk, carrying typewriter, camera, kit bag, across the tarmac and into a side shelter for the in-country arrivals.

An extraordinarily beautiful woman welcomed us when the bus stopped. She wore the familiar national dress. She asked that the round table conference journalists be singled out and follow her. The other passengers went to the main Customs area, where I had been only once, on my first arrival in 1965. There were ten or twelve of us. We followed, awestruck. This was the new Vietnam. The country with the biggest, most successful standing army in Asia.

Into the VIP area we followed her. She bade Jay and me sit at a certain table, in a similar arrangement and on the same hard-cushioned seats I remembered from twenty years ago. The other journalists were seated alongside and around us. For some of them it was a holiday. They were fellow travelling Communist Party members of their nations. They knew nothing of Vietnam except that it was a country that had won a long war involving the US. That is how they spoke of it. That was their attitude. When the rollcall was done, I saw that only two of them were real journalists. A girl from Malaysia, a man from India. The others were invitees. Committed to the cause. Their cause, not necessarily Vietnam's.

I never did learn the hostess's first name. She had drawn six of us together in that section around that single table: the Malaysian girl, Jay and I, the Indian journalist and a colleague from a leftist magazine, and an elderly Filipino journalist who supported the Communist Huk movement.

She asked openly, in front of the others, what it was like to return. I said I was relieved to be back. I nearly said *back home*. I was relieved, I said, even if I could not add I was relieved that I had not been shot by my unseen sniper, hiding out in the airport tower. In some strange way I was also relieved by the familiar scenes of poverty; of the scenes that had to me been freeze-framed since I left. I could hardly tell her that. It would seem a political comment, extremely personal and selfish. So, I pointed to an air conditioner, fifteen metres away, and said, "That's a Carrier air conditioner. I was here when they were being installed twenty three years ago."

She was surprised. She had expected me to say something else. The Indians and the Filipino were almost suspicious. Jay was confident I was right. The Malaysian girl, curious, went with her to the wall. It was reassuring to contemplate that air conditioner, still buzzing nicely after twenty-three years.

A blue and white minibus awaited us. It was by no means a procession. Nothing so military or orderly. The Customs officers had opened a bag or two, but had mostly been interested in watching us arrive. The Immigration processing had been slow and boring, with the old-fashioned system of stamping and looking at the face to compare it to the passport, and opening a wooden crossbar to let each one go through, then dropping the crossbar again. My Customs man didn't want to look in my pockets. He marked down my old Canon camera. He tried some English on me, and I gave a brief two-sentence lesson. We repeated after each other: "I have nothing to declare." So he said, "You, sir, having nothing to declare!" He laughed at this success. He had added the "sir."

Vietnam was looking good. Then our minibus drove to the old double-laned air base entry gates. The park was still there, ahead, to my right. It took me straight back to April 1968.

I had just jumped out of a plane from Da Nang, run through the Service gates and hitched a ride with an ARVN (South Vietnam Army) jeep. A South Vietnamese colonel and two soldiers were picking up supplies, on which I sat. We were at the gate, in line for checking, several vehicles ahead of us.

Ten simple kites flew into the sky. I counted them as they rose. The ARVN soldiers followed my hand, pointing them out. They were nostalgic. They had flown kites, too, as children. We passed through the gates but were being held up by a traffic block ahead. No one was in a hurry, so we watched the kites. Ten cotton lines down to ten little boys and little girls. Shouting. A bit confused as the kites ducked and rose in the swirling wind. An owl-shaped kite dropped as another square kite rose.

The jeep pulled over to the side, near a steel picket fence. I stepped down from the rear of the jeep. Crouched, I watched the kite display. In the jeep, the ARVN soldiers sat back. They wore helmets. I had a helmet but no other protection, so I stayed crouched. The children flying the kites were in a loose group. Mothers or fathers or elder brothers and sisters were behind them.

The wind turned. Most kites came down. The children wound them in. The boy with the owl kite was persistent. He let the line go higher, then wound it back sharply, to the glee of the spectators, including the ARVN soldiers.

The boy walked forward, over a beaten track which South Vietnamese and US airmen used as a shortcut to the airport. He juggled the kite up and down but the winds were against him. A horse-shoe shaped crowd of mothers and father and brothers and sisters stayed back to get a better view. The boy was the centre of their attention, and ours, too.

His owl kite failed, dropping suddenly before he could wind it in. The boy was returning, we were departing. The crowd was awaiting him. Only a few were finished for the afternoon and starting on their way home, holding children with failed kites. A small group of US airmen led by a senior South Vietnam pilot entered the path from the South Vietnamese Air Force, taking a short cut to the airport.

The owl kite boy stepped onto the US airmen's path, ten yards ahead of them, onto a small jumpjack mine. A tree took most of the blast, the boy took the rest. It blew his foot off and bloodied him all over. It was not a cinema version of an explosion. It was short and sharp. A thump. Silence. Then the child's long scream of shock and agony.

The ARVN soldiers jumped from their jeep to crouch beside me, guns at the ready. Waiting. Looking to the colonel.

The crowd backed slowly away, leaving three people standing like statues. Mother and father and sister of the owl kite boy.

The ARVN colonel looked ferociously at me and his men. No! Stay!

The whole park might be a minefield.

We eased slowly over to where the family stood, transfixed in fear. He ordered me to hold the little girl. The soldiers held the parents. Kneeling, we brought them all down to our level and held them firmly as we watched the footless, blood-spattered boy try to walk to us.

Behind us fifty or sixty Vietnamese stood back, ordered by our colonel to stay perfectly still. The boy's screams held us all in helpless pity. He was a walking detonator.

Unable to walk he limped, then hopped, then fell down half-crawling over the grass, whimpering for his mother whom the ARVN soldier now had in a tight grasp, his right hand over her mouth. He held her tight as the bloodied boy crawled along the main path towards her. My little girl had fainted in fear, or horror. I put my helmet over her face, then slid down behind her. We were spoons on a deadly oval. I had nothing else to protect her with.

The bloodied, footless boy, still holding his owl kite string in a small wooden bamboo cross, called for Mama and Papa to help him. But they were held tight by the ARVN soldiers. They could only stare helplessly at him. He lifted himself and began crawling again. An agonisingly long minute of slow dangerous progress across what might have been a minefield. One more hit and he would be finished.

Six more of us were exposed to him setting off another mine. Would it be another half-fizzer, like the one that hit him? Or a full jumpjack, rising high to take a slice of everyone? Killing some, always maiming many?

The boy finally crawled to his captured father, who grasped him tightly. We all rose slowly. His father and mother joined and carried him high to the roadside. I carried the little girl. She was tiny and fragile and as light as a feather. My helmet was still covering her face.

The colonel sat in the jeep, ordering by radio some mine specialists to clear the park. We drove fast to a military hospital and made the bloody delivery. All the way the little girl clung to me like a frightened swimmer going down, gripping me painfully, as her father, behind me, stroked her head. When I handed her to him, she gripped him just as tightly.

There were white coats and medics moving around as the boy and his mother were taken in. We returned to the jeep which started, but did not move off. I sat back right, a few feet away from the father now sitting on a small stone wall, eyeless, with the little girl still clinging to him. The radio talk stopped. The colonel ordered us to move. The driver had a wide, nervous grin on his face, of uncontrollable anguish, and sorrow.

In 1988 our minibus with its cargo of journalists drove slowly through the street dividing the park. It looked unkempt but peaceful. There were children flying kites, students lying on the grass, reading. The fence was the same, the trees were the same. The pathway was not visible, overgrown by grass. The entry to the Air Force base was now open and clear. No sandbags, no armed guards, no uniformed men.

I had kept up a murmur of running commentary to Jay, showing him where we arrived from military transport flights, where we took off from between concrete hangars for surveillance flights, where the miles of sandbag protective fences ran. But when we reached the park he had already seen the boys flying kites. All I said to him was, "That's the kite boy's park." He knew the story.

The bus seemed to me to be going unnecessarily fast. I had been used to slow and very deliberate travel down these streets. I wanted to take it all in over again. There was no time to say everything I wanted to say. There were stories in every block but just as I started on one, we would speed through to a new area. So I remained silent for the rest of the way, past the presidential palace, the park across from Media Row, the cathedral, to the Brinks/Rex Hotel, now renamed. Another familiar place, this had once been my home.

6

After only a few hours back in Vietnam I started planning my return and my search. This almost irrational confidence grew as I walked around the hotel, meeting old staff who seemed pleased to see me, and after a quiet hour in the rooftop garden looking at old Saigon. There was not a single new building on the skyline for as far as I could see, and I could see right down to Cholon. In fact without the bright lights of 1968's restaurants, bars and clubs, and almost no motor traffic, it was easier. It *was* an irrational confidence; I knew there were twenty years there somewhere, yet I felt I had just returned after a few months away. The city felt like Saigon, not Ho Chi Minh City, and I knew I could very quickly find my way around.

Even stranger, the Vietnamese staff were startled that I had not physically changed in twenty years. The photos of me in Da Nang could have been taken a month earlier. So I took up the old relationships with my friends and the city itself, treating the war, the invasion and the revolution as a good excuse for not coming back sooner. For my unfinished job.

We booked into the Rex Hotel, and the room keys were being handed around. I asked if we could take 421, a room I had worked in and lived out of for quite a spell back in one April during the war. Jay was sceptical about my claims that nothing much would have changed, so we had a little bet. He would take the key and see the room and come back while I did all the form-filling. He returned, and I began describing it.

"First of all, it has a massive key. I've seen that, so that part doesn't count. You got to the room by walking down the north wing, overlooking some old tin-roofed buildings. Ahead and above you are the huge water-coolers. You entered by opening French louvred cream-painted doors with curled brass handles. It has a very high ceiling from which a fan was suspended. Two single beds with T-bar wooden frames for mosquito nets. There is a small annexe, well lit, with hard divan chairs, which I used as my workroom. The toilet room has a massive old high-sided bath with big brass taps protruding into it. The vitreous china wash basin has similar taps and an unforgiving spotted mirror.

"There are at least two tables, one high, one low. One will have a vase of flowers on it, the high one will have writing paper and a pen on a pad. There will be at least two Thermos flasks, one with tea, the other with cool, clean drinking water. The floor is tiled, smooth and cool."

Jay was not giving anything away. "Go on." he said.

I couldn't think of anything else.

"You missed the portable fridge," he said.

"I had no refrigerator in those days."

"OK. You win. That is exactly, precisely, definitely, positively it. And you've got the bed nearest the door and the morning light."

He said I probably felt cool about knowing all that. He was in a happier mood. All those stories he had asked me to tell him again and again when he was eleven and twelve and fourteen and sixteen started to fall into place, the details were now realities. The kite boy story had been sad; perhaps the brighter stories would keep the balance.

He asked how I came to be staying in the hotel. I told him I had come for a meal at the officers' club at the Rex, and stayed on, too tired to move.

During that April, all those years ago, I had been on more missions than was wise. In one spell I had been on ten missions in eleven days, from the "Iron Triangle" near the Cambodian border, in the Achau valley, on hills with just numbers out of Da Nang, and had finished by getting a call to go to Cam Ranh Bay where my request to go on fighter-bombing missions in Phantom jets had come through. I was very fit; it was becoming difficult to put the pictures together but I knew for certain that a big attack was coming soon and I wanted to see as many battle areas as possible to try piecing it together.

For the Phantom missions a series of tests were involved, for the journalist flying would have to be the navigator, there being only two seats. I parachuted, I was swung on simulators for G-tests, I was sworn to secrecy for two years, I was to carry a gun, a packet that contained a list of Vietnamese language questions I was to ask if I baled out and made it safely, and a featherweight map in exquisite detail, showing not only the northern part of southern Vietnam and western Cambodia, but all the Demilitarised Zone and well into the south of North Vietnam. I was tested in the G-suits, given the clearest instructions on ejecting. It was a professionalism in briefing that left anything else I had previously encountered looking a distant second best. I hardly spoke a word during all these tests.

A single stray bullet into a wing of a Phantom flying at the speed of sound would start a tear that would in seconds pull out into a long hole and our projectile would start to break up. We had seconds to eject. I stayed in the camp several days before everything was right.

The role of the secrecy clause soon became evident. We were to go over the much abused DMZ and even into North Vietnam where massive flows of arms and men were heading south. My hut was on the edge of the splendid long airfield, not far from the hangars. A simple cot in an unadorned hut, with one window.

The engines started up before dawn. I had slept from ten the night before and felt myself to be well prepared as I looked out on the strip. All I could see was flame from the jets warming up. It was an eerie yet exciting sight, like grounded comets immobile on an airstrip. Long spiralling jets of flame coming from sunheads.

On our mission that morning there were just four of those Phantoms which would form a team. Air Commander Major Ken Dean was taking me on board in place of regular navigator Flight Lieutenant Joe Santos. That was according to the white stencilled names just forward of the pilot's seat.

Ken I knew as a professional. His squadron's other pilots spoke highly of him. He had flown in Korea. He was approaching "double-ace" level. An ace had 100 missions. He and all his pilots were in top condition. The rule was that nothing but the mission in hand would be discussed on air. The targets were gone over and over again.

We howled away down the long Cam Ranh Bay strip. Under each wing there were two 500-pound (227-kilogram) dark-grey, finned bombs. Forming an upside-down triangle was a bright silver napalm canister. Two such triangles of explosives were under each wing of the three Phantoms.

When they got out over open sea they dropped the napalm.

They would not use napalm. (The South China Sea has today on its sea bed hundreds of canisters of napalm, eroding away. The Soviets have oil wells out there now.) Nothing was said. It was their code.

With that weight gone, we could go further or faster. It was a bleak, overcast day. Low cloud cover made the missions almost impossible. We stayed high. The radio crackled in code. The arms and men were still flowing, it would be better if we stayed high. We were to interrupt that river of arms to the south.

We stayed there for a long time. Fuel was running short, but that was not their problem. Just the cloud.

We swung back a bit and into my view came what seemed an immobile Boeing freighter, not unlike a fat 707. We braked back and sat underneath this plane which had lowered from its belly a long straight pipe at 45 degrees from its body.

It was my job to talk simple directions into my helmet microphone: left, down, right, up. None of this starboard and aft nonsense. The long pipe closed into the female grip of our fuel opening, and the refuelling began. After suckling for four or five minutes, the pipe withdrew and we snapped shut our fuel cap.

We continued the mission, but nothing more happened. We returned to base, defeated by cloud.

The next morning, we took off again. This was Ken Dean's 199th mission. Again, the silver canisters dropped harmlessly into the sea. Again, the cloud cover stayed. And once more the mission was abandoned.

The next morning I looked out at 4 a.m. into the darkness and saw what was now familiar to me, comets burning on the tarmac. Intelligence had given a new appraisal. The old mission was intact, but there was now an adjunct to it. That is all I was told.

We flew north in the same formation. We came in from the sea, over North Vietnam. "By the way," Ken said to me, "that .45 you have. I take it you've gathered that it's for defending yourself if you come down in the north. They come with pitchforks and bamboo spears and all that. White men parachuting into North Vietnam are not well treated. Do the best you can. Save the last bullet for yourself."

He actually said this: *The last round is for you.*

I had known this, even if I had buried it, subconsciously. None of them had shown the slightest interest in sidearms. It seemed a small price to pay for being cut up and beaten, or just humiliated and put into a stinking prison and further beaten up and tortured. The choice was mine. I thought I would try surviving the beatings.

We bombed a couple of bamboo bridges. The North Vietnamese troops had withdrawn during this bombing. It would be up to them to replace the bridge — the locals would do it for them in twenty-four hours — or ford the streams.

A radio crackle came again. There was a North Vietnamese machine gun nest from which mortars were also being used. They were in the Demilitarised Zone and hitting buildings, including a small hospital just south of the DMZ. A "neutral" staff had been hit, some killed, some patients killed. The neutrals were European, Irish, other girls who had volunteered for duty in children's hospitals, only to find themselves in heavy demand for any hospitals.

We swung south. For the first time we went through the sound barrier, using rocket assists pinned to our tails, so to speak. There was a shudder, then silence, as we left our own sound behind. On the ground they would have heard the sonic booms. At about 27,000 feet we began the dive, many miles from the target. Faster and faster my instruments ticked over until we had reached twice the speed of sound. Diving, with rockets burning and gravity helping. The machine gunners' nest was just that, a former B52 bombhole perhaps, with a dozen men busily firing and mortaring into this little town.

They didn't hear us coming. Had they looked up, they would have seen just a black speck coming towards them. They didn't look up — we had left our sound far behind.

My job was finished for the moment. I had a few seconds to watch. To aim was to point the Phantom; it was nearly as simple as that. We dived in a straight line from on high straight towards them. Ken released the 500-pounders, ticking on *Explode*! as they went down, just a few feet below us travelling at the same speed.

We gently lifted from them and they continued on their way towards the men blasting the hospital. We pulled away in a stomach-lowering climb at four or five gravity pulls and swung around just as the bombs hit. Bits and pieces flew out. There was a cloud of dust and smoke.

We circled again. Nothing was left of them.

We had four bombs left. We left for the next target. The ground reports reached us in another radio crackle. ". . . Thank you all" was what I heard. We dropped another couple of bombs on another couple of bamboo bridges, then returned home to Cam Ranh.

The others had landed safely ahead of us. When we pulled in, the two other crews were waiting for us, headed by a photographer I had never seen before.

All were awaiting Flight Commander Ken Dean on return from his 200th mission. The other two crews, four men, were proud to be there: it had been their 100th mission. They held aces from a card deck in their hands, but the boss, Ken, had no need to hold a card. If he had done he would have held two aces.

Like the fifth husband of a movie star, I got flow-on fame. I had navigated for three missions only, yet the photos would show me in there with them. I went back to my hut and wrote and wrote.

I felt decidedly sad in leaving them. At dinner with them I didn't ask about the napalm. I never heard one of them once call the Vietnamese "gooks" or "slopeheads". They were worried about the war, they were the men who would not tolerate napalm. They also would not tolerate the killing of innocents in hospitals.

Two weeks later I was to drive into an ambush at ground level. The first cabled condolences for the dead and congratulations for my escape came from the *Washington Post*, and the 559th Tactical Fighter Squadron. They had given me, on departure, a small wooden-backed plaque with several metal badges on it. They sent on a cigarette lighter with their insignia, to Hawaii.

I flew on to Nha Trang. The township is on the east coast of South Vietnam, a brief helicopter ride north from Cam Ranh Bay. I came to Nha Trang on a Caribou transport plane a few days after my Cam Ranh Bay Phantom missions, from Kontum, in the central highlands, with a lawyer, David Sharp, who had been writing for the *Bangkok Post*.

As we were landing in Nha Trang, the Viet Cong opened up with a mortar barrage, scoring a direct hit on a big fat oil storage tanker just off the end of the airstrip. Then they opened up with automatic fire. We began sprinting as the next mortars landed closer to the Caribou, lighting the hundred yards to the terminal with their blasts.

It was said I made it in ten seconds flat, which meant the sergeant from Nebraska made the distance in nine point five, wearing heavy boots and carrying a tape recorder he told us he wanted fixed for his lonely nights back in Kontum.

The planeload of us lay on the concrete floor of a little hut that served as the terminal, hands over our heads, while the attack continued. In the middle of the blasting attack a telephone just above me on a wall began ringing. It was one of those old-fashioned rings like telephone girls would make by turning a handle quickly. Someone was turning this handle long and hard.

We were still under attack. David grinned at the incongruity of it:

"It's probably for you," he said. I was going to carry the joke further and answer, "Palmos here" after I reached up and brought the phone to concrete level, but I thought, one joke in the circumstances was enough.

"Yes," I answered quietly.

"Press camp here. You got an Aussie Frank Palmos down there? Journalist?" Sharp heard all this and could hardly control himself. The mortars were falling and there was automatic fire and we had seen several new young soldiers who were frightened. But in emergencies often the most frivolous of comments seem hilarious, heightened by the surrealism of the moment.

"Say, what's all that noise down there?" the voice shouted.

"Incoming mortar shells exploding," I said.

"*Whaaaat?*" Between gunfire his voice could easily be heard. He had an audience of perhaps twenty, prostrated on concrete. Gradually even the more frightened of them were looking over and seeing the irony of this crazy call:

I said, "Can't you see the black smoke from the bonfire?"

The camp was a couple of miles away but the oil storage tank fire was big. The billowing black smoke was killing a pleasant Spring evening's air.

"Christ. My slanteyes told me it was the Chinese setting off fireworks," he said, "and I've just sent two men down there to get you."

A few minutes passed. The incoming had stopped. The VC had hit and run. The jeep men arrived and began to pick up our bags and move on. A truck was coming for the others who seemed quite content to stay on the concrete floor. The oil fire was glowing fiercely, throwing an eerie glow into the room.

The jeep men were moving quickly because they wanted to get on the road before the Vietnamese came out again after the attack. But we had only gone a couple of kilometres when the streams of motorcyles and old Citroëns came onto the roads, so we were forced to dawdle along for the last miles to the camp. The population sensed the attacks would not continue.

The soldier not driving kept mumbling to his friend about "Yella". A minute after we arrived and were signing in the desk man shouted to no one in particular: "Come on, yella!" We signed in by torchlight.

"We been expecting you from Cam Ranh. They told us about you. First Aussie here for months. Last one we had drank twenty cans in one night. Didn't he?" he asked the last question into a darkened room. There was a murmur of confirmation and perhaps some approval for this beer-drinking feat.

"Could do with a can myself," said Dave.

"Bar's open."

A gloom had settled over the large room. For the first time I saw some small lights were burning. The windows had been blacked out. We at first thought the men were worried about a further attack. But Dave discovered they were waiting for the yellow caution light to come on.

"Lousy VC. Put in a few stinking mortars, now we got no movie," said the jeep driver.

His pessimism was misplaced. A few minutes later there was a low growl from a siren, a camp guard swung the door open and looked in: "Yellow alert men. Remember that is CAUTION at all times. Thank you and goodnight."

And on came the movie.

John Wayne was shooting Mexicans. Another war.

7

On the first morning of the Conference I met James Pringle at a makeshift post office where we were both buying New Vietnam stamps. He had just returned from a walk to his old office in what was the Media Alley, facing a park onto which the former presidential palace also faced.

He said he stood looking into the old office, which still had the same doors with a draw-to steel outer door. A dog was out front. A man either emerged or came by who in his words, was "quite hostile" towards him. He had seen enough. By that time we had both been for short tours of old Saigon, the new Ho Chi Minh City.

I described it in my first articles filed as a "freeze frame", a city that had hardly changed in twenty years. The sandbags and the barbed wire had been removed, the buildings needed paint and maintenance, the absence of weapons of any sort was welcome — even the police carried only traffic-directing batons — but it was a city almost untouched since 1968. Apart from a very small number of ancient Russian black sedans, and five or six new Lada Niva 4WD vehicles, we could have been in a time warp.

At the conference the fellow-travellers were lost. These sycophants asked questions such as: "Leader, what is your view on Imperialist Encirclement?" and "Please summarise the Progress of Progressive Peoples." These brought chilly, indifferent responses. The tone of the conference became clear: the leaders of New Vietnam were there to field tough questions from independent journalists and to get their new policies across. Open Door.

Then the awaited questions came, from David Storey of Reuters in Bangkok, Amando Doronila of the *Manila Chronicle*, Clayton Jones of the *Christian Science Monitor*, Keith Richburg *Washington Post,* Rosnah Majia, *Utasan Malaysia*, Barbara

Crossette of the *New York Times* and Kawanishi Kazuo of the *Mainichi Shimbun.* If this was to be a serious press conference, their questions had to be answered.

The round table conference took on a new look on Day Two when Vietnam's Foreign Minister Nguyen Co Thach delivered his speech, which included the usual claims that the West was to be blamed for the present state of poverty and backwardness in Asia, legacies of colonial rule, a nominal attack on the United States, a call for normalisation of relations between China and Vietnam — who in 1979 fought a limited war on the China-Vietnam border. He then said Vietnam was ready to forget all the past problems to get moving again. He avoided the questions best answered by the new leader. But the new directions, after having giving explanations for the failure of the system, were now to be explained.

Day Three saw the arrival of the new leader, Nguyen Van Linh. For those around the press table who had never been to Vietnam, the interpreters helped with pronunciations: the name "Nguyen" is pronounced "Win", in English. The main speaker, the secretary-general of the Communist Party of Vietnam (CPV) was first of all not a "secretary" as Westerners understood the word, a person who takes dictation for a boss, but in fact the leader, president, or prime minister of Vietnam. His name, Nugyen Van Linh, was pronounced "Win Van Ling". This was the man we had all been waiting for.

When this newly elected liberal leader came to power in 1987, he promised the nation that he and his team would bring Vietnam into the modern world, that they would open the nation to international view. The past sacrifices were never to be forgotten, but the needs of the now vastly more populous nation of sixty million people — twice that of the thirty million in Vietnam at the turning point of the war, the Tet Offensives of 1968 — must now be attended to. He spoke openly of Vietnam's economic failures, the need for change, the need for international economic joint ventures, and gave his word that New Vietnam would honour its promises and become a part of the international community and take its chances in open competition. Today, he reiterated those themes.

After the preamble Nguyen Vanh Linh invited joint ventures in New Vietnam, asking other nations to recognise Vietnam's acknowledgment of international interdependency, ensuring capital profits for investors, welcoming economic co-operation between Western countries and Vietnam.

The message was clear. Vietnam was standing by an open door, prepared to do business with the world, and preparing its own people for the experience.

The press conference was not easy for Linh. He was confronted by skilled and knowledgeable journalists who asked how Vietnam would cope in an Asia with China, Taiwan, South Korea, Malaysia, India, Singapore, Indonesia already competing for markets. Japan had already won in Western markets. "We will take our chances," he said. "It is the only way."

And so the press conference continued. There was an interruption for an historic interview. I had asked the organisers to bring to a secondary press conference the leaders of the Tet Offensive attack on the US embassy on 31 January 1968. A suicide squad had attacked and occupied the embassy for some hours, a headline-winning move that embarrassed the US and Allied forces.

I had made the request as a test of the New Vietnam claims that they would answer any questions. They came through. The press conference was a success, with much new information coming to light. In 1968, the number of raiders had been put as high as one hundred, but the spokesman, a military historian who helped plan the commando raid, said that only nineteen men took part, eighteen and one driver. Only one of the eighteen who went in and held the US embassy for several hours survived the day, apart from the driver.

The speaker was General Nguyen Tuot. He was the first Viet Cong general I had met (and coincidentally the man who would help me from that day through 1988 and into 1989). It was his first meeting with the free press and he smoked nervously as he told the story of the raid, meticulous in his detail. It was this attention to fine detail that saved us so many weeks of going down wrong trails, and by the end of my personal search we were to become firm friends.

My opportunity came during question time when Nguyen Vanh Linh told a story about his own family during Tet. He and his wife and children had lived in their favourite family cottage not far from Cholon. Midway through the Battle for Saigon he was ordered by the party to move to Hanoi.

He was then relatively junior but slowly making his way up.

They had a special task for him there. But his wife refused to go; the cottage was dear to her. Normally he gave way on these decisions to his wife, but this time he was firm, and reluctantly they moved. The next night the cottage was obliterated in a bombing raid, along with many others. They had all escaped by a narrow margin of time. That was his personal story.

I asked whether I could return to Vietnam on "another personal story" that required research and then approval for a film crew. He knew the story I had to follow up was the ambush of the Western journalists. He could not help with any information about the man, but said he would guarantee visas for me and my film crew.

He did better than that. Before the assembled international press he said, "You shall make your film. I give my personal guarantee."

As the conference progressed I took time out to re-acquaint myself with the streets and life around the old Saigon market. It was something I would do again and again with Viet, my contract cyclo driver, throughout 1988 and 1989, perhaps a form of proof that now everything was safe. On my first visit for twenty years I stood outside a small restaurant where I had been when finally the market was declared too dangerous for any Westerner.

US dollars and the US military notes were not widely used on my first trip to Vietnam in 1965, nor was there much barter trading of quality military clothing for local produce. I used the piastres, and imitated my Indonesian pasar bargaining habits which covered, to my pleasant surprise, more than half of the game. I was able to walk around freely and get some excellent fruit. Indeed, the whole market was very well organised: sectors for vegetables, fruit, flowers, meat, fish, fuels like charcoal and spirits for lamps, artwork, and so on.

By 1968, however, the market place had become less attractive. Surrounding the entire, very large block of the central Saigon market were sidewalk stalls selling US military clothing, C-rations, aid items marked "not for sale" or "a gift from the US people." In 1967 in both the main and street markets the Viet Cong had dropped grenades into shopping baskets carried by people close to any uniformed soldiers, killing and maiming scores of them. Only the very foolish ventured back, and they were not welcome for obvious reasons.

8

After I had been guaranteed visas for my film crew, I had several days to plan and do further work from my handy former office at the Rex. Furthermore, the earlier offer of help had been confirmed. With terrific efficiency, the national archives were opened on a public holiday for me, and the director of the archives, Huynh Ngoc Thu, provided me with much of the normally banned material I would need to get started.

The Saigon papers of 1968 brought out to me for translation by Madame Thu served to remind me of the atmosphere of those times. Each paper carried seven or eight graphically illustrated cinema advertisements, and I recalled that the Vietnamese would pack out cinemas showing war movies of a particularly gruesome type. Stories of Asian warriors using 'Killer Blade 447' (the mayhem one hero was inflicting on the populace, his 447th victim being his last). Simple stories they were — of bone-crushing, blood-letting, limb-slicing, beheading, torture, spiking, stabbing, murder by stealth and double-crossing.

The cinemas in those days had the whole range of John Wayne movies and the same John Wayne Mexican-American epic I had seen in the Nha Trang club started up there some days later. It seemed strange that they were showing war movies, even if they were set in the nineteenth century, when there was a much bigger conflict going on outside.

More positively, access to these archives enabled me to begin researching confidently. I discovered a phoney interview in the *Saigon Post* quoting a "Reuters man" saying he had been to the ambush site on road 95, which was obvious disinformation to get the Viet Cong off the hook. Other good material began to come to light, including new material from the South Vietnamese army records.

To keep the momentum, I decided to visit the ambush site. Madame Thu knew the area well and gave me detailed notes on a map, marking the main roads in and indicating the old 1968 boundaries. Many street names had changed. She gave strict directions to a group of four cyclos, mine, one for my son Jay, and two others for two US university students. These two students had ignored suggestions amounting to official warnings not to go to Vietnam and had come as part of a group of ten or twelve led by their lecturer, a Vietnam veteran.

Jay had struck up a friendship with them, a boy and a girl of twenty-one or so, and told them a little about my strange search for a killer. They were keen to come. As far as I was concerned, the more the better.

We rode three kilometres to Minh Phung circle, which I knew well. From then on it was a series of ups and downs through streets with changed names and numbers, looking for the ambush site. Every moment was fun for them. The cyclo drivers liked the job. Two of them were former South Vietnamese Army soldiers, though neither of them had fought in the Cholon area.

When we got into Road 46 and Road 48 I had difficulty collecting my thoughts. The streets were full of people, yet the ambush site had been emptied of them ten or fifteen minutes before we drove in. Recognition was difficult.

The heat was starting to get to me. That was unusual.

I asked to go up and down one street several times to get a look at the angles, then on a whim asked to take a small cross lane into the next street Road 46. And I found it. A forty-five degree corner, the ambush site, and perhaps one thousand people in the strip from where the ambush had taken place to where I joined the refugees.

My head was buzzing. The day was very hot, the street noises overbearingly loud. From the moment we arrived in four cyclos and I stepped out to take photographs of the corner I had run around, and the site itself, we were besieged by scores of curious people.

The three kids stayed in their cyclos while I walked. They were having a great time. Jay came out once to help me with a photograph, but returned to where everyone around the three cyclos was testing simple English greetings. We had not been mistaken for Soviets, which had made it easier for them, but the crowd was astonished to find three young Americans in their midst.

I walked to the ambush site, and attempted to stay calm while taking photographs. The focus didn't seem to work. Holding the camera still was difficult. I started to see heat haze where there was none. I started to hear threats in everyday talk on the streets. I tried to calm myself by raising the camera and taking another shot or two, but I began to feel dizzy.

The sounds made by a teenager hammering the rim of a bicycle wheel became rifle shots. The shouts that came from a vegetable stall as people bargained loudly I heard as threats. After only three minutes I felt endangered, and could not stand being there any longer. I quickly walked through the busy crowd gathered around the other three and asked to go back to Minh Phung. Fast. I asked Jay and the two others to follow me.

Viet, my cyclo driver, was on his first long drive for me. He set off and we got fifty or sixty metres up the road when he slowed. We looked around to see the others still there talking peacefully to a large and growing crowd. I kept thinking that if a fanatic began firing, they wouldn't have a chance. We waited, moving slowly along, until we saw the other cyclos pulling out to follow in the distance.

Viet pulled in on the main road of Minh Phung and we sat down in a small streetside stall and took a cold drink.

I'd been in trouble. Now, back on the wide boulevard, I felt comfortable. It had been my first time into the backblocks in twenty years. Very slowly the other three came up the narrow streets and into the main road from the ambush areas. They were laughing, all of them, the three cyclo drivers and the three Americans. They all joined us in a cold drink of a local lemonade.

They stayed together as Viet and I went ahead, leading the way to the heart of Saigon, to the Rex. They were talking about what a great day it had been. As I overheard them talking about the trip, I realised they had not seen or heard anything threatening. For them, it had been just a trip into a little bit of history; for me, an episode of imagined danger.

I decided I needed a beer in the safety of the hotel. I would do some more homework to feel better about paying my way on this extraordinary visit. While Jay joined the American students' group heading for a new little restaurant, I took a handful of old pages I had written in 1968 and went to the roof bar. Pen in hand, pretending I was doing serious work, I drank the beer and began to read.

They were the wrong notes for the occasion. I should have been out and about like the students were, looking at New Vietnam instead of reading this old material. But I was stuck in the war years, familiar territory that seemed so much more real to me.

The first pages I turned over were an awful recall of a firefight where I had worn desert boots which I later threw away. It read:

They were killed in the morning, at 9.30 a.m.. But what were we going to do about these eighty bodies in the graveyard? Grinning recent death at their fathers six feet under. And what was I going to do about my only pair of soft-soled boots? The boots were drenched through with warm blood and other little things that oozed from bodies. Worm things that slid out from long, jagged holes in their sides. And pieces of bone from their skulls that lay smashed on their bodies. Sometimes not quite attached to their bodies. I suppose I could lift my feet higher. The troops with me had boots and just crashed through the garbage of skin and bones and blood that lay before them in the graveyard. Some of them looked like sixteen-year-old boys. The mess in my boots was starting to gel.

That was all these pages said. I had forgotten the fight. Guerilla war was strange like that. There were at least three occasions when I saw major firefights in cemeteries. Another on a racecourse. A lot of small actions took place in market gardens just north of the town. Odd places.

The next page I recalled well. It had been written in Saigon after the official press briefings called the '5 o'clock Follies'. It was there the assembled correspondents in Saigon were given a daily briefing on the events of the war. It was originally called a daily briefing on the progress of the war. The word "progress" was dropped by late 1967.

I was rarely in Saigon for more than a week at a time so I attended only twenty or thirty of these briefings, called Juspau briefings. The first one I went to taught me that "ten clicks" meant ten kilometres. Public relations men or real soldiers would give us the review of the day. The meeting had been devised to stop the avalanche of demands for answers from the US command in Vietnam, abbreviated to MACV (US Military Command Vietnam). To have us all attend a nightly briefing was very sensible.

When Neil Sheehan came to Jakarta briefly in 1965, switching from the UPI newsagency to the *New York Times*, he told me about briefings, and the words used to disguise reality. By 1968 there were several lists of these strange words in existence. After several "Follies" I wrote a page with the help of some other correspondents entitled, "What the Major really meant to say." It read, with the clue being what was said on the left, and what was really meant on the right, like this:

Five clicks: five kilometres
They levelled their ordnance on them: They aimed at them
There was vertical envelopment of the area: An attack by helicopter gunships
Enemy camp base in an inhabited area: A village
Enemy command post: A pagoda or hospital accidentally bombed
Jungle munitions factory: The local blacksmith's shop
Rounds impacted in an inhabited area: Village shelled by mistake
Columns of enemy soldiers and porters: Some armed, some unarmed people
Vicious terrorist aggression: a counter-attack
Severe disruption to civilian life: Halting supplies to downtown bars
Enemy troop concentrations: Two or more Viet Cong suspects
Estimated number of enemy killed: An unnatural upward progression of numbers
Putting a hurt on them: Killing or wounding the enemy
South Vietnam Army patrol missions: Search and Avoid missions
Pacification: Making friends with the fucking people
A Cong: Almost any Vietnamese at a great distance
Enemy: Anyone killed in an attack
Enemy in disguise: Any civilians killed in an attack
Response to impact: Twisted or mangled bodies
Severe response to impact: Just bits and pieces of bodies left
Acute environmental reaction: Shell shock

There were others I noted or picked up from news sheets. The defoliation units had a big sign exactly like those signs in national forests saying ONLY YOU CAN PREVENT FOREST FIRES. This one said: ONLY WE CAN PREVENT FORESTS. And Vietnamese civilisation was described as, "the handed-down ability to carry two baskets of rice with one stick, and lift one grain of rice with two sticks."

That night I had the worst nightmare in some months. It was the same death-rattle growing in volume. I was awakened by Jay holding me firmly and speaking softly to me. "Dad, Dad, wake up. It's all right, it's just another nightmare."

A lot seemed to be happening in this January week of 1988, in the Rex Hotel. But it was a lot of 1968, and not much of 1988. I was physically immobile, with just one visit to the ambush site and a few walks down the renamed Tu Do street and Le Loi Boulevard. Yet I felt I had travelled so many years in those days.

The idea of the search became ridiculous. Futile. My thoughts turned to the plan that Jay and I would go to Cambodia. We would see it through different eyes. For me it would be the last time, for him a chance to see a devastated country close up, perhaps visit the Genocide Museum, the high school converted by Pol Pot into a vast torture block. He could go to college knowing a little about Vietnam.

His mother had told him I would have nightmares. She should know. She had the backlash of so many of them in our broken nights. Sarah Lawrence College couldn't have prepared her for that.

We travelled overland by bus through the devastated fields of Cambodia, across the majestic Mekong River. As we waited, Jay had gone into market places and spoken the best he could to the people, and the Vietnamese soldiers leaving. He had sat for hours with the correspondent of my old newspaper, the *Washington Post*, Keith Richbold, based in Manila, talking college courses in the US.

For me, the land had lost its verve and its productive greenery. We visited the Genocide Museum. There were three or four thousand photographs of people staring at us, their expressions telling us they knew they were soon to be tortured to death. No one came out alive from Pol Pot's prisons. They came out as bodies: burned, drowned, hanged, electrocuted, or beaten or starved to death. The drowning rooms, the electrocution rooms, the hanging places, the photos of men and women and children in progressive stages of death, were all there for us to see.

Who was this photographer? Who was this man who ordered photographs taken for some macabre record of such brutality? I hoped he was dead. More likely he was up on the Thailand border being sheltered by Thailand and fed and armed by China.

Jay was puzzled by this idiocy. I told him not to worry. I can't understand it either, although I know how it comes about — international politics. We walked out through the preserved high school killing grounds. The barbed wire was still in place, the hanging poles still in place. The torture chambers and the pictures of the dead in place.

We went to an evening supper and listened to some political speeches about the new stability in Cambodia. We stayed in the royal guest house, another place of bad memories for me from earlier years. Yet I slept soundly. On this occasion at least, Jay had no need to help me through the night.

We flew to Angkor Wat, and saw the monuments earlier kings built to their religion and to themselves, using slave labour.

Jay walked and climbed in awe over this great monument, and talked with Indian architects who were restoring it for the UN, and Heritage bodies. We could not drive back. Pol Pot's assassins were still hiding along a certain road, and killing someone every night. We would have been a prime target, twenty foreigners in a bus. We took a plane out, high over them. The plane was flown by Russian fighter pilots, who took it low and swung it hard. Jay was thrilled by the turns and the low flying, but I certainly wasn't interested. I was looking forward to a quiet flight home, to Ho Chi Minh City that is.

We got home safely. Not a care in the world, it seemed, after those early minutes of fighter-pilot manoeuvres. Then a minibus, in the dark, back to the Rex. Back past the kite boy's park, through darkened streets. The normal streams of bicycles had at this hour dried up. We saw just the push-carts of a few soup sellers, their wagons lit by small kerosene lamps. This time I expected to comfort Jay through some nightmare, but he slept soundly.

I was awake by six in the morning and began writing again. As the day lightened I decided to continue my search. But I had done as much as I could this time. I would see the town, begin a news feature for the *West Australian* and take it easy. Lots of those delicious Vietnamese soups, and some tourist shopping with the little money I had left.

Such was the start to the search. It would not be a simple matter. I had no idea how I would fund it all, I just had a conviction that it could be done. It would take a long time. But from then on, having decided, it would be no more than some manageable hardship. Nothing new, or so I thought.

9

On Monday, 17 October 1988, I arrived in Hanoi for the first time. During the trip, I had sat alongside Denis Farrell from the Australian Bureau of Statistics, in Hanoi for the second time as part of a rolling team to help Vietnam carry out a census. His estimate of Vietnam's population today — between sixty-five and seventy-five million — seemed to me like the odds against bringing my search to a successful conclusion. After all the deaths, turmoil and movement of people that Vietnam had experienced in its recent history, tracing a man who killed four journalists in an ambush in Cholon, the Chinese quarter of Saigon, on the morning of Sunday 5 May 1968, looked impossible.

I was last off the Thai flight 682 at Hanoi, an airport in such sad shape that it is hard to believe it served the north so well during the war. Immigration officials in dark confessional-like boxes slowly processed the passports. My visa showed I had arrived a day earlier.

I was extremely patient. A young uniformed man carried my passport to a table where, on a long backless bench, seven identically uniformed officials sat. Then followed, without rancour, a discussion about my passport. It was something to break the boredom. My passport started at one end of the table in the hands of man wearing a uniform of low rank. "This man has been to many places," he said.

I sat only a few metres from the other end of this table, five metres from the most senior man, who would be last to see the passport and comment on it. It was clearly going to be a long process, so I produced a packet of Triple 5 cigarettes and left them with the senior man. He took one, then handed the packet down the line of seven. The yellow packet lost seven cigarettes on the way down, crossing with the passport at about man three.

As each one took a cigarette he closed the packet again, carefully lit up, puffed, then passed the packet on. Smoking made the inspection a little longer, but finally the passport got down to the senior man. He read it through, nodding his head. He looked over to me and nodded in a firm but friendly way. He then handed the passport down the line, and again it passed the cigarettes on their way back. Only seven remained in the packet, for everyone had taken one out on the way down and one for later on its way back. The chief thoughtfully offered me one of the seven. I politely refused. He took one and slipped the packet into a drawer.

My name was called and I was ushered through. A beautiful young girl with a metre-long pigtail approached as I emerged. She introduced herself as Mai Huong. "Just call me My," she said. Mai was to be my interpreter. The luggage room and customs were in chaos. A French diplomat was complaining loudly about something that had gone wrong, and half a dozen Asian businessmen were swearing in English. But my bags were right there, and chalk-marked already.

I picked them up and walked right through. Like a class in school the uniformed officials on the same long bench waved their hands in a friendly gesture as I went through. Patience, I knew from past encounters, worked best in this society, and today it had worked again. I was the last off the plane and the first through Customs.

Bomb scars were still to be seen around Hanoi, though nothing overshadowed the essential beauty of the countryside. From the airport to Hanoi is a very long drive, about forty kilometres directly, but fifty or more with the usual detours. The town was very much worse for wear. It must have been lovely in past times when there was tranquillity and order, and it was possible to appreciate the graceful architecture. Peace, money, and a system that can ensure these are fundamental to creating a civilised environment, but none of them is available at this stage in Vietnam's history. Despite courageous attempts to beautify the houses by covering their facades and roofs with green creepers and other shrubs, they still look run down.

At the hotel I stepped into my room and saw it with Western eyes. French plumbing from 1900. Brass fittings stamped "Lyon Soeurs 1887". Poor electric power, 40-watt light bulbs, a mess of plugs and outlets. A floor of linoleum that had been cheap even in 1930. A bed of natural fibres that was as hard as it was outdated in the West.

I unloaded my gear onto the second bed, swept the mosquito net into place over my bed and took a look at it as Asian eyes might see it. A secluded place of great peace and comfort, something only the very privileged could have. I had water where they had to go to the well. I had power when they had none, or had it closed down after 10 p.m. I had a mosquito net where they had coils smoking through the night and I had a room to myself where their coil-smoke had to do for five or six bodies. I had clean sheets and a blanket where they had ten-year-old covers. I had an aspirin for the worst of my sickness whereas they had a balm for most ailments and nothing at all for the pains and hunger and poor nourishment.

I had money to walk the street and sit on my haunches and eat a fine soup where the soup makers had sat for hours waiting for a little money to come in, protected neither from the cold nor the rigours of the long walks home. I had strong leather boots and warm clothing where they had little but a thin jacket over their summer clothing. I had only to walk into a dimly-lit corridor to ask for new, hot tea and the semi-sleeping staff sitting on hard wooden stoods, head down on stone benches, would respond.

Who and what was I doing this for? For me? Some lingering quest? Some personal story? — War Writer Finds Viet Cong Who Shot friends? And if I *were* to find the man, would I find myself capable, or incapable, of vengeance? But what about all those friends killed in the war, didn't I owe them something? Or was it just to be a holiday from humdrum gardening and bringing up children? A tour of newsworthy North Vietnam, and some slumming in yet another failed Communist country? To work out my little mental devils, then return forever and be able never again to bother with Vietnam?

Lying on my bed, I began to feel ambivalent and confused. As a diversion, I turned to thinking instead of the possibility of establishing a news agency bureau in Ho Chi Minh City; maybe bringing in two young people from the US or Australia and training them. I mulled over this plan until at last I felt that I might get some sleep.

The Press Centre in Hanoi, which holds a team of trouble-shooting worldly-beyond-their-years information officers, was my first stopping point, as it is for most visiting journalists. Here, the first question, which every journalist except me answered to their satisfaction was: "Whom do you wish to see? Can you provide a list for us? I responded with: "I don't know exactly whom I wish to see. I know only what information I need." This had the effect of causing understandable puzzlement. As a correspondent I had always mapped out a clear list of interviewees, and left space for new, unfolding or unexpected stories to break.

I was here with four weeks to spend on a program that I hadn't defined for them. I had deliberately not attempted to do this sort of formal preparation. What I really needed to get hold of were names. But to simplify matters I sat down and typed a list of institutions to visit, identical to one I had suplied to the Foreign Office several weeks earlier. Typing it now seemed to make it more acceptable — National Archives, National Museum, Vietnam Newsagency, Vietnam Journalists' Association, Military History Headquarters.

That was fine. We would begin with the Military History Division, they said. There was one question I would not put on any but a mental agenda: How many of the Vietnamese working for the Western newsagencies as backup for TV crews were agents? There was at least one, who I had suspected for many years, but then he might have told lies simply to avoid pressure. Many of them made the transition a little bit too easily, escaping the sort of retribution one might normally expect, when the Liberation forces entered Saigon in April, 1975. After thundering about the Reds for ten years, they seemed to turn to writing about the glorious fatherland's victory with great alacrity.

Before the official interviews, I had an informal talk at the Press Centre with Foreign Press Service director Nguyen Cong Quang. "If you find this man, your name will be inscribed forever in the Vietnamese society," he said. It was just one of the more appealing votes of confidence he gave me. When he asked me whether I would make a film if the man was not found, I replied that I would. With a feature film we could always make up the ending. But with a documentary, the audience would be bound to be disappointed if it was not revealed who the man was.

He told me of other projects he had known about: "But nothing like this. This one has the best story of all". Later that day, dinner was suggested. Denis Farrell and Keith Chapman, UN Food and Agricultural Organisation (FAO) agronomist who worked out of Bangkok, invited me along to a restaurant called the 202. There we were served a delicious meal of stir-fried vegetables, stuffed river crabs, and small plates of hot and cold delicacies and sauces. Keith spoke of the potential of Vietnam: "This land is capable of feeding one hundred million people easily and then exporting some, yet I feel on some days non-thinking officials are going to stand in the way of their own people and ruin the FAO projects. On other days I am confident we will win through. When I visit the Delta I'm reminded of how wealthy the land is: it looks like every single plant has a name, individually planted . . . that's how skilled they are."

At the 202 we met a Swedish woman who sat at a table on the balcony with her pretty three-year-old daughter, awaiting her husband. Another Westerner told me the husband worked in the Swedish paper factory, that already had the stamp of disaster ringing through its plant.

"They're not really experienced in giving aid," he said. "But a few of them get to escape from that grey place." He didn't like Swedes or Sweden. He was from Canada, but rarely lived there. His job was to travel the world and advise on engineering-related aid projects.

A phalanx of Australian workers arrived. They were here to do maintenance work on, or to renovate, some parts of the embassy. They were accompanied by a pained-faced lady from the embassy who clearly saw another long evening of duty ahead of her. And she was right. The men unloaded from a cooler thirty or forty cans of Australian beer and other goodies, and each of them contributed to a six-inch high stack of Vietnam dong which they handed over, uncounted, to the restaurant owner, whose task was to tally up the millions of dong and arrange the meal for them.

The restaurant was clean, but very simple. Naively, I thought there would be a dozen like it in Hanoi, but they soon set me right. "Only three places with decent tucker," they told me: "Chacca, 202 and 69". The meal was better than I'd thought possible. As dinner progressed I put to Keith and Denis that it would be best to pretend I had not been involved in Tet but was simply doing an investigation. It would make questioning easier and give me the advantage of being able to tap the source, when needed. They agreed. There were times when each of them had had to adopt similar strategies to get a project up and running.

We rode home in cyclos through the dark streets. Rain had then begun to fall seriously. I was beset by tiredness and hoping for a peaceful sleep — to start having more idiotic nightmares at this stage would make the going very difficult.

On the next day I was called from the hotel's breakfast room to meet a young man from the Foreign Office Press Centre. He'd been assigned to me, not as an interpreter but as a form of courier, for it was easier to walk the three hundred metres from the press office to the hotel than trying telephones and having to hold on interminably. He'd been marginally briefed. All he knew was that I was looking for a Vietnamese soldier who had fought with the National Liberation Front during the Tet Offensives.

While I was being fetched he had obviously discussed this with the hotel's manager who immediately said to me; "I don't think you can find such a man down in Ho Chi Minh City today. We had many sacrifices in that Tet battle." The press officer was slightly alarmed by her frankness and quickly came in with some comforting words: "Of course we will do everything we can," he said.

He was a little worried I might have objected to this breach of protocol. On our walk to the press office I reassured him by saying that I knew press assignments were not to be discussed, but in my case, the situation was different. The more Vietnamese who knew about it, the better. I was being over-kind. I doubted if that would help me in Hanoi. (And so it was to prove, for I met few men or women who had been further south than Da Nang in 1968.)

It was in Ho Chi Minh City that I needed the gossip to spread, but that was some weeks away. Whatever help I would get in Hanoi by having the search more widely known would come from officials. I did not want it to become a matter of Being Kind to the Journalist on a Hopeless Mission, but instead aimed to create some puzzlement, a lot of curiosity, and maybe some sympathy for a search that might appeal enough for them to afford me some help. The last thing I wanted was a series of assessments that said the mission was hopeless and that the journalist should be treated tolerantly until it dawned on him how ridiculous it all was.

Reactions in the Foreign Press Centre alone took roller-coaster rides, as did my hopes. The older generation of former journalists and news assistants, those people who helped gather news, repair clandestine radios or run courier missions carrying underground newspapers from village to village, mostly claimed that, although good records were kept, none were kept on individuals.

They regarded individual searches as not very practical, being more concerned with the New Era in Vietnam. Or so they claimed. But as the events unfolded I discovered the "older generation" was another term for loyal party men, the very people who needed to be quietly removed if Vietnam were to progress. Their preoccupation with generalities and avoidance of anything particular or individual was nothing but an admission of almost total ignorance of events around them, a sure sign of indoctrination and acceptance of the "need to know" principle.

They said we had probably been ambushed by one of the various People's Defence Force units fighting at street level during Tet or the Battle for Saigon. All the postwar searching for missing comrades had been done long ago. The final ceremonies had been held, and the New Era had been heralded in. This search sounded to them like the problem searches for US troops missing in action, and the last thing they wanted was more fuss about finding bones or graves.

The reaction from the younger generation, those who would have been just born or were infants in 1968, was quite different. They knew precious little about the Tet Offensives from a personal standpoint. History books told them about the Spring Offensives (Tet) but didn't quite explain why Liberation didn't come until seven years later in 1975. They spoke in awe of many generals, colonels and heroes whose names were known now as historic military figures, and knew many of the Communist Party leaders. But the stories were told to them — as they were to me for some months — in political language. There were offensives against the enemy and there were great sacrifices, but very little detail.

This younger generation had read some poetry and some short stories from the front lines, but again, these were not couched in very personal terms. The art from the era showed a similar politicisation. The search for them offered a new insight into their own war of Liberation. They understood none of the realities of tens of thousands of missing soldiers and civilians. They knew nothing of what the older soldiers knew: ninety per cent of the missing could never be found. They had been blown to pieces in bombing raids or ground attacks.

Despite government officials telling me they would help in any way they could and then declaring the search was hopeless, I gained some encouragement. Their overall attitude was more important. I didn't mind them saying it was hopeless provided they did the best they could to answer my questions. As long as I was allowed to investigate, any mistakes in questioning would be mine.

At this point I set out on a difficult line of enquiry, but full of confidence that I would at least be able to get unit numbers and other military information — even if the path was blocked by dead and missing men.

10

Tuesday, 25 October, 1988. This morning, all the progress, the hundreds of days of research and preparation, the wonderful promises made by friends in Ho Chi Minh City and officials in Hanoi, were to be put to the test. A full morning was set aside for an interview with the Director of the Military History Institute, Lieutenant-General Hoang Phuong. This would be the first true test of the practicality of the search, as distinct from any personal or spiritual endeavour involved. I had no doubt that Secretary-General Nguyen Vahn Linh had spoken more in encouragement and in hope that my search could succeed, but he would not have had time nor the resources on hand to think about the chances of success.

For convenience we met at the Foreign Press Centre, where I was able to spread out my writing and recording equipment and where regular tea and coffee was available. Any sticky translation questions could be tackled by simply going downstairs to a translation pool and several reference books.

General Phuong made an impressive entrance. He proceeded to unpack his notebooks, briskly and without waste of undue energy, and began to speak just as directly.

"I know from Foreign Affairs and several other Cabinet level sources about your search. I admire our leaders very much and respect them for their past as well as their present activities. And several of them only last night again spoke of your search . . .

"They can ask me to help all I can. And I shall ask certain specific divisions and branches to do all they can. On that, I give my word . . .

"I will do all I can. But I will also tell you now my assessment of this search: It is hopeless."

So General Phuong stared at me with a half smile on his face.

I sat utterly cold. Cups rattled as the first round of tea was served.

It wasn't an auspicious start to the meeting, but at least he was still smiling.

I had put in hundreds of hours on research, letter writing, discussions with anyone who might be of assistance as I weighed up my chances. There was Evan Ham, for instance, a filmmaker from Brisbane who had helped me plot the interview pattern, saved me many hours of formal letter writing by paving the way for me with his own contacts in Hanoi. He had boosted my confidence by figuring that "some success would be likely".

But now, here was General Phuong telling me it was an impossible mission.

"It is impossible because of a number of things. First, of all the battles you had to choose, it was the second Tet Offensive where the losses were as great in percentage as any others, but in numbers much, much higher than usual. It was an historic battle, and our records of that battle will be as good as any other, and because it involved Saigon, perhaps a little better. But there must have been tens of thousands lost without trace in those early months of 1968.

"Well, let's cheer up. Let's hear the information and the questions. We still have to give you the help you need. Many others may disagree with my assessments. But it can't be worse than impossible," he said. The man telling me this, I felt from the background briefing, was certainly in a position to know. He had joined the Communist forces in 1945, taking part in what is called the August revolution. This was directed against the French and Allied forces wishing to re-establish French rule, at the same time as the British were paving the way for the Dutch forces to retake rule from the Japanese in Java. When the French and other colonial forces returned to their former colonies, however, they found the time bombs left by the Japanese: national freedom movements led by Western-educated intellectuals.

The Japanese had trained locals in security forces, taught limited use of weapons, and when the surrender came were often only too happy to hand over their weapons to the locals rather than to the Allies. General Phuong's life suddenly became that of a revolutionary. The French attacked. The nationalists withdrew to the provinces. The long war began.

In 1949 at Dien Bien Phu he took part in the battle that finally removed the French from Indo-Chinese soil. Not only was he an historian, he was part of national history.

"The mix of the practical and the academic is ideal," he began again from another angle, "but I have to be always on the alert not to be subjective. So I consult frequently with my colleagues and those like General Giap, who was the founder of the Vietnamese Army. He is a living volume of history, so we consult him frequently. There are others from the Dien Bien Phu days, generally around seventy years of age, with whom we consult regularly.

"Only yesterday (24 October) I returned from a northern province where some retired, aged revolutionaries live. They love the hills and prefer to live their last days in tranquillity. This seems to have sharpened their mental capacities, for their recall of even small battles has been a remarkable help to us.

"But very rarely have we to get down to such fine detail as you need. I am concerned about that. I have no doubt our complex structure of historical divisions and branches will soon locate who made certain attacks at what time of the day. But the sacrifices! So few are left."

In speaking of historical divisions, General Phuong was referring to the fact that each region of the Vietnamese Army has its own Military History Research Institute, and that within each Institute there is a Provincial History Committee. As well, each army corps bigger than a division has a History Research Committee working full time. And each branch of the armed forces, Infantry, Air Force, Artillery, Marines and so on, has its own History Committee. Furthermore, with each Division is one officer who keeps track of the historical work.

The thought that I might have to deal with so many different levels, and all that entailed, was depressing to say the least. And when I asked whether there might be an outline history or provisional history of the events of that period on which I could draw, I was told "No". Completed histories and publications were many years away.

As the interview continued I did discover something of interest — namely, discrepancies in the reports of the launch of the biggest battle in the Vietnam war, the Battle for Saigon, or Second Tet. Hanoi National Library archives staff produced for me every newspaper printed in that period, including the leading *Nhan Dan*, the Army newspaper whose editor I was about to interview. The newspaper in its editorials spoke of the battle starting on 4 May. Yet the underground correspondents of the Viet Cong in the battle reports always said the morning of 5 May was launch day.

Both were right. They were using different calendars. In the south the calendar of the previous month had only twenty-nine days. The northerners were using a calendar with thirty days in the previous month. Phuong took up the story: "This led to a lot of confusion. The second Spring Offensive details (Battle of Saigon, or Second Tet) were strictly secret. People got different orders at different times. Hue and Da Nang, for example had attacks started by the time they started in Saigon." The important point was that, by the Western calendar, the Battle of Saigon was in full swing in every part of the south of Vietnam, by midday on 5 May.

We returned to the problem of the search. Phuong felt "by reason of odds over twenty years" the man I sought was long dead. The platoon he was with would have certainly taken more than fifty per cent casualties, because that was the average casualty rate in the heart of that battle, and would have soon merged with another unit, either losing its original number and name, or losing its earlier identity because of the merger.

"So you see why I say it is an impossible mission. But do carry on. The historians in Ho Chi Minh City will help all they can. Personally, I think it is a great idea for a film. Showing people fighting each other, then becoming good friends again. I like that. I think our people would like that," he said.

The suggestion that we make a feature film of the search was raised independently by dozens of senior officials who knew only that I was doing a job of journalistic investigation. I discovered later that almost none of the battles had ever been the subject of features, but that instead there had been "theme" and propaganda films. It seemed the Vietnamese had their own nightmares to ignore.

And so ended the first important meeting on the trail. Apart from being told I was wasting my time and should consider a fictionalised account of the story, I did acquire some useful information. I was given some potentially useful names and details and told how to get the correct passes for my interpreter Mai Huong when we were in the south.

Mai Huong's fiancé was awaiting us when we emerged. He

would take Mai home on his motorcycle. I was in a reflective mood. I felt a degree of depression edging in, and decided I should try to fight it off.

I took a walk along the edge of the Lake of the Restored Sword then turned into some narrow streets. Teenagers were arriving on bicycles. The girls wore deep red lipstick and pretty showing-off dresses. Some of the boys had jeans but most had cotton trousers cut to look like modern jeans or as seen in magazines from Bangkok. I heard Abba, Madonna and the Little River Band. The kids had crowded deep into tiny cafes to escape the public gaze, but they waved frequently to me because I was Western, and they aspired to gather in a Western feeling, looks, music, fractured English, at those meetings.

The August Cinema doors were wide open and customers were flowing out after a double feature, a Rumanian spy story and something that seemed to portray Castro meeting Lenin, all dubbed in Vietnamese. It was something to do. Cuba and the Rumanians, whose people are the victims of two of the most unsuccessful social experiments in history, were passing on celluloid strips of irrelevant imagery to Vietnam, itself in the throes of an unsuccessful trial of Marxism-Leninism. The six o'clock bell had just tolled when I entered the hotel. Denis Farrell and Keith Chapman, taking one look at me and understanding that mine had not been a good day, offered dinner and drinks. I was grateful, to put it mildly.

11

Soon, no matter where I was or how successful the day had been, I was feeling that perhaps the Vietnamese assessment of my project was the correct one. My mind seemed split between Western mental habits and what I was encountering daily in Vietnam. "Hopelessness" was really an unsuitable word, my Western training would tell me. Be an opportunist. Take in what you can, see what you are allowed, absorb the information. If it looks like being a hopeless search, then make the best of it. Make some friends, sell some stories. Add the experience to the old Vietnam war years and think of it as a counterbalance.

Loss of hope was stupid, my Eastern training told me. It was a word only to be used for impatience. Had I been impatient in my first years in university in Indonesia, living in suburbs and villages, travelling slow salt boats to the outer islands, I would never have lived as an Asian. I would never have acquired the capacity to speak and read their languages, step from their life into a Western life in one evening then back again for the next day's studies. Certainly I would never have had the privilege of meeting or working with all those great men and women who had struggled to drag their once colonial nations into the new world.

Back in the hotel after another day of people telling me I was wasting my time, a Japanese correspondent literally caught me by the shoulder and took me to the bar, got me a drink and told me about his marvellous TV story: he had tracked down the source of sandalwood in north Vietnam and had filmed some villagers who had done some dance for him which had never been performed since the war. He had convinced his Tokyo bosses to send in a four-wheel-drive for the expedition and the vehicle had then been given over to the Vietnam Government on completion of the film.

Evan Ham had asked me to deliver something to this journalist a couple of days earlier, so I knew him well enough. He also lived a floor below me in the same hotel so I saw him a dozen times in the first three days. He asked about my project and listened carefully as I told him about it.

"That's no hope," he said.

He asked me if I had a big farm in "Austra-alia". I told him I had indeed had a farm only three years before but it had been destroyed by bushfires. He asked for details. He had never known anyone who owned a farm. I told him my farmhouse had been destroyed, along with five thousand trees. I had lost my house, my furniture, my trees, my flowers, my vegetable garden, my fruit trees, my water tanks, my favorite wildlife, kangaroos and wallabies and koalas, my ducks; the four or five hundred birds which lived on the farm, and the several laughing kookaburras which came to us daily were also all dead.

His English was good. Yet he could not comprehend broad acres or wooded hills except in national reserves. He was a Communist Party member of old, now resigned, but still feeling his role in life was to bring some equality to society. Suddenly he saw me as a big landowner.

"But you have your land, still. You are rich. Very rich!" he said. "Did you make your money in the Vietnam war?"

I asked what money.

"To have a fifty hectare farm, of course."

A fifty hectare farm in Japan could only belong, in his mind, to a very wealthy man. I told him I had lost the farm entirely. That I had bought the farm with my savings from ten years' work.

He was sceptical. The land would be worth many millions in his society. He was pleasantly drunk. He was friendly, but puzzled. He asked why, with my money, I had not brought in ten or fifteen thousand dollars, which would ensure success to any search, as it had for him. I told him I had little money left after that farm fire, that I had a family to bring up, and money was tight.

"Then you will not succeed," he said.

"But let's drink to the success. If no success, no matter. In Vietnam today it is very different. You will never find a soldier from 1968."

He had been there four years, in that same room in the same hotel. He had recorded on film every major speech and a dozen human stories of schools restarting, generals retiring, the Cubans building a hotel for Hanoi, birdlife on the Hanoi lakes. He spoke twenty or thirty command words of Vietnamese. He hated the language. He wanted to speak more English.

He was an industrious dullard. He hated the successful Japanese businessmen who would come in and fix deals and remove themselves, not because they were businessmen, but because they could remove themselves, when he could not. He regarded the Vietnamese as Things to be Filmed. He would begin every new exchange with me by saying: "No hope on this one." I found a polite way to remove myself and went upstairs.

Just as I was sitting down to write, a roomboy knocked on my still open door. He brought in my notebook, left on the bar where the Japanese and I had been.

He was the same old man who had spoken broken French with me on my first day there and we had since "spoken" as much as one can, together, over the several next meetings. I had given him a nice work shirt, which had left me with only four for the rest of the Vietnam visit. He asked me in very polite, but broken French, if the Japanese man was a friend of mine. I replied that journalists talked to each other.

"After all this time he still knows nothing," the old man said.

My next contact was Major General Tran Cong Man, editor of the *Nhan Dan*. Although the Army's newspaper, it is the best available because it is edited by a professional journalist, who was trained in real journalism before he took any rank. The other national publication is the Communist Party of Vietnam daily, which even mild-mannered, sycophantic public servants don't read, no matter that it is delivered free to them. It contains all that is not wanted in a newspaper. Instead of news, it is full of ideological ramblings.

One would have expected this, too, of the *Nhan Dan*. But General Man has managed to successfully guide the paper through the most turbulent years of the Vietnam war, as well as the disappointing postwar years (among the strongest critics of the politicians are many military men who did their share to win the Vietnam war, but now watch in dismay as the politicians send the nation into decline).

General Man's office was always busy. It would look busy even on a quiet news day because it is in the heart of the old town in

Hanoi, with a tramline running close by and a passing parade of heavy freight trucks. Within the newspaper grounds itself — the office is an old colonial-style one, a former government department — the business of publishing a national daily from such cramped quarters adds even more sound and colour to the external traffic noises.

Our session began with General Man sitting quietly and listening to the interpreter spell out clearly my own background and my present interests. (Even when we were able to use some English or French in everyday conversations, the use of an interpreter is much safer for formal interviews.) From the halls of his memory he began to recall. His first words were: "Ah, yes. You were shot by mistake."

They were not really his first words. They were his last words to a preamble, but Mai Huong had taken the final statement as the strongest and used it to open her translation speech. It had a dramatic effect, because Man was so positive. He said:

> You will need some help, and as a fellow journalist I will try to help you. You were known to me before you came from discussions we had here in Hanoi some days ago and I found the project fascinating.
>
> Fascinating but very, very difficult. I will give you my summary first for I am starting to recall this incident and this is a period I shall never forget for it was a most important part of the war.
>
> My summary is that the man himself is dead. That if he was an outsider and only joined that platoon a few days earlier just for that attack he may have been known by a false name. That will make it harder.
>
> The historians will tell you some figures, but I know the facts first hand and the facts are that very few survived that hottest part of the battle there in Cholon on that day. So, difficult, yes. I never use the word impossible.

It was a wonderful start to the interview. After being told by a military historian that I had no possible hope of finding the ambush platoon or the leader, I had spent a long time lying awake at the hotel pondering the next thirty or forty days.

Having come through what I had considered would be the toughest parts — getting in, getting permission to search, and even finding top-quality help — I was now facing the realities of the matter. It had not been a pleasant night, but I resolved to continue. I had no intention of returning to Perth after just a few days in the country, given the months of work I had already put in.

And it was then I made another sensible decision. As much as anything else, this was, after all, a work of investigative journalism. I would remove my feelings from the daily scene and search for a platoon that had ambushed a civilian jeep from which one man had escaped. The other man was simply a fifth man. If I had an advantage it was being able to ask the "other man" from time to time what other inside knowledge he had.

Adopting this approach helped me in a number of ways. First, it kept emotions at a distance. Second, it encouraged me to listen very carefully to even the most discouraging opinions on the search. Analysing them was not difficult when one understood the talents or the disciplines or the character of those expressing them. And third, it allowed me to examine my own evidence and question it.

I had always, for instance, said the man used a .45 Colt automatic. That brought raised eyebrows with some military men. Historians saw no significance in it. Yet when I agreed to take a look at some handguns in the military museum "to make sure of the gun" I found the Chinese-made K54 to be smaller but almost identical to a non-expert in firearms to the .45 Colt. (I would later find not a single Vietnamese soldier in the Cholon area ever remembers seeing the .45 Colt used instead of the K54 issue.)

General Man said he had always thought the shooting was an accident. That shooting and others usually involving one person he had mentally noted as "clear mistakes" because of mistaken identities. He was certain that even now, if anyone remained alive from that day, that the platoon members would not know they had killed journalists. This was going to be important, for he devised a plan to help me smoke out some of the soldiers or civilians who might have lived in the ambush street in May 1968.

"I will write a story asking for anyone in that area at that time who witnessed jeep ambushes, and say that we need more details for our historical records. If I signal to them who the people were in that jeep he will feel guilty and never come forward. I assure you, we will get *some* information."

He was very keen at the prospect. Though more than sixty years of age he could still feel excited by the hunt, he said. It reminded him of his early pre-war days in journalism.

"We have done this hundreds of times for Vietnamese seeking family, lost people. Frankly, mostly without success, and we assume they are dead for there were so many thousands unidentified. This is the first time we have done a search for a foreigner. It is fitting it should be for a war correspondent."

He then had me go into fine detail about some parts of the battle. Man had an incredible capacity for listening to and absorbing detail. He was seeing the battle through foreign eyes, not through those of his correspondents. And he was seeing and hearing what unexpectedly became the savage centre of fighting on Day One of the ten-year war's most important battle. He had followed the war from Vietnam News Agency and Liberation Front radio reports as well as his own correspondents and even today remembered the exact day, and often almost the hour, of incidents. I began to get comfortably confident that the military archives, although kept by people who seemed pessimistic about my chances, would yield great results for me.

We had long overshot our interview time. Copy editors and secretaries came through, asking Man to check stories and sign papers, and he did this with a few moments of concentration, before turning back and listening or questioning with the same concentration. Interview times were not sacrosanct for him. The newspaper was, but he could stretch his time provided the work got done.

My young interpreter was obviously fascinated by the man (whom she had visited on other assignments before, but when he was being interviewed, not when he was cross-interviewing) and enjoying the flow of stories from battles she only knew about from folklore and briefly written references. Mai had been four years old when the Battle for Saigon had opened, and only eleven when the war finished. To her delight, the editor included her and made extra translations from French for her benefit. General Man went on to ask about the soldiers' clothing, their footwear, their weapons, their ages, the way they moved. I was most frustrated that I could only answer half the questions.

How close did he come to you? Two metres, perhaps a little more. And he missed with two shots from a handgun? That tells me a lot. He was almost certainly Defence Forces. A lot of them were hopeless shots! I was to hear that time and time again, always followed by a huge laugh from the regular soldiers. They would then say: "But the party men were the worst shots. Terrible. We would never rely on them because they hit the wrong thing."

Tran Cong Man rounded off the interview by dismantling my picture of the ambush and the men and reassembling that picture. A change here and there, a suggestion or two. "Keep the two pictures in mind. Finally the real picture will emerge. In the meantime we will keep in touch. After another month or two — nothing will come quickly, after twenty years — you will find yourself getting closer and closer."

It was sage advice. Almost to the letter, that is what happened. He also played the percentages: "Perhaps the man you recall wore boots. I would say he had rubber sandals. Be prepared to change the mental picture you have had down these years. Reports I made in the heat of war and reports by very good correspondents had to be changed, for the mind plays tricks in very hot situations. Mostly you have a good picture."

As to the strategy of staying detached, pretending that it had all happened to someone else and that this was just another investigation, he fully agreed. He had to do this on almost every major story he covered.

Mai and I were silent for a long time after we stepped out into the light of day and the noisy traffic. She had new pictures of the war and war reporting in her head, I had a second, well painted word picture of the people "most likely" to have been involved. It was well past noon, five and a half hours without food. The rest of the city had sensibly stopped for lunch, and so did we. I took a bowl as big as a military helmet full of chicken and spiced noodle soup, washed down with some bitter-sweet tea served in thimble-sized cups.

No Hanoi soup lunch is ever silent, particularly if you are a foreigner, dining with a very curious and friendly people. But my answers were mechanical. This was the first taste of the reality and the thrill of the search. It was no longer an academic, historical question. It was a piece of the war, which seemed so recent that it still lived in Man's word pictures, that no matter how arduous and time-consuming it would be, it would be very exciting and rewarding.

We had come by cyclo. The full name of this three-wheeled vehicle is in Indo-Chinese French — *cyclopousse*, meaning the driver pedals you in this modified bicycle with a seat slung between two wheels. The two cyclo drivers joined us for the meal and their presence and their spirited conversation kept others around me busy, so I was able to have time to go over the interview. The final cost of this magnificent lunch for four was approximately thirty cents, including a packet of Lotus Flower cigarettes for the drivers.

The next stop was the Hanoi National Library. The drivers got an after-lunch siesta time, and we got another view into the war as seen from the north, in 1968. Stepping into that library was an experience in itself. Unchanged since its inception around 1930, it has even today the long reading desks, hard wooden benches or single chairs, padlocked cupboards with see-through doors containing special books, hand-written card-systems of that era. One card we drew showed no one had taken this certain publication out to read since 1969.

Mai Huong asked for the *Nhan Dan* newspapers from 1968, and as a backup anything else published, cultural magazines, literary weeklies or other Hanoi newspapers with just local circulation, to be brought. While awaiting the retrieval of the newspapers, I looked around. There was nothing new in being the only foreigner in the place, but something new in seeing so many people — perhaps forty to fifty so intent on their studies that only a few in the immediate area even bothered to raise their heads to look at us.

That was to change. It was then my turn, when the papers came, to become so absorbed in the reading that I ignored the library protocol. I was able to pick out key headlines and certain contents and got to work photographing these articles, asking questions for more details from Mai as I did so.

To take the photographs I had to stand on benches or chairs. I was being as quiet as I could. But if Mai found something new she would whisper up to me and I would reply as best I could in whispered English. It was this whispered English, not my standing on chairs, that brought so much attention. Whisper in Vietnamese and everyone knows how to ignore it; whisper in English in a Vietnamese national library and everyone listens.

Slowly a shadow passed across the newspapers, and into my viewfinder slid the chief librarian. Mai had not noticed. I moved the camera aside and looked down to see her looking first at my boots, then slowly up to me. In slow, precise English she said: "It is not allowed in this library to stand on furniture, please."

No matter how red the national flag, my face was an equal to it. From my vantage point of six feet above all other readers, I could see them looking at me. Not so much with disapproval, but with cool surprise. Some were looking at my face, some at the camera, some at my boots.

Who wears boots in Hanoi? Sandals yes. Light scuffs. Slippers. Bare feet. But not R.M. Williams Outback Australian boots. For longer than was comfortable I was the centre of attention. As Mai started to quietly apologise for her guest's behaviour I nodded politely to those looking at me, and as I nodded my apologies they nodded back and went back to their books, though I could tell even then they would be asking after we left: What was that person? Not a Russian with those boots and dress jeans. Why was he so excited?

But we couldn't be stopped now. I took the librarian into a window box area and politely explained I was an Australian journalist doing research and would she accept our apologies. Yes, she would. Please take your boots off and you may use the benches, not the chairs. "In case you fall," she said. "And your other newspapers are ready for your inspection."

From table-top up, she seemed to be wearing a workaday formal blouse not inconsistent with the national dress. She in fact was wearing Bangkok or Hong Kong designer-style jeans, with zippers down the legs and studs and various flaps. Perhaps not jeans, but baggies or jodhpur trousers with fashionable little pointy-toed shoes. But she was certainly, Mai later assured me, the control person in the national library. I was beginning to reassess the allegedly sober and conservative picture everyone painted for me of Hanoi. At twenty-eight or thirty years of age, she must have had an extraordinary talent to be where she was, and obviously determined to maintain her individuality in a stuffy environment.

What we got in there that afternoon was a living word-picture story of the war as they saw it through 1968. For safety in recollection, I photographed as many articles as I could. Some of them were short reports from UPI, AP, Reuters, Agence France-Presse, but most were reports from their own correspondents on the front, and commentaries from writers in Hanoi. There was considerable war encouragement and propaganda, but strangely very little from the Communist Party intellectuals.

The headlines always proclaimed victories, but the contents were very telling. For, despite their limitations in equipment, the correspondents were often able to have their reports of certain battles in the pages of the following morning's newspapers. Not human pieces. Not colour pieces, but stories that recounted the size of the battle, the intensity. Predictably, casualty figures, other than those from the Western newsagencies giving numbers of Allied and South Vietnamese losses, were rarely mentioned, except to say that many "heroic sacrifices" were made.

I had taken my boots off to do the last lot of photographs. I had placed them near the exit door. We were there two hours. In that time many people left, and most of them stooped for a moment to feel and examine the boots. This led me to offer another apology in simple English to the librarian. "Think nothing of it. You are welcome. There are rules," she said. So, carrying my boots, I left. She was not in the least interested in the era we were researching so excitedly. I found that mildly curious.

We rode the cyclos back first to the Foreign Press Centre, then continued alone to the hotel not far away. Mai, even though she was tired, was now showing deep interest in the story. But she was conservative in her comments. All she said, more than once, was, "This is not like anything I have worked on before."

At the hotel I dropped my recording gear and camera behind the counter (where a small photograph of Ho Chi Minh was illuminated night and day by a tiny Xmas tree light, unseen by those on the other side of the reception desk) and took a walk.

In a small park nearby, with a working fountain as its focal point, I sat and watched teenage boys play a sort of soccer with badminton shuttlecocks, kicking them back and over a high net suspended between two bamboo poles. Late-teenage or early-twenties girls and boys sat on a few park benches staring into each other's faces, and discreetly holding hands behind the benchbacks. Two groups of adult men played gambling card games on the sidewalks, inviting me to join them, and laughing when I told them I could not understand the game.

I thought it very peaceful and most unusual at the time, but in my next weeks in Hanoi I would find this a very common combination of evening play. It was all very new to me. But these people had adapted to what we saw as extreme poverty and lack of opportunity; they were living and coping within a system that they tolerated, but not necessarily loved. Having nothing to compare their life to, they simply got on with living as they knew it. Love, gambling, sports, gossip, communal soups, were just fine as they were. Aspirations included a bicycle, perhaps a motorcycle.

To supply the gamblers with cigarettes a street seller sat by them on a small wooden stool, hand-rolling cigarettes made from bits and pieces of other cigarettes. These very thin sidewalk-rolled cigarettes were then sold into the circle of card-playing men for less than one cent each.

The six o'clock bar bell had long been rung when I returned. It was dinner time and Keith Chapman, Denis Farrell and a newcomer, David Heyman, awaited me. Not to dine there, but to go out. They each had by any standard very good stories to tell on their work that day: How many people are there in Vietnam? Sixty-five million? Seventy-five million? How to get a census moving in what we would consider a disciplined manner. That was Denis Farrell's work.

It was Denis's second trip to Hanoi, and as I read him he would return again and again to ensure this challenge was met and the census completed. For Keith it was the planting of lychees in the mountains to the west of Hanoi. I never did get there, but his descriptions of the people and the terrain and the opportunities for them, lychees or other crops, live with me today. He worked easily with the farmers, despaired of the bureaucrats.

David, an Englishman living in Los Angeles, was in Hanoi for a "different holiday", as he put it. Having been paid out handsomely from United Artists in Los Angeles, he had some time and some money. Not to burn, but to learn. Denis knew the place, so he called my driver, My. "Dak San," he said. Then he left matters in My's hands.

I had 'inherited' My, whose full name was Dong Xuan Mai, easier for a Westerner to pronounce as Swan My, from Brisbane filmmaker Evan Ham. My, the chief cyclo driver at the Hotel Reunification ranks, had four or five regular clients each year, mosly for just five or six days, but in my case a whole month.

We asked My to take it very easy. It is embarrassing enough to have a fellow man pedalling you without asking him to tire himself. The becak (pedalcab) drivers in Jakarta had, when I first arrived in 1962, a working life expectancy of about fifteen years:

from twenty-five to retirement at forty, and then to the scrapheap.

It was extremely pleasant rolling along the near-empty streets in the cool evening. First, to a restaurant near the Hanoi Hilton jail. No, a mistake, said Denis. Ah, Swan My knew what he meant. We moved on to a second, then a third and a fourth. Sorry, not the right one, Denis said at each. Exasperated, he chose the fifth. (The next day I discovered that "Dak San" meant not restaurant, but "special dish".)

12

At the round table press conference I had attended earlier in the year one of the Vietnamese journalists in high profile was the director of the Vietnam News Agency (VNA), Do Hoi. Do Hoi, pronounced Zo Hoy, was an experienced campaigner for the Ho Chi Minh forces. Although he was in Egypt when the Tet Offensives began, his colleagues and later his employees were in the thick of things.

One of the most likable of personalities at the conference, he ensured that foreign correspondents there were given as much help as possible. Do Hoi often had two or three of us back for a coffee or later in the day a drink or two, and during one of these meetings he invited me to continue my search in Hanoi later in the year.

He had been most realistic in his appraisal of my chances of getting material from the VNA files, but he thought it a good story. "More important to us is you newsmen coming to visit us. With all your experience we can learn much." That was an extremely generous comment. And just how generous it was I was to learn this time round in Hanoi when I met his reporters.

If the reporting of the Vietnam war raised all kinds of moral and ethical, social and personal questions for Western reporters and photographers, it meant something entirely different to their Vietnamese counterparts — duty and sacrifice.

I went to the VNA headquarters, an elegant if rundown building near the Foreign Office's Press Centre, for two meetings with Do Hoi's journalists. Their organisation had operated all through the war, more often than not on a shoestring basis. It served as an outlet for government responses and propaganda, but mostly as a news gathering outfit. Always short on materials, machines and paper and trained reporters, they had no easy time. The files were sparse; a lot of the paper had been recycled. But more impressive than that was the fact that the group I was about to speak to had between them been on more than 250 firefight missions.

Do Hoi had cleared a large meeting room for us. A long table, with tea, coffee, a stack of cups and saucers. A plate of nuts and dried titbits. Ashtrays and opened cigarette packets for the smokers. A pitcher of water and glasses for everyone.

He opened by saying this necessarily would be a "composite conference" because the four invited journalists, and counting himself as the fifth, had over the period 1964 to 1975, served more than thirty-three years in total working down south during the war.

For some of them the war had begun in 1962 and for others it had ended with terms in Cambodia as late as 1983. An average of nearly seven years each. When the various journalists reported their involvement periods it had been simplified to each of them serving at least five years between the major escalation in 1964, and the entry into Saigon of the victorious forces in 1975. Only Do Hoi himself had not been there in 1968, for the Tet Offensives, but he had more than nine years on the road, in all.

At my first visit I had brought two typewritten sheets, one giving the background, the second listing questions I needed help with. They had done their homework well. Do Hoi gave me the bad news first, then a summary of what they had to say. It was a "composite response", as I would soon see, because everyone had contributed.

The story went like this: No one in Hanoi, around that table or in the VNA or any others they knew of working in Hanoi now, was on the spot in the Minh Phung area on 5 May 1968. There were reporters with those troops, not necessarily the ambush platoon, but with troops who filtered through that sector. They arrived with the troops on the outskirts of Cholon just after midnight and started moving into Cholon proper at about 4 a.m.

One of the reporters present remembered seeing at least two of four of those colleagues going in before he headed off for his own assignment towards the radio station. He thought there were four reporters in Cholon that morning, in the "hottest part" of the battle, and all were reported killed. Some months later they learned three had been killed, and the fourth badly wounded by a rocket. He was nursed to some health in a Saigon hospital but was never again to regain his full health.

It was weeks before any of them knew about the four Western journalists being killed in Cholon. None of them, at the time or in final recall, was in the least surprised. They had had advance knowledge that Cholon would be the centre of the main fighting, before the expected even hotter fighting in the heart of Saigon itself.

Between 31 January the first of the Tet Offensives, and 11 May, including the withdrawal after the major Battle for Saigon, or the Second Tet, they had attended services for seven journalists killed from their own side.

There were two accounts of the number of their reporters involved in those offensives. Hence the difficulty in getting it all right for me at that interview. But using the "composite" form, we all agreed to take the details and sort out the facts at a later date. For example, one man was definite that twelve journalists had been assigned to certain wings of the attacking armies in both Tets, and only five had survived them. Of those five, apart from himself, he knew of only one other still alive.

Another said he was with a party of eleven, seven of whom were journalists, the other four were radio operators and announcers or "operatives", and of that initial eleven, only five survived the attacks.

It became clear at this conference that no one had ever kept track of the number of Viet Cong employed or North Vietnam Government journalists killed during the main ten years of the war, between late 1965 and early 1975.

"We were shot at or targeted by the enemy forces as a matter of course," they said. "Some of us were in uniform. At least we were in camouflage dress. Without complaining, we can say we were often worse off than the regular forces because we had to carry our reporting equipment and were often used as pack carriers for the forces."

On that morning of 5 May there had been perhaps twenty-five journalists moving in with the forces. At least four of them had gone with the "Sharp Edge" forces into Cholon. At least four had stayed back. They were radio news journalists who would come in around 7 May or 8 May and go straight to the radio station with prepared victory speeches, and the means to keep the news flowing.

The others, and this included those before me at that interview who went with other wings of the army attacking from the south and the east and the airport area, were regarded as a separate wing. They carried a mixture of gear, but all of them said they carried at least twenty kilograms of ammunition, hand grenades, rifle-fired rocket heads and other explosives, for the groups they were accompanying. On top of that base pack, they carried radios for reporting, and, depending on their roles, movie or still cameras, and cans or rolls of film to see them through a week.

They were sitting ducks. On the morning of the ambush I had one of the heaviest cameras then available to professionals, a Mamiya C103. It weighed perhaps two and a half kilograms with bits and pieces. A few hundred metres away were the Viet Cong's journalists carrying in twenty kilograms for others, and then another one or two kilos of their own gear.

No matter they were as they claimed "doing three jobs", in helping their forces liberate — as they called it — southern Vietnam. They were carrying more than twenty kilograms each, then stopping every fifteen or twenty minutes and sending in news reports. Seven months later, recalling how heavy my five-year-old daughter seemed after a long piggy-back walk, I brought out the bathroom scales and weighed her: twenty kilograms. I had carried her just three kilometres. Some of these journalists had carried more than that for about twenty kilometres from the evening of 4 May to the start of fighting on the following morning. Now, this is not a lot for a fighting man, but for a man expected to duck in and duck out of firefights and keep reporting, and help wounded men, it's tough.

When I mentioned that at the conference, they all laughed. On their way down from Hanoi they had carried at least thirty-five kilograms. "We were much younger then. And hardly ever under attack," was their explanation of how "easy" it was to walk for between thirty and ninety days down the Ho Chi Minh trail, from Hanoi to just west of Saigon.

One of them was extremely proud of his sixty-day walk. He had an academic background, in botany. "On the way I used exactly thirty different types of herbs for food or healing. I noted them all and left these notes at the resting stations on the way down for others to use as they came through. Many of them, from inside the Lao and Cambodian border, were new to us. I was the guinea-pig and if they worked, everyone got the benefit." He was happy to accept that if the herbs were poisonous he would have fallen sick.

The conversation swung back to Cholon. None of them was unhappy to have missed it; the losses were too great. None of them could have anticipated it, but on the grapevine they had heard someone in the Viet Cong had gone over to the other side around 1 May and had informed the South Vietnamese and US forces of the impending attack. Cholon was to be the centre of the attack. It was always going to be Cholon, anyone could see that. But to have it confirmed was helpful to me.

That they knew of no one alive from their ranks who survived Cholon was some sort of proof, and any Westerners in Cholon that morning would be in danger, they said. It was not a time when anyone would stop to ask questions of identity.

Why? Because it was assumed from their side that the Viet Cong colonel who went over to the other side would have betrayed their plans. They could not change at that stage. I asked why that would make it different; I said the South Vietnamese or US forces would not tell the Western press that an attack was expected. This comment caused genuine surprise, even some disbelief, because their press were very much a part of their war effort.

I explained. We were not attached to any forces. We were independent journalists, sometimes given intelligence briefings, but never given advance notice of attacks or strategy. We had to fend for ourselves.

The meeting then fell into silence. Do Hoi, who had international experience, was left to mediate. They could not quite comprehend my statement, and wanted some clarification. Do Hoi, knowing what was puzzling them, called for tea. "A moment of reflection," he called it.

To explain fully was impossible; the systems were so different. Even then, with reforms and new freedoms beginning to appear in the satellite nations of the USSR, such as Hungary and Poland, it was almost impossible for them to comprehend that a newspaper company first of all needed no licence from the government. It was equally difficult to understand that young people from high schools or universities could choose to go into journalism and go into training environments that were not controlled by government. If the government did not own the newspaper, who did? If the government did not provide the direction of what to report, who did?

Who, for example, paid for foreign correspondents to come all this way to Vietnam? They knew when we were on missions we stayed with the troops, and ate the same food as the soldiers, came in and left by the same helicopters. Who arranged all that? When correspondents were killed, were their ashes not sent home in military fashion? The questions were endless, and mostly unanswerable in that short time. Only Do Hoi had an understanding of how the Western press worked, and it was even then with difficulty that he explained that, for the moment, his colleagues should assume we had no help from the "enemy forces" (US, South Vietnam, other allied forces such as South Korea and the Australian and New Zealand troops) except as "residents in bases".

The matter was never quite settled, certainly never fully understood. But Do Hoi's explanation helped stop some of the questions. It was not the time to get into the differences in philosophies.

Yet they would arise time and time again, in this search. No one said it, but it was implied at least in the early stages, that it was only natural we were ambushed in Cholon on that morning because we would have been wearing camouflage uniforms and carrying ammunition and weapons. When the question was finally asked of me I told them we had no weapons, were wearing civilian clothing and were in a non-military jeep.

That was the first occasion of several I would hear the comment, which came this time from two of them simultaneously, that any vehicle carrying Westerners would be regarded as an enemy military jeep, probably carrying intelligence officers. "Soldiers go in trucks. Everyone knows that!" they said. And behind the jeeps would follow armoured cars. Sometimes tanks.

That was their experience. They had not been exactly on that spot in Cholon. However, by 1968, they had on average been down south for three years each. They had been in scores of encounters, mostly in small jungle firefights; but their experience included several close to towns, and two or three on Saigon's outskirts. When the jeeps came through they were followed by armoured cars, or armoured personnel carriers came first, then jeeps with the officers who then directed air attacks.

The enemy had never treated them differently for the simple

reason that they were in camouflage uniforms. They were always with the troops they were hoping would win the particular battle.

Between battles, many of them went into Saigon. Only a few were born in Saigon. Of the journalists I interviewed, all had been educated in Hanoi, then joined the News Corps because of a call-up. Fifty of them had gone into one training session. One man spoke for them: "I already had a wife and three children near Hanoi. In 1964 there was a callup for journalists and fifty of us attended. All of us got through the course. The Government gave us training and at the end of the course, we were all sent to the south. We travelled in small groups. It took us nearly a hundred days walking to get there, to Tay Ninh province. We went in and out of the Cambodian border several times, on the way. Some went on to the Long An province. We were all then within two days' walk of Saigon."

Many had come through Laos. All of them had been in and out of Cambodia several times to get to their southern destinations. The trail then was no bigger than a well used track in the jungle, protected by the canopy of trees for most of the way. There were "reception points" where permanent staff met them, fed them, told them the news and sent them on their way.

"Not quite as easy as that," said one of the journalists. He had started with a huge load of explosive and ammunition, and food, and delivered much of that as he went. When he got further south he found he had to pick up equally big loads to carry further south.

Journalists they were, but pack mules they became. They were an appendage to the army, and were never in doubt, for they were fighting for the cause. "There was so much resistance down south, we had to do it this way. For example, many villages were avoided because the people were not trustworthy," they said.

I called for a break. Tea, coffee, water, whatever. I had heard a lot of good strong information about who was where during the Tet Offensives, and I had been shamed by their workloads compared with mine. Do Hoi and I had worked together to put aside the philosophical differences in what journalists do in totalitarian as against Western government systems, for the moment. And Mai Huong had now been interpreting for more than two hours.

Do Hoi and I then, in a mixture of Vietnamese and French while the others had a cigarette and coffee and ate titbits, decided we could arrive at a better picture of Cholon by getting the

With President Soekarno of Indonesia, 1965.

With Indira Gandhi, Jakarta Foreign Correspondents' Club, 1969.

With General Than, who led the Tet Offensive attacks 1968. His first meeting with a foreign journalist, Long An province, South Vietnam, late 1988.

Left: In Honolulu 1968, two weeks after the ambush.

Long An, November 1988. General Than, showing Tet attack maps of 5 May 1968.

Teaching the Foreign Office staff to use a word processor in Hanoi, September 1988.

Right: My Hanoi interpreter 1988-89, Mai Huong, Hanoi 1988.

VNA (Vietnam News Agency) journalists interview, Hanoi, October 1988.

Two of the Viet Cong leaders during the Battle for Saigon. *Left:* Hero of Vietnam, General Tang. *Right:* General Tuot, now head of 7th Army Military History Division.

Left: My Ho Chi Minh City interpreter 1988-89, Minh Ha.

With Co Van Cuoug at our meeting after twenty-one years, Ho Chi Minh City, 15 January 1989.

With Co Van Cuoug and General Tuot.

journalists to build up word pictures of themselves and their work and then homing in on what they recalled of Saigon at that time.

Do Hoi thought it also a good moment to see if we could get, for example, a fair estimate of the number of journalists killed on their side. This had never been done before. We had another hour or two, and this was the ideal time to mix the stories. What we had to avoid was the philosophical differences between the opposing sides.

But it didn't go that way. I asked first, describing it as a "round-off" question, why they did not question themselves as to why those villages did not want them in, as they came down south. The villages were not happy with them and their Communist philosophies? Perhaps. Or did not want them ruling them from the North? Perhaps. It took another thirty minutes of talk, in which they repeatedly said these people were "unaware" and "not enlightened", before we could change the subject.

It was easier when we got back to their story. They carried into the field from these bases in the south not only ammunition and explosives and small arms, dried food, sugar, concentrated milk and herbs they found along the way, but news as well. They were actively reporting, using their radios, to the Viet Cong headquarters in the south, and these reports were being relayed to the north, from bases they had not yet reached.

They now lived underground. On the Ho Chi Minh trail they had been able to walk freely, for the chances of them being attacked were very small. But only at the bases, eighty kilometres apart, had they been able to rest and sleep safely, usually in camouflaged shelters. With smokeless kitchens, lookouts, the cover of jungle canopy, and the fact of being in Cambodia, meant they were safe.

The Americans might have known they were there, but were not allowed to bomb them. The Cambodians knew nothing, or didn't want to know. This was the time of Sihanouk, who had started his anti-American crusade. Laos had always been a sanctuary. Cambodia, whether Sihanouk liked it or not — and he appeared to agree — was also a haven for the North Vietnamese Communist forces pushing their troops down south to bring down the US-backed South Vietnam Government.

"We were losing our independence," the journalists said. "It was our duty to report this, and to help everyone in the fighting."

They lived underground for many years, literally underground. Not under the same ground, for they were forced to move sometimes only after one month. They had whole "apartments" underground; ten or twelve very big rooms, and another sixteen or eighteen smaller rooms, off those passages. If they were on flat ground the complex was quite deep. If they were in "safe" jungle areas, the complexes often opened onto hillsides. But always they were protected by a layer of earth above them.

"Who dug these rooms for you?" I asked. "We did," they said. "We could never trust to ask local villagers to come in. Mostly they knew nothing of what we were doing. They might have thought just a few of us were there, when in fact there were more than sixty or eighty of us."

They had dug the jungle complexes using normal shovels and just thrown the dirt around over a wide area. On flatlands, they had dug the dirt and at night taken it far away, and spread it thin.

Occasionally I had to stop the conference, to allow the interpreter a break, or to adjust my tape-recorder, or just to have a coffee. We stopped around this point, and I felt compelled to ask if I was hearing a battle story, or a journalist's story.

"Apart from two or three intelligence people there, and they moved about, all this was done by journalists or our assistants," they said. They dug all the trenches, did all the aerial wiring, the lighting, the repairs on their equipment, and had guards to shut off the sending of news when any enemy planes or troops came near.

They often stayed in one group for months at a time, hence their great affinity when they finally met again in Hanoi. Journalists would then be called, one or two at a time, for specific missions, and they might never be seen again. "Not that we assumed they were dead," one said. "But if they were headed for the city [Saigon] we would count them as being dead."

On the other hand, it became apparent, they also considered themselves sooner or later dead, even in their underground hideaways. "The enemy had very excellent spotter planes. In the jungle we were safe. Our aerials were strung between trees, as they were on the flatlands. But in those places we had only to worry about smoke from our kitchens. By the time we journalists arrived at jungle camps we were safe."

In sum, this information brigade played almost the same role as the journalists hired by the US, ANZAC, or other armed forces. They were there to tell the army's side of the story, not really to gather information, and certainly never to question events or the origins of information.

Those attached to the military were either indoctrinated into the cause, or generated artificial enthusiasm for their causes. Many of these men had been trained to fight and did an extra job on the side, that of reporting the war and spreading favourable propaganda. Not once in all the interviews did I hear of or read reports that indicated a setback. The terrible losses of the Tet Offensive, for example, had not been admitted by late 1989.

Despairing of getting any further with such men, I began looking for some answers from older press guides who might have operated at a higher level.

13

A meeting with two elderly and apparently distinguished press guides was arranged for me. They had served under the French until the Japanese invasion, then served under the Japanese. One was a Japanese specialist, the other a very experienced man who spoke enough French to get by. They had worked with press or government for forty years,

Only later did I realise that this interview had been arranged with the best of intentions, but without any prior research.

Before the meeting, I spent the morning down town, that is, in the old town. My hotel, the Thong Nhat (pronounced Tong Nyat) or "Liberation" was on the edge of this area.

Justin Jordens, an Australian university student who had spent time in Hanoi and was by 1989 working in Kampuchea and learning that language, too, had given me a few nice stories about new streets words in Hanoi. "Quan Khu", which means literally "zone", was now being used to describe gang zones in Hanoi.

The gangs in question were largely made up of the grandsons of old soldiers. His younger generation liked to dress in semi-military garb and stage mock battles in the streets. The craze spread quickly. There arose "Military Zone 1" and "Military Zone 2". Gangs were named after their area's number, or arbitrary divisions. The toughest of these gangs were those around the Hai Phong harbour, but those in Hanoi were pretty fierce, too. The gangs' uniforms evolved from military styles, but modified for fashion, consisted of khaki army shirts, blue worker pants, both worn very loose to give a baggy look, black rubber sandals and sometimes peaked military caps.

Conservatives regarded the gangs as hooligans, and were puzzled, as most adults are, by their emergence. Hardly any of the members of these outfits could have had anything but blurred memories of the bombing of Hanoi, or the wartime atmosphere, and it was less likely they had been in the south, even as children. Yet this strange legacy of the war, the military displays, the blatant propaganda displayed in museums, appealed to them greatly. It was an easy slang expression to remember or identify: "Kwan Kew", like "Jets", or "Banditos".

I saw dozens of them in the small back streets of the downtown area trying on Hong Kong- and Bangkok-made imitations of US street wear. The polished teenagers wore jeans and upmarket gear. They went for baggy clothing and oiled hair, and although Justin had said they wore mostly sandals, by the time I arrived they were getting into sneakers with high raised rubber soles, to add an inch or two.

They were extremely friendly towards me and tried out their few words of English. A couple of these para-military "delinquents" walked with me halfway back to my conference point and left me to return to their jobs. As they left a middle-aged man in a bookshop watched them go. He said in French, "They're make-believe soldiers. What else can you expect in a country at war for so long?"

Despite the poor start, I was still buoyant because the two promised interviews seemed certain to bring rich rewards. For months since January 1988 I had been told that these two particular men, now retired, would be helpful. Evan Ham in Australia passed on the story that they had both known Ho Chi Minh personally and would have inside knowledge about all major events.

As each new contact in Hanoi boosted these men more and more, I began to feel confident. I would get all the Tet information from them because one had been in Saigon in 1968; I would get more stories about Wilfred Burchett because they had been Burchett's translators. And so on.

If that bit of morning touring brought insights of a socially interesting kind only, it was at least much more than I got from my interview with the two press guides when it finally took place. The two retired officials used up four valuable hours without providing me with the slightest piece of useful information.

It was not a matter of failing memories, for both had good recall. They had both been very low-ranking workers for the French, the Japanese and later for the Communist Party. They had been in the most amazing places in the south, and in

Cambodia, when really hot battles were being fought, yet they had spent the duration of actions holed up somewhere and could never give a detail of any significance.

Theirs was an unending tale of propaganda. A view from under a rock. Tet, for example, was an interesting time because they were translating materials in radio stations. No, they saw no action, but they would be able to tell me where I could get copies of these speeches, and so on.

There was an anti-American tirade. The US bombers were hitting the Ho Chi Minh trail and bombing them inside Cambodia. Illegal, criminal! Surely it worked both ways, I replied. You were using another country as a sanctuary for the delivery of arms. That was different, theirs was a justified and glorious struggle, they responded.

The whole interview broke down. In an attempt to put a little life into it, or at least to wind it up pleasantly, I told them the Foreign Office had said they were among the most experienced people in Hanoi, and they had met many leaders and early war correspondents. No, they hadn't actually met any leaders. Not Ho Chi Minh, although they had seen him several times at meetings. One said he had met the leader of the Japanese Army, or was it deputy leader? They had never met any of the famous men I was scheduled to meet down south, so I couldn't even get an advance picture of them.

The last attempt to retrieve the situation was made by a young translator who said everyone knew they had been longtime friends of the crypto-Communist Australian journalist Wilfred Burchett. Could they tell us of some of the missions they were on in the south, particularly around the times of the Tet Offensives.

One said, "Ah, yes, another Australian journalist." There was a long silence, then the other one said, "I heard of him, but I never met him. But I met another foreigner, Wolfgang Schmauzer, and a team of Japanese TV men. I prefer the Japanese because I speak Japanese."

The interpreter and another trainee official still wanted to hear about the other one's friendship with Burchett because this old man's reputation rested on his intimacy with professional names and past leaders. "Well, I met him once. In the south. He came into our camp, in Tay Ninh, I think. He had been in Cambodia. He was a very nice man. We shook hands."

Describe him, they said. "Well, he was a fat man with a fat red face and had only a little bit of white hair left. He was always sweating and I helped wash a shirt he had and we hung it out to dry. We all had some rice together. When he had eaten and his shirt was dry, he left. A jeep came for him and he went into Cambodia again."

What about going on missions with him, they asked? No, there had been no missions, replied one of them; he was required to work behind the lines, serving his government the best he could. He was very proud of his work and his sacrifice.

I thought there would be more Burchett stories coming up. In Tim Bowden's account of the life of cameraman Neil Davis, *One Crowded Hour*, Burchett is quoted as saying he saw Davis go past with South Vietnamese soldiers as he, Burchett, was in hiding with some Viet Cong. He claimed he stopped the Viet Cong from firing on the ARVN soldiers because he recognised Davis with them.

Davis checked his diary and sure enough, he was where Burchett had said he had been that day. Burchett had been able to go in an out of sanctuaries in Cambodia with Communist forces. Although a dedicated Communist supporter — he didn't live long enough to see the systems crumbling, or the parties fighting among themselves over the spoils of Indo-China — he was a very canny reporter and made himself very wealthy by selling his stories to the Western press during the Vietnam war. But he did not live long enough to enjoy his money.

I said that as a young man I had interpreted several sessions of the Asian Games speeches for Wilfred in Djakarta in 1962. He had come to write about the impending victory of the Indonesian Communist Party, and the PKI's display of martial arts — "Dance: The People's anger against Reactionary and CIA Agents' Forces" (which meant the armed forces who kept the PKI in check) — using sharpened bamboo poles and parang knives to show the people they would be dealt with harshly if they did not side with them.

But the invitation for the one man who had met Burchett to speak about him and to give the junior officials a taste of the real war, and hear good stories of great men in action, was a failure. They had asked what he had then experienced while with Burchett.

"I never saw him again. He never returned to that camp and I never went on a mission. My job was to ensure people were given the truth of the war."

We emerged into the cool evening air, the old men staying behind over tea and cigarettes. I was flanked by the junior officials, one a trainee, the other starting into a fourth year. They both started to speak at once then halted to sort themselves out.

"What we just heard is amazing," said the trainee. "From my first weeks we were told these two venerable officials had retired with honours and were known for their friendships with many famous leaders. Whenever they were asked they said, 'Yes, I knew him'."

They had probably built these fellows up themselves. Or others just above them had. The truth was no one had ever checked with *them*. The officials had never bothered to correct the rosy and ever-growing stories about themselves, but merely answered yes, they knew this or that famous individual.

An Australian cameraman who had been in Hanoi several times before me had brought me similar stories. "You've got to see Fathers N. K. and N. H. S. They are a mine of information. They were personal assistants to Ho and Giap, they led Burchett everywhere and did his translating, and they know just about everyone who was a big name at Tet. . ." Almost as an afterthought, he added, "They were right in the middle of Tet."

When I arrived in Hanoi I was told the same stories, by at least three officials. It was established legend in the Foreign Office. Yet no one had checked. No one had ever asked them to be explicit. These stories turned out to be simply not true.

In Vietnam, it is relatively easy to assess the amount of genuine knowledge, information or experience any potential source has. One begins by asking for an overview of something. If the person is simply a fool, a gush of propaganda tumbles out. If his indoctrination is at war with some native intelligence, you get small but often very useful data which, added to a lot of good guesswork, allows you to expand and fill in the picture. But if the person had a high rank during the war, you could begin by assuming he knew why, say, the Tet Offensives had to be started when they did — for international leverage at no matter what sacrifice — and you could assume he was now under pressure to start looking for reasons why his promises about Socialism benefiting every man, woman and child, and a job for everyone, had not only remained unfulfilled but were followed by worse conditions than ever.

The sad old men had never lied. They had perhaps been a little devious in saying they knew Ho Chi Minh or had interpreted for Burchett. They had simply not known much, down the years, of what was happening around them. They had accepted the Communist Party line and so much of their "international awareness" came earlier from that strange and warped picture of the world China used to broadcast in the interests of the exported revolution, and later from the Soviet Union.

The elders had never been outside the country except to sanctuaries in Laos or Cambodia. They had never seen how other nations and peoples functioned. What was hardship for others was to them normal. One of them at the start said: "So, you think food is in short supply now. In the Japanese times it was ten times worse", only to be corrected by his associate saying, "But what about the famine of the foothills? We ate grass!" And so on. The level of hardship was somehow related, through twisted logic, to heroism and victories, not the result of mismanagement or greed or leaders' power lust. These attitudes were arrived at after the prolonged absence of any comparisons, of materials or information.

Several hours later, after midnight, I wandered into the streets to take a break from transcriptions and using the word processor. There had hardly been a soul abroad at 10 p.m. on previous evenings so I was not surprised to find the streets empty except for four street sweepers.

Three of the four were women, wearing cheap black cotton trousers and blouses, often patched. They wore breathing masks and even at night, the familiar conical hat to keep their hair clean.

The system in Hanoi is for the manual workers to sweep the refuse into piles, then await a truck. Woman after woman looked up as I went by. We exchanged pleasantries and they giggled and were polite. But their demeanour was subservient.

A few months earlier Justin Jordens, my Quan Khu gang informant, had stopped in a little shop where these cleaners had sat down for some tea. They had called him "sir" from the start, although just in his twenties he was hardly their senior. He tried to get them to lower their level of address but they asked if he attended university. He replied that he did, so they said, "Well, you see. You are a sir after all!"

After having wasted time interviewing the two veterans, it was almost a relief to spend time with and talk to the street cleaners. They at least could offer pleasant company and honesty.

The next day I was in the Foreign Office when one of the two elders called to me. He had come specifically to see me and had been waiting for a while. He brought out a small pack of papers in an old Second World War courier pouch made of webbing. Inside it he had kept for several years a number of press releases proclaiming the victory of Dien Bien Phu. "I did those translations for the world press by myself," he said.

I could hardly help being moved. There were five of them, covered with official rubber stamps. One had been signed by General Giap. "These are treasures to me, part of our history. For the museum, when I die."

14

So far, I had conducted the search along very regular lines. I knew that would have to change or I would get nowhere, yet I didn't quite know how to alter the direction, and nor did I want to pass up official interviews in case they should finally yield something.

I decided to travel outside my search boundaries. Instead of sitting in cafes fretting over the impasse I had reached, I would begin again at street level; it was just possible that some unsung survivors of the war could provide some new approach or ideas. As much as I could do with those, even if nothing turned up it would be refreshing to talk to some ordinary 'non-official' Vietnamese for a change.

Hanoi's old town has streets named originally after the activities of those who worked in it. Silversmiths lived in Silver Street, tailors worked in Tailor Street, and so on. These days the city is much changed, although there are some remnants.

The French introduced a kind of architecture that is still quite impressive and with the Vietnamese- and Chinese-style shops between these bigger buildings, one day this old town will again be very pleasant. It has an atmosphere of industry that I found attractive. Although I was happy to ride along the bigger boulevards and the various tracks around the lakes and the Red riverside, I was drawn back time and time again to this old part of the town, where for the price of a coffee, it is still possible to sit outside and enjoy life flowing past without being stifled by exhaust fumes.

One little corner shop became a favourite of mine, but I had been there four or five times before I met the owner. On one afternoon, a beautiful woman delivered some crusty French bread to my table. She looked at me closely, smiled, withdrew, bowing. Then came the owner, who said his name was Ky. He had been told this strange Australian journalist had become a regular. He said he was an old soldier, though when I said he didn't look old, he agreed that he was only fifty-five.

Ky spoke modest French. He proudly reminded me that his name was "international" because in French it meant a place where boats tied up, and in English something that opened a door. It was small talk, and he continued it by saying he would one day have a sign incorporating all three meanings into a sign for his shop. In Vietnamese "Ky" means eccentric, strange, and wonderful. He was still puzzling how to fit this in with a key, and a quay.

After that little chat he seemed at ease. He shyly asked if I had been in the war. I said I had.

"Ah! The war," he said.

Had I been to Kontum down south? Yes, I had.

Ky then said: "I killed many Americans in Kontum province." He didn't say it proudly. It was all he could think of to say to continue the conversation. He had never before met a Westerner. He had just killed them, with his platoon, when in uniform.

Ky said he had always been puzzled by the Americans. Some of the troops he had attacked were sensationally courageous. His group hardly ever made kills with them. They were older soldiers, Marines perhaps.

"And those Air Cavalry. We always feared them. But the other ones were easy. They were no problem. We hardly ever lost on missions against them." The "other ones" I presumed were the conscripts.

"Oh, those Americans, the older ones, they were very good," he said.

He repeated this a number of times. But it was the younger ones he wanted to know about. I told him I had an old, very short story, a vignette really, among my files back at the hotel. It might help explain the difference between the professionals and the conscripts. The story was from 1968 and had been written in Kontum province. He interrupted me: "That was when I was there!"

Ky wanted no more talk then. I should return tomorrow and have soup and more good bread with him. He would prepare something special for me. But the following day I couldn't come.

He pressed and was anxious, before we agreed on the day after tomorrow.

When I got back to my hotel I searched the files on disks on my little portable word processor. It was there. A skin and bones story, written on my little Olivetti back in camp at Dak To in Kontum that night. I had called one soldier a Negro; I changed that to Black. Not a story to be carved in marble, it was one of a hundred pieces like this I had written in Vietnam, more as a kind of diary than anything else. Now it would have a readership of two, or an audience of two, for Ky could not read English and I would have to try to relate it to him in a mix of languages.

Two days later I went to the Key-Quay-Ky coffee shop. I was there early, before noon, and Ky was a little embarrassed by my sudden arrival. I had caught him making the special table setting for us. I pretended I hadn't seen the special arrangements so held up my hand and said "*nam phut*", signalling I would be back in five minutes.

It was then I got the feeling we could be in for a very long talk. Ky had half-curtained off a small area at the rear of the shop. The usual number of customers were there at the front, being handled by the girl who had served me a week ago on my first visit. Ky had scrubbed down this little section. The table was spotless. Crisp French bread surrounded the centrepiece, which was a tall thin vase with a single carnation-type bloom. There were chopsticks, spoons, Chinese soup spoons, little paper napkins folded star-shaped, and an open flat jar of mixed chillies from which an aluminium scoop projected. To one side there was an open, still full packet of 555 English cigarettes and a simple clay ashtray.

I had brought a box of chocolates and some photographs of my families in Australia and the United States. Children at school, beaches, a Vietnamese restaurant run by a former Saigon family, and similar scenes. He bade me sit down, and I looked around further while he was away for a moment. Above me was a shelf where there were more flowers, a couple of empty copper shell cases now etched with delicate bird and flower motifs. Between them was a black and white photograph of a handsome young man, framed in a funereally ornate steel frame which showed a few rust marks. The man was staring straight ahead, solemn but proud. He wore a high-collared black jacket with no insignia, but pasted over the base of the photograph, before it had been framed, was a series of stripes and battle signs.

It looked looked just like Ky. It had to be a lost son. A young man now long dead. The setting for our talk was bright. I was anticipating a pleasant talk and hoped it would not turn morbid.

Ky returned with two huge bowls of noodle soup, broke some bread, and effectively declared the meeting open. No dark clouds appeared. Ky spoke happily. I showed my photographs; he said nice things about them.

Yes, he was married and had three children, all of them still in high school. Just the three. Good. It was not a dead son. The man in the photo was his father, hence the unadorned uniform. He had been a guerilla against the French, in the north. So I thought.

I asked further about the family. Sisters? Brothers? One brother, he replied. A wild young boy, three years his junior. He had two sisters. Identical twins. Both school teachers, one in Hoa Binh, the other in Ha Nam, both towns just south of Hanoi. He started to tell me about their children, but I let that information slide.

"And the brother?" I asked.

"He is not with us anymore," he said.

It was the brother. The man in the photograph, for certain.

The meal was sensational. He repeated that although as a young boy he had seen many French people from a distance and picked up their language in the classroom or from other Vietnamese, he had never met a Westerner. He was especially surprised to have now encountered one who had been in the war, no matter that I had not been a soldier.

He talked about the hardships of the jungle in Kontum province, the raids by the Phantom jets, the respect he had for the professional American soldiers and the luck they had fighting the younger men. I did my best to keep up this war talk, but he had such superior knowledge of weapons, and the unit numbers on both sides that it became a one-way talk for most of the time. He knew all about Iroquois and Chinook helicopters, M15s, B41 rockets, C-rations, and other shorthand of weapons and transport and materials.

I had been advised to bring a bottle of whisky as a present for his sideboard. The chocolates were the best I could manage, a gift from a friend just in from Bangkok. I need not have worried, for he himself produced a bottle of whisky, late in the afternoon. He was not offended when I said I did not drink whisky, and there soon appeared several large bottles of cold beer, just for me.

After a decent interval, I asked again about the brother, how he was lost.

"He went to the other side. Frankly, I tell you, he is far away."

I assumed his brother was dead, and that this was his photograph from earlier days.

"But tell me this story of yours," he said. I said I would do that right at the end. I was now interested in his brother and asked him to tell me that story first. We had plenty of time. He was, thankfully, not in the least morbid.

Ky slid the curtain aside to let more light in. It was closing time. He left the main shop door open, to catch the dwindling light, and to watch the traffic outside. He commenced to tell a story, using the third person.

When the mining of Hai Phong harbour had started, many of the better-performed soldiers had been called back to help in the defence of Hanoi and the Hai Phong harbour. Floating mines were being placed in the sea all around Hai Phong to stop or slow down the flow of arms and materials to North Vietnam, from Soviet, Chinese, Cuban and other ships. All the friendly nations, he said. There was a call for volunteers to go out in small single-motor powered boats to locate these mines. By "locate" they meant drive into them and explode them.

The men who did this were heroes. Awarded medals before their missions. Before each of these singularly suicidal operations, the men involved were given their memorial ceremonies. Their photographs would be placed on a small altar, before the assembled family, colleagues and officers in the forces. Candles would be lit around the photograph on the flower-adorned altar. Eulogies would be spoken, as though the man had passed from them. His heroism in the upcoming act of killing himself by driving into a mine would be included in the eulogies. The "dead hero" would then, that night, start his last journey.

He had been present at one of these ceremonies. It had been eerie, he said. A man alive spoken of as already dead. "They then put on their dark clothing, left everything worldly behind them for their families, and departed."

I avoided looking at the photograph.

I'd never until then heard a Vietnamese speak of death by

saying someone was "going over to the other side". I was familiar enough with this idea at home, having a Greek father and an Irish mother, lots of versions of the Ferryman taking you on your final journey.

The man in the photo had been his own Ferryman. He had finished his story, it seemed. "Now, tell me about Kontum," he said. I fished out the twenty-year-old story. This is what I had written:

We had been waiting for one hour for the North Vietnamese army troops to come along the narrow track that followed the brook, which aerial intelligence said was their supply track. Sometimes. We expected to wait another eight hours but that didn't matter because they would be coming with small elephants to carry their heavy cannon. We would certainly hear them coming and would be safe because we had mined the track on both sides and buried trip-flares at each end of the ambush, which would show them clear as day when they tripped them.

We were waiting easily because there were ninety men in the company and all well-armed and well-protected in trenches. If the stars were with us it would be a turkey shoot. All were well-armed except me, the Warco, as they called me, parlance for war correspondent. I was another small problem for them to protect; on the other hand, a man who might take a photo of them that would be published at home.

None of us had seen an elephant carrying cannon before, and we were impatient for everything to commence, although we might have to wait another eight hours. That was what intelligence told us; they would certainly come through within that twilight to dawn period.

While a heavily built black South Carolina soldier was near the brook checking the plastic bombs set into the bank, he upset a trip-flare and sent a rocket one hundred feet high, leaving a flat cloud of thick, white smoke that hung in the valley for ten minutes.

I thought the North Vietnamese would certainly see the cloud and we might as well give up now and go back to the top of the hill to the base camp and sleep a comfortable night in real trenches instead of lying here in shallow trenches in the valley in the jungle. But the young company commander from Philadelphia said it didn't matter. We would replace the flare and continue waiting for them because they might not have seen the white smoke from the other side of the hill, up the valley.

While the South Carolina man was re-setting the new flare he accidentally set that off, too. A second cloud of white smoke went up and hung in our little valley as the fog was beginning to descend. "Same thing," said the young company commander. They might confuse the smoke with fog. They might not be around the hillside and might not have seen the smoke. When the South Carolina man came back I asked him, "Don't you think the Charlies would have seen the smoke?" He said: "Probably not, because the company commander says they might not be around the hillside yet.

"We will wait for them Charlies and their elephants to come deedley-boppin' along this here trail and we'll give them such a big blast and have elephant steaks for all."

He said what they did not know was that as soon as they set off the trip-flares we would open fire from our side, and Claymore mines and shooting would probably kill half of them, and the others would jump into the water and when they did we would blow them to the top of the hill with all that plastic bomb set into the banks of the creek.

"And there will be some sort of good story, for a correspondent like you," he said. "You don't have a trench. If you like, you may share mine."

But I declined because I wanted to stay clear of the Claymores opposite the brook bank. "Claymores will leave you plenty of elephant steaks," I said, "though I have never seen an elephant steak myself."

The trenches were near the river bank. I moved to higher ground, but still on the perimeter of the company, made a small place, then came down the hill again. The young commander from Philadelphia was reading for the fourth time, he said, a long letter from his wife, who was now living in Wilmington with his mother. He had himself written the fourth page of his daily letter that he sent to his wife and his mother.

"We send the letters out with supply helos and they sometimes make it in five days. Would you believe it? Five days from the stinking jungle out here in Nowhere, near the Cambodian border."

He concentrated his energies on his letter writing and when he had finished he read about the Philadelphia Phillies in newsclips from their letters and wondered why they had made so many errors and so few runs in the last three games. When he had finished reading he looked up and said he missed his wife and missed watching the Philadelphia Phillies and he would be going home soon anyways.

He was my size, medium slight. My height, medium high. My color, medium olive. My face, medium Irish. We could have swapped clothes and the hand-held radio. But he had a moustache, to make him look older, perhaps. We couldn't have swapped eye-wrinkles; I had some years on him. He said, "We will all stay awake, all through the night waiting for these bastards with the elephants." He said he had never seen an elephant in the jungle and that he had written to his wife and mother, in that night's letter, that tonight they would blow up some North Vietnamese, who were the enemy, and some elephants, who were carrying cannon south.

"But I didn't tell them these are only small Asian elephants," he said. "That would spoil it for them."

He then went to sleep.

And so did the deputy commander, who snored, and snored very loudly. I know, because I was finally the only one awake on our part of the hill and I was not even in a trench, but lying on my back and looking at the Orion's Belt stars and brushing off little fat, round spiders that dangled their web-lines down to me looking for food. Or whatever it is that jungle spiders look for when they lower themselves on gossamer from leafy bamboo trees in the middle of the jungle, just a few miles from the Cambodian border.

Then a second snorer began.

Oh, he was a champion snorer.

The deputy commander was more of a soprano.

The second snorer was a deep bass. At two in the morning he could be heard all over our hill and along the brook and probably around the hillside.

No elephants had come yet.

No North Vietnamese had been heard.

So, I wriggled over to him, through the dirt and put two fingers around his nose and squeezed the fingers gently together. He snorted, turned his head and then stopped snoring. Then I crocodiled a little further over the hillside ground until I reached the soprano snorer, the deputy commander, and applied the same gentle treatment. The nose squeeze worked again. He stopped snoring and did not begin again.

But I guessed even the elephants had heard it down our valley. I did not sleep because I expected us to be attacked. We might not be the attackers. There had been so much white smoke drifting up from our little valley, and so much snoring noise.

At 3.30 a.m. the Phantom bombers came in, on radar-directed bombing missions to hit a hill behind us. Had we called them in earlier on a pre-emptive? Had another company on a similar hillside north of us wanted to hit them before they came south? They were distressingly close. The Phantoms dropped 750-pounders through the fog, north a mile from where our company slept in ambush. This went on for thirty minutes.

I was wondering about the Phantoms and the spiders when I first heard the North Vietnamese chip-chip-chopping through the jungle, ever so quietly, on the far side of the brook.

There was one with a jungle knife ten metres forward of his comrades and when he could not push the bamboo aside, he cut gently into the blocking branch. That is how I read it. I am sure they did not speak but used hand signals. The bombing had finished beyond the hills. I think I would have heard their whispers, in the clear night, only thirty metres away.

After five or six minutes they had pushed past the ambush site, well clear of the trip-flares and Claymore mines and plastic bombs in the brook-banks and the 94th Battalion's company troops. If they had elephants, they had left them around the hillside, for another night. If there had ever been any elephants.

They had passed down several valleys while the Phantoms were dropping their 750-pounders. Whatever they were carrying south they got south, that night. A delicate night's work for them, though had I been a soldier and not wanting them to go south that night, I would have opened fire at the sounds of their chip-chopping.

But I am not a soldier. I let them through. Who would I turn to? Everyone was asleep. Would they snore if I went to awaken them? Invite attack? A whole company as easy targets from men well-hidden, well-prepared. Wide awake.

I let them through, then I went to sleep. The stars were fading by then. I was awakened at dawn by a laugh. Someone was saying the correspondent has slept the whole night through. He is not used to the jungles.

What should we do now, commander?

He said, "We will take the Claymores, leave the trip-flares and explode the plastic bombs."

They took the Claymores, left the trips and after some "Shits!"

and "Damns!" they blew the plastic bombs up. The infallible, last-resort plastic bombs that were ready in the brook-banks for the North Vietnamese when they jumped into the stream after the Claymores had made elephant steaks.

"Someone went past last night," said a young corporal, who had been looking over the area and found tracks.

"Screw the Charlies!" said the young commander from Philadelphia.

"Men, pack up and head out," he said.

So we packed up the ground sheets and the grenades and the rifles and letters and chocolate. And buried the breakfast tins. And headed out up the valley and started a long climb to the safe base camp at the top of the hill half a mile away.

"You know what I miss most?" said the young commander as I walked beside him, "I miss the Philadelphia Phillies. I have only weeks to go in this lousy war. I might get home and catch the last games of the season. I have written my wife."

The translation through three languages had taken me some time. Ky was adept in keeping the line of the story, despite interrupting me after every second or third paragraph.

He rose to close the door and lit a small lantern, more to help with atmosphere than to add to the light from the single 40-watt bulb burning over us.

"Yes, that explains a lot. I must tell you sympathy. They should not have been put there in the first place. After all, this is our country," he said.

For me it had been a most pleasant afternoon. I had enjoyed the talk and the food. He had at last met his Westerner. Not a US soldier, but someone who had been with them, someone who understood his stories of the fighting. I had just one other question. To confirm what had been hinted at, I suggested to him that he probably felt very proud of his brother having volunteered for that suicide mission in Hai Phong harbour. For his part, Ky laughed, and laughed and laughed. He was a little drunk.

"Why do you say that?" he asked.

"You have a photograph of him, above me," I said.

"That is not my brother. That's me! I am dead!"

A little unsteadily he stood up and brought the framed photograph down. "This is me. Dead!"

I had stood up with him, and sat down with him. Now the

photograph was between us. It was definitely time for another beer. He took a whisky.

"My brother unfortunately deserted to the other side, to the enemy," he said.

It was in Kontum province that he last saw him. Trinh, his brother, had joined him only for three or four uneventful weeks, then disappeared.

It was assumed he had deserted. Ky had argued against that, saying he might have been killed or wounded by enemy bombing, and lain dead in the jungle. But the evidence was strongly against that.

Ky was looked on as a former hero and campaigner whose brother had deserted. No one would say it to his face, but he felt something more was called for to show his loyalty. He had returned after a five-year tour of duty with a magnificent record. In Hanoi no one had questioned his loyalty. The shadow was only in his own mind from Kontum, where Trinh had gone over to the other side.

When the mining of Hai Phong had begun he had not yet been married, but now he wanted to marry. It was the most difficult time of his life. He felt selfish because his war duty was over, yet the war continued. Had escalated, in fact. The bombing of Hanoi had started, the harbour was mined. The war seemed to be going well for them when he left Kontum. Now it seemed the national objectives of freedom from foreign intervention were even more distant. The enemy was bringing the war into their backyard.

Ky had had mental problems. He expressed that well by twisting his fingers in his ears. Not as dramatic as it should have been, for he was now in his darkened coffee shop, and holding a glas of whisky in his other hand. I laughed at the sight of the man before me with a glass of whisky in his right hand and a make-believe gun of insanity in the left hand, both held high around his ears, performing all this with a big laugh.

"And so, I decided to die for victory," he said. "My sisters were OK. Is that how you say, OK? Well, they were OK."

He volunteered for the mining missions in Hai Phong. His sisters were aghast, his parents were unforgiving. His father was so against it he wrote a farewell note which his mother had brought — a sort of eulogy, saying how he had been such a good child — to the farewell ceremony at the harbourside.

His mother had come, but being frail, she asked a neighbour to be there with her. The neighbour sent a beautiful daughter of twenty-two to help "the old lady nearby" to the ceremony. Her name was Thu. Autumn. Dying leaves. So Ky met this girl when he was about to die, a girl who was caring for his mother at his own funeral.

"These ceremonies were held on the harbour. If they held them in Hanoi perhaps someone would not be able to keep up that spirit of heroism all the way to Hai Phong," he said.

So, to maintain the verve and the spirit, they were kept close to the small boats they were meant to steer into the floating mines in Hai Phong harbour; from here, they would be able to leave their memorial ceremonies and go right in.

But this meant the families had to travel from their villages and towns to these special services. It moved Ky that this young girl had accompanied his mother by bus over a rough road for several hours to get to the harbour. Her beauty moved him even more.

That Thu had looked at him as a hero gave him a new inner strength, and he decided he would die with her love in his heart and her image in his mind. His mission would also remove the stain of his brother having gone to the other side. He would show himself a worthy son to his mother and his father, no matter that his father did not understand. And a hero to this beautiful girl, and for his country.

Down on the shoreline he was placed at the helm of a very small wooden boat, powered by a slow, old-fashioned string-pull-started motor. He had been shown photographs of the mines, then shown unexploded mines on a beach further south. He would recognise them.

Ky moved slowly away from the beach. It was the typhoon season. The skies were overcast, but muted moonlight gave him silhouette vision. Normally he would have hit a mine within thirty minutes. He gave himself about twenty minutes, driving straight out.

But nothing happened . . .

The clouds occasionally cleared, leaving a big shining moon for a minute. He saw no mines. He saw many big ships behind him in Hai Phong, and he saw in front of him, at a distance, several other ships in single file, like cutouts from a book, flat against the horizon. Between the ones far at sea and the harbour he had left there were the mines, which were his mission.

He circled and circled, hoping, yet not hoping, to hit a mine.

"I ask you to excuse me," he said. "I could not see a mine."

Ky was by then very cold and wet from the spray and wind.

"I loved that girl so much. Yet I had only met her one time," he said. "Whatever I would do would be spectacular for Thu!"

He kept circling until finally, when he thought his petrol was running out, he saw a shape.

"Like a box in the water. Like the photos of the mines. This was it."

He rammed the box. The bow of his little boat hit the box with a great thump. He was thrown out, but was strangely alive. No explosion. The boat and the box were nosing away from him, and at each bump he expected an explosion. None happened.

He began to swim towards the few lights of the harbour. He got tired. He lay on his back and watched his boat and the box bump along, the moonlight behind them.

Then the explosion came. The box and the boat had pushed into a mine. He was by then well clear. Ky continued to swim for thirty or forty minutes, and eventually waded ashore. Exhausted, he slept on the dirty sand near a pier.

In the dawn several men came along and picked him up. His uniform of hero told them everything. They fed him and nursed him, for several days. Ky assured them he was all right, so they put him on a bus to Hanoi. In Hanoi he walked around unnoticed. The city people paid him no special attention. He walked until a soldier asked him if he needed help. By now Ky had been four days away and long dead.

He walked the final three kilometres to his parents' house. His father answered the door, and surprised, embraced him. All he said was, "So it should be." He awakened from a short deep sleep to find his mother looking over him, in tears.

There followed a meal, and the story. Everyone fussed over him. Neighbours were called in. Little gifts came. By late afternoon he was feeling at home. At ease, healthy and alive. In clean clothing he went to the front gate to savour the feeling of life after death. He wore simple trousers and a black pyjama top. He watched as people went by, thinking up the revival of his story for his senior officers, of how his mine was exploded, yet how he lived.

Then Thu, in drab worker's brown skirt and light-brown shapeless shirt came into view. She swung a small drab bag.

Coming his way. He remembered all that was beautiful of Thu, and his final hour. The afternoon seemed perfect, although he suddenly felt unattractive, embarrassed.

Thu walked quietly past where he stood. He nodded politely. Thu returned the greeting and walked on a few houses, to her door. He had followed her with his eyes all the way. She turned. Thu looked back. Ky nodded recognition. Thu fainted.

His father then called him a hero. His mother was just glad to have him back. The military unit had respected his victory in exploding a mine, and living through it. He was given back the photograph of his death in victory. No more was said of his brother, who had deserted. Ky had quelled all such doubts on his family's dedication. Ky and Thu had courted, and married, under an umbrella of bombing over Hanoi.

"You have seen my wife," said Ky. "*She came to my funeral.*"

It was the same beautiful girl who had first served me in his coffee shop five or six days ago, and who now left us at our back table.

Our coffee shop afternoon drinking had left him quite tipsy, and by now I was a little overconfident also. Wanting to round off the story, I asked if he ever found out what happened to his brother.

What had happened after he had "gone to the other side?" I asked.

He answered by counting off on his fingers a series of statements, as though they were attributes or sins.

"First he got to the enemy side.

"Then he got high rank.

"Then he got to California.

"Then he got a lot of money."

He spoke freely about him now. They exchanged letters occasionally. I asked if his brother knew Ky had volunteered his life for him because he had defected in 1968.

"So far I have not told him," he said. He implied that it might bring him bad luck. Besides, the war was now long over. They had made their separate decisions.

"I am the lucky one. Without him going over I would never have had such a wife. Just a poor simple soldier like me would never get such a beautiful wife and mother."

He smiled slowly. Then laughed, and laughed and laughed. Thu came to his side and he held her hand. He fished out the box of chocolates I had brought from behind his chair and presented it to her, from me.

Some simple soldier.

15

In October 1988, in the company of Mai Huong who had been with me right from the start in Hanoi, I travelled down to Ho Chi Minh City to continue the search. We flew down on Vietnam's only airline, Hang Kong Vietnam, on a Soviet-built version of a Boeing 723. A few weeks earlier an identical plane coming into Bangkok airport during a violent electrical storm, crashed killing seventy-three passengers. I had been booked on that flight, but had cancelled at the last moment. The memory of that was still close enough to bring about, for me at least, a sombre mood.

My plan was to meet and talk with General Than, now living in Long An, and in 1968 commander of two of the five wings of the Tet Offensive's Battle for Saigon from 5 May. After negotiations, and somewhat to my surprise, he had agreed to an interview with me.

At Ho Chi Minh City we were met by Minh Ha, a French-educated interpreter who had been at high school in Hanoi during the worst of the bombing raids, before spending some time in France. It was Minh Ha's first assignment on the search so she preferred to follow proceedings and help out rather than take the lead. By the time we three had travelled to Long An she was as captivated by the search as Mai was.

For transport we had a Soviet-made car, a Volga. The Volga looked like a well-kept version of the British-made Ford Pilot, but inside and in performance it was like those cars the British produced during their "I'm all right Jack" days, when workmanship was quite poor. The seats were now collapsed in on themselves and we felt like children, desperate to see the view but only getting our chins to window-ledge level. The villagers must have thought the VIP car was carrying a poor Western veteran who had had his legs shot off.

We travelled the busy road to Long An, being passed by long-wheelbase Chevvies which I remembered were used at airbases as baggage pickup trucks. With huge V8 motors still running well, their pickup trays now converted to carry twelve or thirteen passengers covered by a flat-top tarpaulin, they made light of the roads and zoomed past giving us a buffeting.

However, we were at peace in our collapsed seats and our motor was ticking over nicely. We used the time to discuss the interview. The girls were puzzled by my change of plan. Minh Ha was just catching on to the search, but Mai Huong had sat through hours of very technical discussions on the Tet Offensives and other battles. So technical had the discussions become that we carried with us an old IBM punch-card giving us precise translations of military ranks from *dai trung* (general) down to *bing nhi* (private) and a big list of other military terms. We'd been in a maze of information, thirty to forty hours of it on tapes and transcriptions and handwritten notes.

The Battle for Saigon (Second Tet) was clear to us from a technical and political standpoint, but the people involved were still being called by their functions only. When we had tried to fill out this information we got not evasive answers, but standard replies that individuals were part of a team, the team was part of a platoon, the platoon part of a regiment, and so on. For me, the men remained faceless. It was not an evasion of facts, but recall by men who genuinely felt that way. Personal quests like mine were not something they were familiar with.

We had all had splendid results despite running into various dead ends. It was apparent after each interview that golden or black moments of history previously unknown to the interpreters were being revealed, giving them a new understanding of their country and their peoples. Equally significant to them was the fact they were meeting very famous and formerly powerful figures; no longer mere footnotes in history books, they were able to listen to them discuss not politics and slogans but real men and women, hour-by-hour fighting, withdrawals, losses, accidents, a strong enemy, hardships with food, health.

Not only Mai and Minh Ha, but military men had lauded General Than, so I expected to meet a very special man. I would try this time to get a composite picture of the men who were in Cholon that morning of 5 May. I would not worry unduly about the battle strategies, but about the type of men in those Tet firefights. What sort of men were they? Sitting around in hiding discussing the move into Saigon within a day or two, they must have known their chances of survival were slim. Often under a tree in relaxation before the battle, each of them would be thinking they would see only four, not nine, of those friends again.

Than, now retired, was General Than, Commander of the 6th and 7th Regiments in the Battle of Saigon. He was the Commander of the Long An Army (the province that folds itself crescent-shaped from six o'clock south to 11 o'clock north-northwest around Saigon) and although all five wings of the attacking forces were important, three were crucial, and he was commanding two of them.

General Than and his aides greeted us warmly on arrival, mid-morning. He was now the Chairman of the People's Committee of Long An, retired from active duty.

Than was tall for a Vietnamese, perhaps 1.75 m, strongly built, and with quite broad shoulders. A wide forehead, very bright light brown eyes. Mobile, mostly smiling lips; in military terms he was a father figure. By the time our very long interview was over, I told him if I'd been a young colonel and had my choice, I'd have fought under him. He wore loose-fitting light grey trousers and shirt. No adornments. No rings, no watch, no patches or battle emblems, no collar studs.

General Than knew the purpose of my search, asked a few questions on the results so far, and then asked how he could help. Behind him he had pasted up the original attack plan from 5 May with arrows showing attack directions of all five wings, and overlays with other military information on it concerning forces of both sides. Right from the start I knew I was going to like the man and enjoy the interview, for he had tremendous recall and a deep love and sympathy for fighting forces. I was to hear him frequently include men of all ranks and nations in his comments.

At last I had a man who would speak plainly. So often I heard the euphemisms "foreign enemy" and "puppets" and "those opposing progress" and other names.

Our session began without ado and, I thought, positively.

"Let's not make this a monologue. Put questions to me at any time," Than said.

Encouraged, I said, "After a general talk on the battle I would like to concentrate on a description of troops who followed the sharp-edge commandoes in on 5 and 6 May. Their ages, their schooling, their military training, what their attitudes were, and where they are likely to be today."

"Fine." Than replied. "Your questions already interest me. I'll just talk away and you make notes then we'll have a summary."

It was most sensible. I would perhaps get some information I didn't need, but I was more likely to hear information I couldn't have predicted.

What I got from him exceeded my wildest hopes. Fifteen minutes into the meeting with him I was for the first time truly confident of a successful result to this whole enterprise. Confident of finding whether any of the ambush platoon members were still alive, confident of an answer, if not of finding a particular man.

General Than had not only agreed to see me, but had prepared well for the interview, something most others had not done. Usually there were fifteen or twenty minutes of fencing around to see if I truly understood the cause and the sacrifices, and another fifteen or twenty minutes coping with obsequious minor military rankings trying to win merit with their seniors; there always seemed to be some junior officer explaining that they had followed their instructions closely and had wanted to win freedoms as spelled out by the something directive by the something party of the previous month.

Than continued by saying: "You want to know about the second Tet from 5 May? It was a terrible battle. The Americans fought courageously against us at the important Y Bridge. Both sides lost many good men in that week."

He then went on to give me details of a kind I could hardly have expected and which, in a way, made me feel very privileged. He allowed me a view into the very heart of the dragon that was the North Vietnamese army in those desperate days of 1968; or, if one tries to be more dispassionate about it, he let me see how an operation of war was conducted efficiently and, in the end, successfully.

He said:

> Saigon was the brain centre of our enemies. When the offensive was launched on 5 May our forces were broken into five wings. I was in charge of two of those wings, south and southwest of the city. Southwest was Cholon. After the first Tet (in which the US Embassy was held for a few hours) the enemy reinforced Saigon.

Even then the South Vietnamese forces were not sufficient to hold Saigon. It was the US forces we were concerned with. They controlled an area of ten kilometres around Saigon. The South Vietnamese forces were left to protect the inner heart of Saigon. Our aim was to get as deep as we could under cover into the heart of the city to liquidate the South Vietnamese forces.

We had two "leading edge" regiments, crack troops, to penetrate the heart. One came in through Cholon, where your ambush took place. We moved in darkness, from late 4 May through the early morning hours of 5 May. The second came in to the Y Bridge [a point at seven o'clock south-southwest pointing to the heart of the city] which was most strategic. I was directly commanding seven infantry and two artillery companies and overall I had a division in my charge.

One battalion went to the Y Bridge and had to be spread around by 4 a.m. The majority of other companies under my command had the job of surrounding the US forces. Working by night, in full uniform, fully armed, they had a very difficult task, as you can imagine.

We had to keep one kilometre from the US forces there. They were very strong. We had to surround the US forces at a distance, to immobilise them. To keep them from helping the South Vietnamese forces, which we thought we had covered, in the heart of Saigon, our real target.

We had to fight, penetrate, fight, penetrate, into the city. Our strategy was not to kill the Americans, but to isolate them. When the "open fire" order was given at 6 a.m. the Americans were taken by surprise. By those tactics we put them under pressure. We were to hold them to their territory to prevent them joining the ARVN (South Vietnamese) forces right in town.

I could see by their varying response they had no idea what size force was attacking them. We were keeping those US forces ten kilometres south of the town from joining the real battle.

To clear the way for the US forces to get to the heart of Saigon, they had to cross the Y Bridge, where already one battalion had placed itself under cover of night. By the end of the fighting this battalion had been awarded, not once but thrice, Heroes of Vietnam honours.

The US forces, therefore, could not use the Y Bridge. So the US commander inside the city sent a battalion to remove our forces from blocking the bridge. It became a duel between two battalions; our battalion just south of the Y Bridge leading to the city, blocking any US ground forces from the south, and their battalion coming from the city to clear it. We knew it would be a battle with many losses.

> The fight lasted many days. A real duel. The Americans threw everything at us from the air and the ground. But we were well entrenched. [*One only has to see this Y Bridge over the Kinh Zoi River to see how hard it would have been to dislodge them. Under the southern edge of this strange high flyover bridge are hundreds of solid, small buildings, offering cover and protection.*] Finally our battalion won. It was a rare phenomenon in any war for one battalion to liquidate another one entirely.

General Than had been there all through it. From the perimeter of the US bases down south to the Y Bridge. He communicated with a BRC25 radio. He gave orders in code. Battalion commanders got sealed orders on the specifics of the attack or defence only naming *n* hour to start. Then by radio at the last moment they were told *n* hour was 6 a.m.

I had watched this terrible battle for the Y Bridge, which reached its height in the two days following our ambush on 5 May. Those newsagency reports of reporters watching battles from the top floor of the Caravelle or Majestic hotels were deadly accurate. From the balcony of the Majestic Hotel each evening we watched the two battalions fight each other, with US helicopter gunships firing into the south of the Y Bridge. The civilians had all departed by the morning of 5 May just as they had in our ambush area in Cholon.

It did not take long for the General to relate the story of this encounter. What I'd looked for as mere background to my questions had become information very revealing in itself. While he was talking about this battle I reflected on the multiple millions of dollars spent during those mornings of 5, 6, 7 May and the hundreds of lives lost. Here was a man whose capture and information would then have been worth millions, living now in a modest cottage, running a province whose budget was probably now fifty or sixty thousand dollars annually, at the most.

Than was not a man inspired to inflict his personal political philosophies or dreams on others; he was instead a military man with great respect and sympathy and understanding of those forces opposing him, whom he had to defeat. Not once was he derisive of the men opposing him, in fact quite the opposite. He was a man capable of good sense, plain talk and compassion. I imagined him on invitation at West Point going over the finer points of the battle with the US commander who had the job of defending Saigon. Equally, I felt someone owed these same men an explanation, namely the politicians who set these soldiers against each other, never quite explaining why they were to sometimes attack and suffer great losses, and at other times remain immobile; the politicians who let Pol Pot kill civilians on Vietnam borders in 1976 and 1977 before ordering the military men to defend them; the same politicians who would pretend friendship to China while knowing that within a short period they would be at war.

Even the lowest-ranking man in Vietnam, for example, must have pondered the idiocy of having the Chinese as their friends and suppliers in 1975, then being asked to go to the northern borders of Vietnam to defend their country against a massive invasion by the Chinese. Wisely, General Than did not become a party to that nonsense, rejecting a political role after his very successful military career.

We then got to the Cholon ambush. The fighting for Cholon on the first morning of the Battle of Saigon had been very important; though less spectacular than the holding of the Y Bridge it was nevertheless the main thrust. I wanted to know about the people involved. Not the battalion numbers, not the attack plans, but the ranks. Than was more than happy to talk about them, for they were his men after all. He had grown up in villages, he had come through the ranks knowing these men. He had lived and eaten and worked with them. Than described them this way:

> You must understand these people were from the villages. They had very little formal education and very little knowledge of cities. For example, they would hardly know the difference between various motor vehicles. They had travelled in truck transports themselves as soldiers, but would never have been able to drive them or fix their motors. They would imagine only troops like themselves would travel in trucks, and only officers would travel in jeeps.
>
> A Westerner to them would have been an American. They were told Americans had no place in Vietnam. This was not their country, it was Vietnam. Why else would they be here but to continue some form of colonial domination? Once a Westerner rode in a jeep he was to them a US officer. If he had no uniform he was a US Intelligence officer. If the jeep had a white flag, then they were people to be stopped and captured and spoken to. Your jeep was white. That would have made no difference. The car with the West German [*a diplomat killed in Cholon that morning*] had diplomatic number plates which would have meant nothing to them.

The difference between normal number plates and diplomatic plates would have been meaningless.

I can tell you now that the shooting of your jeep was a mistake. We issued orders for men in such jeeps to be captured wherever possible. They might be officers we could have questioned, or traded for our own prisoners later. But your case was different. You faced very junior-ranking self-defence forces. You drove in to our rear lines. Normally we would capture such a jeep in frontal areas. But not right in the centre of our defence forces.

Those self-defence people were not very aware. All they would see would be a jeep carrying US Intelligence soldiers penetrating what they saw as their best defence lines. They could expect armoured personnel carriers and other forces to follow. They must have thought the battle had been brought back into their own territory and the front had collapsed.

These were people who were clerks, students, businessmen, sympathisers, the lowest ranks of our defence. They stored weapons for us in their houses, reported to us, and held weapons for retreating forces. Not regulars, not battle-experienced people. They might have been led by a few regulars, but of low rank. In any event, they would have been in platoon formation and under orders to move, reporting as they went. We had written sheets and sheets of reports from their radio reports in Cholon and not one of them mentioned "Press".

There were several reports of US enemies killed. Those reports were wrapped into whole reports with final numbers of those killed. Very accurate reports, in numbers killed. The men who ambushed you were 100 per cent certainly self-defence forces who were very surprised to see you in there. They would have expected bigger forces to come behind you, and they probably had orders to move on.

I interrupted him to say the ambush had been quite professional. They shot the jeep's motor first to stop the jeep, then fired on us. "Agreed. Four or five in a platoon would have been in charge of these forces. That is standard ambush procedure. But your interpreter tells me one man came out to shoot the wounded, yet he missed one man with two of his shots. That was common. Some of those self-defence forces were political activists, students, doctors, tradespeople, shopkeepers. Not skilled with weapons."

During all this time General Than had been referring to original attack maps, showing the usual thrust arrows with battalion numbers and other information plastered all over them. Tea and coffee, some cigarettes and fruit had been served. Because of his persuasive storytelling, we felt were in the battle with him, while we were also in this long room as students of military history.

He asked Mai Huong how I had escaped from the ambush. She told him I had been wary of possible confrontation as we drove down against a stream of civilian refugees. I had moved earlier from an inside rear seat position to be sitting on the left-outside rear of the jeep. She said I was not familiar with that part of Saigon, but from experience in Indonesia I had felt in danger and had warned the others against going further.

Than said, "They were already too far in, Road 46 was our territory."

Mai continued, "Our guest here today jumped clear and pretended to be dead. The other men in the jeep were killed or wounded. When the man was sent to finalise the killing he shot two others, but two bullets missed."

Than wanted to know how all the soldiers had behaved. We had plenty of time to go into details, he said; besides, it would tell him a lot about the men.

I said they had been very surprised, perhaps alarmed, when we drove into the road which they'd blocked off with 44-gallon drums. They had obviously not expected us and might have been concentrating on avoiding being hit by the helicopter gunship whose rocket-streams we had followed in. When they saw us they shouted loudly and took cover.

There had been perhaps fourteen or fifteen of them, but only five or six exposed when we came quickly around a corner and drove almost up to them. Most of them had the typical black pyjama uniform. All had seemed armed. We reversed the jeep briefly but they opened fire.

He wanted to know what they had hit first. I told him despite the attack I could tell the automatic rifles were shooting into the front of the jeep. By the time they had begun on the four occupants I was well behind the jeep, peeping over my left arm. Already I could see one dead, and one wounded. One of them I was never able to see from my low position, and the fourth was the driver who after being wounded had staggered to the back of the jeep.

Than asked what guns they used. I said both were easily identified: an AK47 I'd seen when we surprised them and the second was an older Burp gun with a cylindrical magazine. I remembered they mostly pulled down on firing, but being rested on a drum would have solved that problem. They emptied both magazines but stayed under cover, even while the man I thought was their commander came out to deliver the *coups de grace*. We skipped the gory parts and the appeals for mercy.

"He would not have been able to understand him," he said of the journalist who held out his press card and called "*bao chi*". "I tell you, these people were very simply educated. Even correctly said, which I doubt, the fact of you being in our most vulnerable areas would have told him you were US Intelligence."

He was interested that a second man had not come forward. He asked about the man who finished off the two wounded. I described him, his uniform, and repeated my claim he wore boots. I told him I was counting the rounds from what I'd thought for years was a .45 and he'd spent six, the third and fourth were misses from a short distance.

Did he move quickly? Was he crouched? No, I said. I had a clear view of him despite my posture of feigned death. He was slow and deliberate, always upright. Nearly all middle-ranking men who'd been in Cholon that morning told me I was mistaken in saying he wore boots. But that was part of the reason I recalled calculating my chances. Not only did he look a little soft and overweight, especially around the face, but if I got the start I wanted on him when he was forced to reload; he'd never catch me in those boots.

Than laughed. He asked what I had intended doing about the AK47 and the Burp gun. Those men would have reloaded by then. I said I would run in a straight line from him, from the point of the triangle he formed with them as the base. For them to shoot me they would have to shoot through him.

"And did that happen?" he asked.

"Yes, except that I forgot I had a corner to turn," I replied.

So I waited as he looked at me. He seemed certain I was dead. I jumped as he was taking the spent magazine out and sprinted away. When I got to where I had to turn I was exposed, but zig-zagging a bit. They opened fire and hit a sign above me to the left and they kept firing, but missed.

He chased me. When I got thirty or forty metres ahead of him I turned and saw him still chasing me. He fired a few times, but by the time I got to the tail end of some civilian refugees he'd given up. I took my shirt off and rubbed it in some mud puddles and wiped my body with mud and ran crouched. The civilians let me through without hindrance.

And that was that. I got a three-wheeler in Minh Phung at the end of that street. When I left three were dead for certain.

Than had followed this through Mai's interpreting and by using a good local map which showed the street, and the location of the Minh Phung intersection. That was a "front line" of sorts for them. So we were deep in their territory.

Than then summarised:

> Your description is very true to reality. It usually happened that way. A group of soldiers shoot down a car and a commander to finish the job. But there are here some helpful hints for us. First, the man's boots. Don't concern yourself, I think he could easily have had boots. this was not as skilled an ambush as you think. They were surprised, when they should have been on guard.
>
> They would never have thought the enemy could have penetrated so far, but they should have been more prepared. They were almost certainly the locals, as I suggested earlier but their leader was inexperienced.
>
> The man who came out in uniform and boots probably got that uniform and boots from an enemy. These self-defence forces used whatever clothing they wanted. He was not the commander, I think. He seems to have moved too slowly, standing up straight all the time was not wise, as he showed when you ran — he could have been in their way. The handgun also was not a .45. Almost certainly it was the usual K54. [I had discovered that in Hanoi myself some weeks earlier.]
>
> Although most likely they were village boys as I said, with some locals, they had been mostly away in the jungle awaiting this period. I was the commander there from the very beginning of the Tet Offensives in January until the end of the second wave, more than six months.
>
> Up until now I would never have believed it possible there were foreign journalists in so far behind the lines. Every officer and every soldier was totally aware that in winning this war we could not rely on our own forces alone, but owed it to the international community. We had great respect and sympathy for journalists. In none of those despatches was there a mention of journalists.
>
> From this sad incident I have to say you were the best and most brave fighter in the battle because you did not lose your cool mind and consciousness.

The detail he was able to present reinforced my opinion this had been the most valuable interview so far. We had moved beyond discussions of facts and figures — there had hardly been a political comment made all through the interview — and towards a new understanding.

In my fear on the spot and in my recall, what I had claimed to be a very professional ambush had been rated as a hastily improvised action in which the Vietnamese had ignored some basic principles of safety. Total success was denied them because of their inexperience, or their inability to adjust quickly to the surprise appearance of the "enemy."

If we had been who they thought we were, and well armed, they would have suffered losses at least equal to our own. Later, we would learn that to be exactly the case. Their losses were heavy.

As we were leaving, General Than and his aides came out with us into the sunshine on the steps of the municipal building which housed the People's Committee or local government.

Than was in a bright mood with us, but when talking about the nation, he was sombre.

"Tell your audience if you are to make a film that Vietnam is no one's puppet, or will ever be. We are truly independent. But our nation is poor, starving, very hungry after forty years of fighting. The whole leadership hates the fact of war . . . without which we would not be hungry today.

"I think you know that after Liberation other forces like Pol Pot and China did not let Vietnam have peace. Tell them not to think that because we're good fighters that we are a martial people. Vietnamese, more than any other people, think war is a tragedy."

The girls were moved by that short speech and referred to it several times in our post-mortems of the interview. It was an inspiring meeting for them, to see this historic figure and to listen to his razor-sharp descriptions and especially his assessments of the men involved in the ambush.

We had all heard too much fuzzy, bureaucratic talk, dealt with too many preliminary interviews in the busy city government departments (where it was often better to ride a bicycle a few kilometres than try to get through on the phone), had too many meetings and delays in getting answers to quite simple requests. On the way back in the car we agreed that today great progress had been made.

We took our time getting home. We stopped by the roadside for pineapples, then later for some crispy bread baked in tiny clay ovens near the roadside in what surely are the smallest "bakeries" in the world. From the sunshine and the fields of Long An we returned to the shadowed poverty of the decrepit city.

Even if it cannot be Saigon again, Ho Chi Minh City will never lose its Saigon atmosphere. One of the leaders said after the 24 March 1978 encirclement of the Chinese in Cholon and the subsequent compulsory acquisition of most of their wealth that what was happening in Cholon and other parts of the newly named city was not befitting the name Ho Chi Minh.

But for all their attempts to take the people out of old Saigon, they have failed to take the Saigon out of the people. In old Tu Do Street, now Dong Khoi, Maxim's restaurant has become the showplace for the upper middle class young marrieds, or the teenagers of the established new powers. They have ball gowns, designer jeans, elaborate sweaters which say "By me" on them, very fashionable coiffured hairstyles and lots of money. They arrive in newish cars, before entering the *dansant* (dancing) place where only very modern pirated tapes are played. There is a swagger to their mobility and an aloofness which betrays they are there for pure fun.

This represents a new development in Vietnam, but a familiar one for other parts of Asia. This country is experiencing the emergence of a money and power class, similar to those in Thailand and Indonesia and the Philippines.

And just a few steps away up Dong Khoi street, on the same side, is the first steambath/massage parlour to open since 1975, when the victorious army swept in and these houses closed their doors before they were forcibly closed on them. The steam pipes and heaters and special rooms were unused for thirteen years; they represented a sort of sub-culture in hibernation, now coming to life again.

The general had fought for a system and certain freedoms, he had said. Little wonder he was today not proud of what he saw in HCM/Saigon. A ruined city with cosmetic changes and only the frivolous showing any signs of prosperity.

16

By November 1988, I was part of the Vietnamese Journalists' Association, in the sense that they were passing me onto more and more contacts. I wanted their help in my search for the ambush platoon. In turn, they wanted me to help them establish the figures of journalists and cameramen killed, and so it became a joint effort. It was during one of our now-frequent exchanges that I met Tran Nhu. Tran was one of seven photo journalists at a meeting in a musty but formerly elegant colonial two-storey building on the edge of the heart of the city. Despite the ruinous state of the building, it had a friendly atmosphere. Quiet, well decorated with beautiful black and white photographs in simple frames, swept stairwells, neatly ordered files. With this as their base the photographers were eking out a very modest living in a new world that could hardly afford to pay for creativity when cement and steel and cables and motor vehicles and ships were far higher priorities.

We got together in an upstairs boardroom, once an exporter's office in the days of Vietnam's rubber boom. The tapes from this session eventually took hours to transcribe and while they were helpful in establishing the numbers of those killed, they mainly concentrated on modes of operation and shed very little light on actions during the Battle for Saigon.

Tran's story stood out, time and time again in transcription. It had been friendship at first sight, or so I thought. I was now used to meeting journalists who carried problems from the war. A second photographer in Ho Chi Minh had also lost an eye and now had a glass eye. Another had some fingertips missing.

Tran had a darkened area around a siphoned hole where his eye had once been, forming a frightening upturned cone cavity which, even to those used to seeing war injuries, must have been unnerving. His other eye was a beautiful grey. It looked at me softly throughout our session and I was forced to meet his gaze and smile or just gaze back myself and nod in understanding, despite the horror of the stories being told.

He was a most modest man. He waited his turn, last of the seven. Yet when his turn came, the others spoke for him. He rarely spoke. Tran was in Cholon, in the middle of the hottest battles, they said. Tran was our best cameraman. He was famous amongst us. Tran would always get the best pictures and Tran was utterly reliable. Tran smiled, and nodded thanks to them for the compliment.

Tran was hit by fragments from a rocket, and lost his eye, they said. Tran nodded agreement. Tran was bleeding from the head yet he delivered his film; he then left us and went to the enemy's hospital, they continued. Tran smiled, remembering. Tran, they said for him, booked in as a civilian casualty, giving the name on his false ID card.

Tran said: "I was treated with great care by the nuns." Tran was in hospital, they said. We then lost track of him for two months.

Tran said: "Yes. I was in hospital. I worried about my camera." Tran returned to them but he strangely insisted then he would use an ordinary still camera, not a movie camera. They agreed to that, they said.

Tran said: "It was time for me to give my position as first to others."

And in this fashion the interview with Tran continued. The others telling his story, and Tran agreeing or adding small comments. All the time his grey eye smiling to me, and me smiling back, trying to show I understood. It took until 3 a.m. that night to finish the transcriptions. I reviewed them the next evening at the Caravelle Bar.

It was my habit to put these pages away for a working day and bring them with me to a small table in Doctor Death's eighth floor bar where I was guaranteed a quiet table with a window overlooking the city, and where I could get cold Saigon 33 beer and go to work on the pages with my fountain pen. I asked Doctor Death (named so because he had a face like a cadaver) whether he knew of Tran. "Oh, yes. A wonderful man. The most beautiful and peaceful photographs. I wish we could have some here."

Three or four days later I called on Tran, on a pretence of getting the name of the hospital. "You walked past it. It is nearly in the same street. I go there still to talk to children. It is mostly for children nowadays."

I asked whether he took photographs of them. Almost as the question fell from my lips I regretted it. What was for me a way of giving presents — taking photographs and having them developed in my local Kodak shop and packing them up and handing them out on my next visit, — was in Vietnam a financial impossibility. A single roll of my Kodak Gold 100 was then selling for 20,000 dong, a month's salary for a government clerk, and the processing costs were very high because of the photographic paper.

He replied: "No. Unfortunately I cannot do this just now." It was a poor start to the meeting. I had meant well and wanted to see him again. He let me off the hook with a good suggestion.

"But let's do it together," he said. "You can take the photos and I will talk to the children. I am very good at talking to them. I wish I had some of my own children, but these are my children, my wanted children." He then laughed. "Imagine me, with twenty children! 'You bad one, stop that nonsense' I would have to say. But I did want to have children of my own and because I cannot I become a hospital father. So!"

I asked then for him to return to 1968. When he lost his eye. His beautiful grey eye looked to me still. It shone and shone. Only his mouth and a frown or two could help me read his answers.

"The nurses looked after me very well. We had our false ID cards. Mine was easy to remember, the name of a dead man in my village. The southern régime's soldiers came through to check us all out. I thought I would be discovered and taken away. No eye. That wouldn't matter, they would ask my other eye to tell the story: Which unit were you with? What was the attack plan? Who are those in Cholon you connect with? But they passed me by. The nuns told them I was not to be disturbed. I was a civilian casualty."

He had taken the still camera when he got out because his head was ringing and ringing and he had nightmares. He would never again handle a movie camera. It was time for his junior colleagues to take over. He was thirty-two. He had long wanted to marry and settle in a village like his own. Like the one he remembered, for his own village was now a shambles. Somewhere, sometime, he would find another village and a village girl. They would do just what his dream had said he would do. They would meet and fall in love and go working, him as a photographer in the nearby town and she at home in the village and they would have children. No wars would take his eye out, no bombs would hurt the village. No more bad dreams.

His grey eye was still gazing peacefully at me. He asked if I had any bad dreams. I told him I had had many years of them. But crassly, I asked him to continue his story, to tell me what happened in Tet and when he began again, and where he was, and what the atmosphere was like, and other such questions.

Tran again let me off the hook. A soup vendor was wheeling past and making his call by tapping a drumstick on a hollow bamboo. "Let's have some soup," he said. He followed me down and ordered for me, telling me we had to pay 400 dong each. "That is his price. A very good soup. Cheap even for me."

There was something a little wrong, but I couldn't see it. In the bright sunshine of day, with sharp reflective flashes from passing bicycles and little trucks, he showed what I thought was professional concentration in looking at me with his lovely grey eye.

"In the warm air you can ask me anything. Whatever is black in my mind becomes softer and humorous when there is sunshine. When the children start to tell me their pain I bring them out in their chairs into the sunshine and pretend I've not heard the story and ask them to start again. The sun soothes them. It makes all those stories better," he said.

He was great company. He spoke so softly in a mixture of French, very simple English and some Vietnamese, yet he could have been playing a guitar and I would have understood. As the street people gathered round him I could see the strips of their shadows fall on his beautiful grey unblinking eye.

It quietly dawned on me that he was almost totally blind. He sat in the sun with his usual friends around him. He saw some shadows and some grey movement. In the sunshine he looked very relaxed. He leaned towards me and started his story, his hand on my face as a subterfuge, tracing his hands over my eyes to indicate how he was hurt and put in hospital. He drew his fingers around my face to show how the nuns would check him over each day.

He had tricked his colleagues for years into thinking he was just a little short-sighted. When there were no more photographs to take and no more film and no new lenses and no new expensive photographic paper it no longer mattered.

When all his beautiful black and white photographs of birds and paddies and water-market canoes filled with vegetables and forest shacks and fish jumping in ponds were all hung, there was no need any more for him to raise a camera and stare for minutes and minutes before he finally resolved an image in his lovely, dying eye.

By rote he walked to the office. By rote he sat with them in the bronzed light and spoke of matters in hand. They looked at him, knowing he was in good shape, seeing quite well, and went thankfully away to do nothing very much at all, week after week, month after month.

"So. You know. They still think I see quite well," he said.

As people spoke to him he recognised their voices and turned to them addressing them by name, so they too kept faith in the eye's life.

> I used to have very bad dreams. None of the war. Well, some. Just the explosions, blasts, blinding light. We had an accident when I was just starting to film. Some plastic bomb accidentally set off. I saw it all, and I remember every explosion just like that. White blanket flashes.
>
> Simple dreams. Me at home. Me at school. I never did fish, but my brother did and in my dreams I took my brother's fish and put them on my line. Simple. I had all my dead friends come to see my fish. Men in uniforms crowding around me looking at my fish. They had soup bowls and I put a piece of my fish in each bowl and we all sat down and ate fish and noodles.
>
> My lovely wife then came in and brought more for everyone. And when all was finished I went back to the pond and got some more fish. The group was bigger every time I got back but my wife still shared my new fish around.

"How many in your fish group?" I asked.

"About fifty dead friends," he said.

The soup seller had moved away. A small but busy shop close by was selling schoolbooks and the children who came and chatted around the books made an enjoyable noise for him. The soup seller had left two tiny stools on which we still sat. In the strong sunshine of the narrow street we were in no one's path.

So these are the stories I tell my children in the hospital. Of course I do not tell them my friends are dead. And the fish are mine. As you know I have no wife. Not even a beautiful one that I dreamed of. I come each day from behind Le Loi Boulevard to here. Someone stole my camera the first day I was there. I live on the first room off the street and it was easy for some poor person. Why would I need a camera? But I told them all and that is accepted now. A cameraman without a camera! Imagine that. The illusion became the reality. Day by day they see me without seeing me. Ideas fixed in their minds: Cameraman.

He asked me to tell me about my own dreams from the war. Did I dream of friends dead? Did I dream of my village and fish and birds? Could I tell him about them? I replied my stories were not as clear as his. Even his present daytime stories were better. I was impressed by his ability to keep everyone else in the dark when it was he who was in the dark, all these years.

With tentative hands I ran my fingers over his face quickly, then to his arm and lifted it and we walked, with him leading me, to his room. I promised him I would write something that night about my dreams and tell him about our side of the war. Would he mind, I asked, if I brought a different interpreter than the first one. I knew someone who might understand because she was a lot older and had lived through the war.

He agreed to the change. "But she must not come to my house as you do. They might ask me to leave if they find out about me."

Compounding his problems were fears he would never find another place to live. With his war record he would finally get an apartment but far from the old Saigon city centre he knew so well, where his friends were. In the block at present his was the only room with a single occupant. Families of five or six lived in single rooms and shared toilet facilities.

That night, I wrote twenty pages.

For the meeting I asked an older interpreter to accompany me. Thu, who was forty, had been a bar girl at the famous Number 5 club. At twenty she had perhaps been very pretty but I suspect at war's end she had been a worn twenty-seven because now she had a particularly brutalised-looking face.

But she had the most beautiful voice and an exceptional command of English. She studied the language when not working her stall which sold imitation flowers made of paper and nylon, wooden clogs for weddings and other ceremonial occasions, and a range of ghastly pottery seconds. I was never tempted to buy anything there nor did she expect me to buy, but we talked frequently and I picked up a lot of interesting gossip.

She was perfect for the meeting with Tran. She translated quickly and she loved the practice. She had read hundreds of English books and had a shifting "library" of eighty or ninety most heavily marked. She had a big stack of Westerns by Zane Grey and Louis L'Amour, and various books by Eric Ambler, all thumbed through and underlined as she had searched the dictionaries for the meanings. Her favourite American author was Sidney Sheldon because she identified with his fast-moving, clever women.

I asked if she would mind accompanying me to meet Tran.

Thu said: "Tran? The famous photographer? Certainly. It will be my honour." I gave Thu a present even before we left. She had asked me earlier for any old batteries. She had a GE calculator that needed two 1.5 volt batteries, a torch that needed two batteries, a battered transistor that needed four pencil 1.5 volt batteries, and a tiny Taiwanese-made fan that needed torch batteries, and so on. I brought them all in new packs from my camera bag and gave her two new audio cassettes, which she could sell from the stall and get the other batteries she needed.

But she would not walk with me along Le Loi.

"They will think I have a foreign man, like the old days. I had so much big trouble because they all told the street committees about me. After Liberation all the bars were closed and the girls got political education. Just nonsense."

So we took separate cyclos to Tran's building. There, we found him sitting outside drinking coffee. As I alighted I said something frivolous like, "Ah, loafing!"

They answered for him: "And why not? It is Sunday."

Thu took over, speaking in rapid Vietnamese. They talked for a minute or two, sometimes about me, but mostly not. She took him by the arm and they walked, to a small coffee shop, then sat just inside the door.

Thu was generous with my money; she ordered the best filter coffee, a packet of 555 cigarettes, and had the waiter go for some fresh bread, and, I learned later, some fruit. She rubbed her hands in front of her after ensuring Tran was comfortable, then took from me my printouts from the night before.

Tran was at peace. Just to be manhandled and ordered around and touched by Thu was a delight for him. Using English she was a delight to listen to; in Vietnamese she must have been pure honey for him. She took the pages and sat back and started to read to him. I felt I was intruding, so close were they as she began reading. She read slowly as he stared with his beautiful grey eye into her face. She began by reading the heading — "Soliloquy."

She then translated this as my story introduction. He nodded. Go ahead. "I am telling him," said Thu, "that when I say 'I' it is you."

"I know that much English," he said.

So, she started again, with coffee, bread, all at hand.

Rarely did she look at me from then on, but read the pages I had written for Tran.

I always wondered who killed them.

Not a passing thought or even a recurring theme. One that wandered in through a side door of my mind, prompted by a newspaper reference to Vietnam or journalists being shot or beaten in South America or anywhere. A thought that would flit out in the glare of harsh daylight, or from traffic noise.

The man asking me the question was always ghostlike, in a hood and a cloak, or someone in battle uniform, who stepped through the side door in a dark corner of my mind. The rooms were always dark and in the dreams the questions persisted. I was inside the room, yet I was watching myself.

The year didn't seem to matter. It was the same question as I watched the man lift his left arm, unsteadily holding the heavy automatic. The mental picture freeze-framed. I could not get up from the ground. My legs were too heavy, my arms could not move, yet at the same time I was in control because I was ice-cold, watching him.

I never did drag myself up in that dream. He was coming for me, and I was stuck fast on the ground. Then I was suddenly on the railway tracks in my home town and a train was coming and I knew the train was going to get me for killing tiger snakes that lay on the railway lines getting warm in the morning sun. I had killed them as I was going to school. A single sharp crack across the back with a stick cut from tea-tree.

Everyone of us in those school days had a tea-tree stick and knew to hit the tigers across the back and they would curl up and bite themselves to die quickly and avoid the pain of slow death. Not once did they ever attack us, yet we accepted the bush town folklore that said we had to kill the snakes.

When I was a big boy of seven, I let a fat mother snake go free because she was so slow and harmless but another boy with me hit her with his stick and belted her until the babies came squirming out and he stamped on them and I began to cry and stopped him and one or two got away. But he told the school I was a sissy for snakes.

And so thirty years later I let the snakes live on my farm, telling my two small children they were dangerous and to stand clear. Stand absolutely still then slowly move back. Twice they did it and I loved them for their courage, not for their obedience. But if you see a mosquito, kill it, smack! Such is the lie in life that we live.

Thu was handing my pages over as she finished them. She had no problems with the snake stories. Tran seemed to love them. It was not what he had wanted, but on a sunny morning, with coffee and bread and the warm voice of a woman drumming dreamily through his mind, he needed little else. Yet Thu or Tran did not turn to me. She read, he listened, to my midnight scribblings. He nodded his head slowly and looked sad.

I followed his reactions and at the same time quietly looked over the pages as Thu handed them to me. I had not read my own writing. I had gone to my little Brother wordprocessor and just written, and written. Thu read again:

But I escape. I am so much faster than he is. He wears boots. They shoot but they have to shoot around him and I know this, so I run to the point of the triangle he forms with his own men. But as I run I know I have to turn a corner and give them a chance to kill me. They hit a sign to my left, and bullets in my dreams dance around my feet. He runs after me, but I am faster.

I want to see his face once again, so I turn and look at him as he is shooting at me from his little pistol. I will know him forever.

The mind pictures were as hard to put together as shattered glass. The part about the dreams finished with Tran looking very sad. Thu started up again with my pages. They were about my return home.

We were outcasts in our own country, in our own towns, in our own offices, sealing away the seething and writhing coloured pictures into another room; enclosing another room in our minds. We could seal it off a few months at a time. But the little doors kept opening. Especially at night.

Even someone with a clear conscience awakens at night in fright at the noise of the wind or at the crinkling sound of a cellophane wrapper unfolding in the witching hour telling him in his half-sleep that someone is in the room. A room he knows no burglar can get into, which is a bungalow in the bush miles from anywhere . . .

More shadows fall and suddenly I am menaced again. I menace them back screaming and shouting as I lash out and put a hard right handchop into my wife's body and she awakens in fright. At other times I cannot respond at all and I lie there with deadened limbs and my death rattle begins, growing into a full deep-throated groan which is cut short as soft hand and a soothing woman's voice calms me. Another broken night for both of us. Then a beautiful sleep. Hell closes at four in the morning, letting those queuing to get in have another short curled-up sleep. Until tomorrow night.

Tran spoke: "This is your man? I was there all through that. Surely he is dead. Won't that help you now?"

I said I didn't see him as dead. I saw him now as a greying senior military man muddling through a job in the provinces.

"No. He is dead. Most of them are from that area. It was the worst, just as bad as the Y Bridge fighting," he said.

Thu asked how I had got back into Vietnam. I went on to describe my previous, failed attempt to enter the country, how in 1979 my well received application was eventually rejected after China attacked Vietnam in February of that year and no further visas were being issued. I told her that I had now returned on invitation from the government to celebrate the twentieth anniversary of Tet, nine years after my first application.

Tran and Thu were enjoying the afternoon, and each other's company. My nightmare stories were interesting and not hard to understand. They wanted to know more about the tiger snakes and the kangaroos. And did I always sleep in a big bed? Weren't my parents in the house to help me?

They wanted to know more about America, not the cities, but the countryside. I had said earlier that I had taken my two children for a very long "poor people's holiday" through California, Nevada, Utah, Colorado, New Mexico, Arizona and northern Mexico. Thu was ecstatic. Her Louis L'Amour and Zane Grey westerns had given her so much of the early west's history. The translations from then on were delightfully long. She knew the world of wagon trains and Indians.

"How could you be poor on this holiday if you could buy a car?" Tran asked.

It was a very old car, I said. But a very big one, very long. It was called an American Ambassador Wagon, and it was so long we put a big mattress in the back to sleep at nights. Lots of pillows and blankets.

"How did you get your rice?" he asked.

I said that every second or third day we would get to a big town and I would check the local newspapers and always I found a job for a day. I put Insinkerators into kitchens for $50.

They asked again and again for descriptions of my travels. It took me ten minutes to get out of the Grand Canyon, a full thirty minutes on Arizona itself, its beauty, its harsh deserts, its lovely springs, its wildflowers. Another ten minutes for the story of the snow in Colorado's Rocky Mountain stretch, the story of Silverton, the mountain streams and the wildlife.

When I mentioned Durango, Thu was beside herself with excitement. She had read all about Durango. The Durango Kid, Gunfight in Durango. My thirty-second description of Durango became a five-minute description to Tran. Louis L'Amour had never had a better interpreter. Tran was getting the wild west story of six-shooters and romance, and he loved it.

I reached the part where we were totally without money, with one can of baked beans and a few slices of stale bread and we wired up a small handle to the can and made a fire at the Four Corners of Utah, Colorado, Arizona and New Mexico and cooked the beans in the can.

They wanted to know why I had no money, if I had made $50 only three days earlier. Fifty dollars to them was a lot of money. I said we had paid nearly all that money in getting fuel for the car, and meals. We also called home to Los Angeles every day and that cost $3.

"For $50 in Vietnam we could drive to New Delhi," said Tran.

"We drove further than that," I said. "If you unravelled our roads into one long road we drove from Saigon to Peking," I said.

"I wouldn't want to drive to Peking. Or Tokyo" he said.

By late afternoon these two had become close friends. I was

their reference point. Thu would tell her stories from her books, liberally interpreting from our travels in the West. She was the raconteur, he was the man who put pictures to her words.

He was seeing a movie unfold for him. One with several high points and many happy endings.

He asked: "How did you cross so many borders? Did you trick them like I did by having many false ID cards?"

I told him I didn't need an ID card.

"So, President Nixon gave you a special pass?"

Nixon was the only president he knew. He knew Kennedy because they had been taught Kennedy was assassinated by Big Business. He had learned that in a training course. I told him it was a different president, Jimmy Carter. He had never heard of Jimmy Carter. Even Thu had never heard of him, and she read lots of books.

"So, this President Carter gave you a pass?" he said. "He was a very good friend, then."

I told them I had no need for an ID card. Just a passport to get to Mexico. They smiled indulgently. To them my answer had been a diplomatic evasion of a straight question. Their own leader Nguyen Van Linh had invited me to make a film. The US president had told the border guards to let me through from Colorado to New Mexico. I had been boiling baked beans with my children to teach them frugality.

But however they interpreted these stories, they knew I would fly out in a few weeks, back to safety and wealth. Whereas they would remain with their daily struggles. The afternoon was a wonderful escape from those realities.

Some fruit arrived. Thu's errand boy had brought back watermelon, papaya, mangoes and some oranges. Thu bent down to the basket and made a smaller basket of fruit and placed it in Tran's lap, for later. The remaining fruit we were to eat. We "tipped" the coffee waiter in fruit, a very big tip it was, and very much appreciated.

Thu kept the main fruit basket under her knees, bringing only small portions out for the table. "Otherwise people will gather around us," she said.

Tran, through Thu, said he would make me "a statement", or that was how she interpreted it — it was really a bet.

"You had no nightmares when you were with your children in the Wild West."

I agreed. No nightmares.

"That is so true. I knew that from the stories. That is another reason why I am with my children at the hospital."

As we ate the fruit, the sun was setting on a truly wonderful afternoon. Tran had been read some pages on a subject with which he was only too familiar. They had had their coffee and French bread, and fruit. They had enjoyed interpreting my stories of travels in the Wild West. The Insinkerators added a touch of high technology and mystery. They would always find it difficult to understand that I was out of money and miles from anywhere. A man with a car must be wealthy.

As for crossing ten or fifteen borders with a special ID pass, well, they would respect my reasons for not disclosing my personal relationship with President Nixon and this President Carter. For the sake of my friendship they would let that little fib simmer, but they made it clear they wouldn't swallow that nonsense of crossing with no ID cards or special passes.

Every American they'd ever seen had worn a chain around his neck and a silver metal nameplate with a number on it. The Soviets didn't wear chains but they were never allowed to walk alone. A guard had to go with them everywhere. These points were minor. It had been a perfect day for them.

Thu asked me about Tran's photographs. Which were the most beautiful? She did not translate as I told her of a set of three of a fishing village down south. The first was an early morning misty photograph of men preparing sampans with folded nets with concentration on their faces and small unfired stoves sitting in the stern on a small crossboard. The second was on the wide lower reaches of the Mekong as they fished. The cloud formations were threatening, yet the fishermen were pleased, and vapour or smoke was coming from near the cooking pot. Several fish were already in the catch basket.

The third was their return. Several women's faces, most of them smiling, were clear. But every man had his head down, bringing the fish baskets in.

It was time to go. The sun had set and the coffee shop was about to close. Thu asked me politely if I would take a cyclo home alone, please. She would walk the small distance to Tran's home with him. She felt more confident in the twilight. I could see that.

I didn't take a cyclo. I walked back, slowly, and went in my western way straight to Doctor Death's bar. I had taken my notebook and fountain pen to the meeting, but not written a stroke. The amiable Doctor Death asked me if I could use my influence to get a photo or two from the famous Tran.

"I know a set of three which will go well here," I said.

The next few weeks were devoted to the main project but in the meantime, I put aside a few dollars for the reproduction of the three photographs by Tran. When I finally returned to the old building I found the stairwell clear of the three-set I wanted. Tran was not there and I barely knew the few individuals who were. I asked where Tran had gone, but they had no idea. I asked if anyone remembered the photographs from the stairwell. Yes, they all did.

"What village was that?" I asked.

"Cuu Long province, on the Hau River near the sea."

I had the excuse that I was leaving, so I could visit Tran to say goodbye. It was quite a long walk. I imagined him, almost totally blind, walking the distance, and admired him even more.

But he was not there and the woman could not help me with an address. He had gone, after all these years. Two small children peeped from Tran's old room, wide-eyed at this white man who had suddenly appeared. I looked around the corridor and saw the same families as before.

When I looked back into Tran's old room I sank into a snap depression. Nothing of him remained. Already there were blankets acting as room dividers. At least five people in there, including the two children, looked as though they had been there for years. The room was grubby and cooking smells dominated the atmosphere.

I went directly to Thu's flower-stall. A new woman was there. Thu was away she said, in a village. She had rented the place from Thu.

"Which village?" I asked.

"Down south in Cuu Long. A fishing village."

I reported my failure to get the three-set of Tran's photos to Doctor Death. He too let me off the obligation. "We've had the same dreadful paintings here for thirty years now. I can wait a little longer."

Two months later I returned from Australia and began immediately on all my rounds. To the Foreign Office, to see Lac Long to pick up sandals he had made while I was away, to have a spicy fish soup at the Kim near the market, to see Viet at his old cyclo stand at the Cuu Long Hotel, to the market for fruit and beer for my room, to Madame 17s to look at any new embroidery for presents, then to Thu's stall, on a hope if you like.

The photographs had been the clue linking them. I had worked that out immediately. I knew Thu was fairly well off by local standards and getting a small home in a fishing village would be easily within her reach. But would she be able to tolerate the quiet life, with her background?

Even before I stepped into Hue road she called loudly to me. Cyclo drivers looked amused, thinking she'd hooked a tourist. Tran was there, sitting calmly inside the main room of the stall. Thu brought me in and hugged me. Tran felt his way across the small insides of the stall, and put his hands on my face and asked me to speak. I said, in English: "It's wonderful to see you both together. You silly people, you went and fell in love!"

He didn't understand a word of it. Tran now had his beautifully spoken wife, and lived in his favourite village. Thu was splitting her time between Cuu Long and Ho Chi Minh. She does this still today. "Do you still have bad dreams? Did you find your man?" he asked.

No more bad dreams, the search goes on, I told him.

"He is dead, I tell you. They are nearly all dead from Cholon and the Y Bridge battles. I would have been dead had I not been taken to hospital. But good luck. When it's all over come and visit me in my village. Don't bring your bad dreams. Even mine have gone away now."

17

Tran Bach Dang had been mentioned to me several times during interviews in Hanoi as one man who could give me a lot of inside information on both the Tet Offensives. He had been the Southern Command leader throughout that period.

What that meant was Tran Bach Dang (pronounced "Buck Dung") had been the political leader of the underground forces in Saigon. In that era there were clearly defined roles, not unlike the distinction between political leaders and military men in the Western system. For example, it was always said when referring to General Giap in the north that he had founded the Vietnamese army "on orders from Ho Chi Minh", the political leader.

When speaking to military men I found the going relatively easy. Answers to questions were given in military terms. They had a deep knowledge of the tactics involved, the logistics, and knew their key men as close friends. Quite often generals were able to describe men and their backgrounds and their fighting habits right down to platoon or commando squad levels. Names, villages or origin, their characters.

With political leaders, I got a broad-world view of the fighting. Historical background was essential before going into specifics. Certain battles were linked to political moves by their opponents. For example, when soldiers told me they wanted to win their territory near Saigon, or take Saigon in the Second Tet, they frequently said they were desperate, making a tremendous effort, to take Saigon so that Uncle Ho Chi Minh could see his country free before their leader died.

There was truth in this. But the politicians, while referring to it occasionally, made their first links between a psychological success like the First Tet in January 1968, and the peace talks in Paris. There was the same pressure on them to succeed in the

Second Tet. They were directing their military forces for a political victory. It was never to be a military dictatorship.

It would be a dictatorship for the people and so on, which of course meant the Communist Party of Vietnam; hardly a secret to those outside. It had happened frequently enough, and it had given rise to the domino theory or domino effect which would see, following China, the nations of Indo-China fall one by one to the Communist powers. After Vietnam, Cambodia would fall, then Laos, or Laos before Cambodia and so on. On paper that appeared certain to happen.

But also on paper it looked like the Soviet bloc with its captive satellites would combine with China into one huge Communist power and sit heavily on the top of the world, bulging into Europe, the Middle East, Afghanistan, and Korea and Indo-China. Thailand and Burma were therefore most likely to be subsumed following the complete victory of the Communist forces in Vietnam, that country being central stage for the final showdown.

Indonesia, heading that way in 1965, was an inexplicable aberration because by mid-1966, after an aborted attempt by the Indonesian Communist Party to take over — it had a massive but ill-directed party and was pushed hard by China — had been thoroughly thrashed and it would not be able to regroup for decades, if ever.

Although many political scientists argued against the domino theory, it nevertheless had influential adherents in non-Communist circles in Indo-China and in Thailand and Malaysia and Singapore in general, who found many friends among like-minded thinkers in the West, where the theory originated. More importantly, the Communists themselves saw it that way. Even after the split between the USSR and China, the smaller nations' Communist Parties saw themselves as brothers in arms.

One of the finest coverages of what *did* happen after the Communist forces led by Hanoi marched victoriously into Saigon on April 29, 1975, is Nayan Chanda's book *Brother Enemy — The War After the War* which details the fallout between, first, the Hanoi-led Vietnam Communist victors and the Pol Pot Communists, the Khmer Rouge, then the break between the Communist Party of China and the Vietnamese Communist Party.

Two wars followed. The Vietnamese finally invaded Cambodia and removed Pol Pot, for which the entire civilised world should have given thanks, on 7 January 1979. Pol Pot had killed millions of people — Vietnamese, Chams, Chinese, and his own people — after marching to victory in Phnom Penh on 17 April 1975, twelve days before the Vietnamese Communists had won Saigon.

Less than six weeks after the Vietnamese had removed Pol Pot and the Chinese ambassador and thousands of Chinese military advisers had fled with him to the safety of Thailand, China invaded Vietnam on its northern border, on 17 February 1979. That was the final split. The artificial binding of Marxism and Leninism was cast aside the moment local interests were threatened. Today the former Brotherhood is little more than a history of failed social experiments.

China, Vietnam and Cambodia are unlikely ever to have Communist parties that will get along together. Indeed, by 1993 they may not have any Communist parties at all. And hopefully, Pol Pot and his Thai and Chinese supporters will have disappeared from the political scene.

Vietnam, more allied doctrinally to the new developments in the Soviet Union and eastern Europe, seems most likely to shed its near-useless inherited political system and return to something more original and Vietnamese. Tran Bach Dang was a man from this failed past; he had told the Vietnamese the world would be rosier if he and his upper-echelon Communist Party colleagues had their way. They had their way. They won. Then things fell apart.

Tran Bach Dang, ever malleable in his approach, was today on the attack. He was one of the few people who had sufficient influence to speak openly about the disastrous state of the economy. In 1987, inflation was estimated at 800 per cent. In 1988, when we were speaking, inflation was already at 600 per cent.

When the Communist Party took over they valued their unit of currency, the dong — "comrade" — at US$1. When we were speaking it took (after various revaluations and currency changes) 700 dong to buy one US cent. By March, 1989, the original dong was one ten-thousandth of its value in May, 1975. Even after these revaluations and currency changes, one US dollar brought 5,200 new dong.

Buying dollars was a different thing again. There were still people of substance wishing to buy their way out of new Vietnam who were selling $500 Colonial-era stamp collections for $100, or $70, or whatever they could get, as well as clocks, jewellery, various heirlooms, for a fraction of their price, to the few foreigners in town or anyone else who had dollars.

For a $100 note, in very good shape and thoroughly checked, they were paying nearly three-quarters of a million dong. A huge premium of twenty per cent, but they knew what they were doing. Within a month they would have a bargain, even if they couldn't get out.

Tran Bach Dang would be very open and strong on both inflation and the management of the economy at the end of our interview. But in the meantime, he settled comfortably into the idea of trying to help with a recall of who was who in Cholon in May 1968. He seemed to have been given a good briefing.

We were sitting outdoors around a garden table set in a beautiful gazebo and alongside huge palm trees in a well-kept garden.

He opened by saying, "The man could be dead or alive. More likely dead. Also difficult, because the forces were a mixture of regular army and self-defence forces. But one thing is certain. They thought you were Americans." He went on:

> The level of knowledge of those soldiers from the provinces was very low. They would naturally assume you were Americans. They had no idea of conventions, no idea of diplomats, let alone diplomatic privilege. The idea of protection, diplomatic or press, would be alien to them.
>
> Without a shadow of doubt they would consider you Americans, probably CIA. Had they contacted me I would have ordered them to capture you. For example, in late 1967 the Viet Cong had captured two Westerners they said they were Americans, and contacted me. They were on the outskirts of Cholon and appeared to have some sort of uniform. They had shot the jeep up and set it on fire.
>
> When we talked to the men we discovered one was a New Zealander and the other American. But both were caterers. We exchanged them for some of our own prisoners.
>
> We also captured another civilian American, or so we thought. He turned out to be a relation of President Kennedy's, in Intelligence. So we took him as a POW and I think he was later exchanged, down at Cuu Chi province headquarters. But we kept his jeep. Identification was always difficult.

Tran Bach Dang had conducted the Second Tet operations from the top floor of a Chinese restaurant in Cholon. He was not as surprised as others had been when he discovered how far we had penetrated into Cholon.

"I would think they let you go down that wide boulevard because they could see that you were not being followed by a convoy. I couldn't see that road from where I was, but by the time you got into the back streets of Cholon we had already taken that area and were moving fast into Saigon city," he said.

He had emerged from his "hiding place" to take charge of the Battle for Saigon, as the Second Tet later became known. Where was his hiding place? I asked. "You are the first to ask that question!" Actually, I had asked where he lived while he was the underground leader in Saigon.

He swung around in his chair and pointed beyond his own two-storey colonial mansion to a small house next door. He had lived in there all through the war. What was more amazing was that the house he now lived in had been the residence of a senior US diplomat. At one stage, when Ambassador Lodge had been out of the country, this man (Proctor? he couldn't recall his exact name) had been chargé d'affaires, acting ambassador.

He saw a number of senior diplomats in the big house over the years. He used the house next door as his Saigon base. His regular disguise was quite simple. He had an academic pose, and academic jacket, with leather patches on the elbows. He affected a French-trained air. He wore horn-rimmed glasses, a cravat, a beret, and puffed on a pipe, like a stylised professor.

"The Americans were very friendly people. Once the diplomat himself saw me emerging just as he was leaving for the embassy. He came over and introduced himself and said a polite word, as a good neighbour would."

That meeting shook him a bit. From then on he would first sit in the back seat of the car, pick up a newspaper and begin reading it, before the garage doors were opened. The car would drive straight out into the streets.

He had good reason to change what he saw as a dangerous precedent. His photograph had been plastered on hundreds of walls and poles throughout Saigon. He was a wanted man. The most wanted man, in the view of the South Vietnamese Government.

"There was a huge reward on my head. Approximately $100,000. At one stage I thought the 'wanted' photos of me posted up ran into thousands. They were in every police station or police guard box. But as it happened there was also a National Assembly election around that time, so there were hundreds of other pictures on these walls, as well as pictures of film stars, and my picture became lost amongst them."

From then on he was ultra-careful about his movements. But he still used the house, albeit with more protection than ever before.

"The diplomat had no concerns for his safety," he said. "This was the best protected house in Saigon." He moved his finger from one point to another down the street and around the rear of the house. Viet Cong guards had him covered at all times, five or six houses controlled by them from where the VC had full view of the house. No Viet Cong attacks, naturally, were made in that street or on that embassy house.

"They had heavy guard arrangements. They could have saved their money and their men. This house would never be attacked."

"A few weeks before I had arrived, in October 1988, an American civilian had come on a nostalgia visit. He was a very well spoken and polite man and he asked permission to visit a house where he had often visited a diplomat friend during the war, and had good memories of it."

The American, now out of government service, had knocked on the outer gate and Dang, who had been in the garden, opened the door to him. The man excused himself for bothering Dang, asking if he could just glimpse for a moment the inside of the house. Dang said he could stay looking as long as he wanted. When Dang finally entered the man said he was honoured to have been let in, and said he recognised many things in the house. Dang continued:

> He was very observant about the house. But a few days later I learned he was not observant of people. For I sat opposite him for some discussions and he did not recognise me. I had been introduced as the spokesman on economic matters. He did not recognise me as the same old man who opened the gate.
>
> A little while later Clayton Jones (from the *Christian Science Monitor*) visited me and I gave to him first the fact that I had been in contact all along with US Ambassador Ellsworth Bunker. One of the US's strict rules was that the Thieu South Vietnam government should never learn of this constant contact.
>
> We used a special wavelength for these communications. I still have some of those cables from him to me, and copies of some of mine to him.

> We had a fixed time, 9 a.m., for these broadcasts. At one stage we made contact every six hours. Once, Bunker's representative visited me and brought US dollars to ensure their POWs were fed correctly. We used the dollars for what he wanted.

This special communications radio link was to play a role, he said, in protecting journalists during the planned Second Tet. He said he was "overburdened" with work at 6 a.m. on the morning of 5 May. Tens of thousands of Viet Cong were in place within or just outside of the city by that time. He send a message to the US Ambassador which simply said: Listen at 9 a.m. for an important message from us.

> That important message asked the US to tell all Western correspondents and other civilians of a code which both sides should adhere to. We asked them not to drive jeeps. Do not wear uniforms, because so much army clothing was on sale and many civilians used them. No weapons were to be carried. They had to have a flag on their vehicles.
>
> At first I was going to ask the US to tell them to have a white flag. But we reflected that this would have connotations of surrender and would not be acceptable to them, so I said a blue flag, which I thought was sort of neutral.
>
> I thought these requests were important because as the battle unfolded there would undoubtedly be journalists and civilian businessmen in areas where fighting would take place. For there were no exceptions possible on where fighting would take place. It would be in every area of the city.

I said I had never heard anything like the code in all my time there, and certainly not on that day or the next, 6 May. I asked if he had a copy of the radio cable. "Unfortunately not," he said.

The radio cable, in any event, had not been sent at 9 a.m., he said. It had been more like noon, on 5 May. Even had the Americans received it and broadcast it to us, it would have been four hours too late.

I asked if he had any idea why it was not broadcast. "Perhaps because it would have revealed they had a link with us, something that was to be kept secret at all costs," he said.

He then spoke of their advantages, and the certainty that the US and the South Vietnamese governments could not possibly have won the war. For example, he had more than forty ID cards with his photograph on them. When the South Vietnam government introduced new cards with an ultra-violet watermark of a dragon, they had exactly the same plates and processes available to them from inside the government printing office.

There were convinced Communists, totally sympathetic to the Viet Cong and Hanoi's cause within the South Vietnam government, all along. One, a senior military man, had led a delegation to the US to advise on what equipment the US should supply to the South Vietnamese Army! "Within days of his arrival back we knew everything they would get, and how we could and would get some of it. More importantly, we could prepare in advance to combat it."

The VC had another officer in the South Vietnam army who supplied them with US military maps of Vietnam. They were, he said, truly sophisticated and accurate maps done by aerial photography. The scale of the maps meant they had in tiny detail any area covered. Both sides were using the same maps. The VC were supplied with maps down to ten-metre detail.

"We used to tune in to the airwaves and given the codes we were easily able to learn by using the co-ordinates where attacks would take place. Our forces, obviously, would not be there when the attacks came."

He had been protected by a senior politician in the South Vietnam Assembly. "I used to tour in his car, using his immunity, to look over the US and South Vietnamese forces and their emplacements. It gave me inside knowledge of what they had within their perimeters, and I used that knowledge to plan attacks on their installations."

Considering Tran Bach Dang could have been handed in for $100,000, it was a measure of the dedication, or conviction — or was it the level of indoctrination, or the hatred of foreigners? — that kept him safe.

The parliamentarian who had taken him on these tours behind the defence forces lines has since died, of natural causes. But one man who was always with them all the way was the leading journalist of the Saigon press. "The editor-in-chief of the *Saigon Post*, Nguyen Lau, was always working for us. Of course that is well known today. He is a member of our Assembly. But then he was considered a strength in South Vietnam, for their cause."

It was the *Saigon Post* which had repeated a spurious story two days after the ambush of the journalists, quoting a "Reuter's representative" as saying four journalists were on the jeep, three dead, one captured. That was very convenient, for these "sources" then removed a witness, and allowed room for the story then widely circulated, which in general said the journalists had brought on their own deaths by drawing arms and firing on the Viet Cong.

Those who wished to believe it, did. The story was reported in the Communist press of Japan, and by the time some ill-informed and posturing parliamentarian in Australia decided to assert the journalists were armed, he was able to add the extra fiction that they had been wearing uniforms. It had been a very convenient thing to do, removing me as a witness from the site. As it turned out, the Reuters man quoted was not a correspondent, but a Vietnamese office assistant who had never got closer to the ambush site than three hundred metres.

But the *Saigon Post* had fixed all that up for him. It had run the story after a lot of damage had been done; I had reported that the killings, if not at first deliberate, were in the second stage clearly deliberate. "We had them all," said Bach Dang. "Every senior journalist on the *Saigon Post* was with us."

I asked if they had had men on the staffs of Western press bureaus. Might they be still with them, having "escaped" to Western countries and now employed by the same newsagencies? "You will have to ask Intelligence about that. I'm sure they won't tell you," he said, laughing.

Whatever they needed, they had. Information, maps, ID cards, access to top-level briefings, tours of the defence installations, reporters to shape the stories the way they wanted them, and students to run errands and report whenever they wanted them. And a safe house next to a US diplomat. After listening to Bach Dang tell me all this, the expression "an unwinnable war" took on a new dimension.

We returned to the heart of the city, to the rundown centre of town where only two hotels functioned properly, where two others still had cockroaches as permanent inhabitants, but were acceptable if the first two were booked out. Where on one count only fifteen motor vehicles made since 1980 could be seen on the streets and where 1945 Renault rear-engined cars were still being used as taxis. Where near-empty, gloomy government stores had replaced thriving businesses in the main streets. Where four or five thousand people slept on sidewalks within a mile of the central post office. Where only one public restaurant of any cleanliness or quality operated, and only two hotels had kitchens — from the old days — which functioned properly. Where schools go without textbooks that are openly on sale on the sidewalks for ten times their listed price. Where the Song Saigon River is still packed with rusting hulks, and freight movement is a guess and gamble.

This is a city where buildings are dowdy and unpainted, where plumbing is thirty or forty years old and where water is undrinkable from the taps, where there are taps at all. Where sidewalks are wrecked, public lawns and squares are in disrepair. Where on a normal hour's walk any Westerner will be approached four or five times for help for someone to escape the country. Where a telex machine is considered modern, where telephone communications — until Australia's Telecom put in a new system — was a fight on the lines. Where typewriters of 1950 imprint hotel accounts, or are the central machine in commercial offices. Where the aircraft have sixty people booked for twelve seats out and primitive brawling occurs to get those seats. Where small Soviet passenger jets ply the main route Hanoi–Ho Chi Minh, meeting one-tenth of the demand. Where lucky permanent government employees and their families occupy homes and apartments of those who fled or were forcibly evicted, who in turn live in squalor in formerly elegant private residences, cooking on charcoal stoves.

In our final minutes together Tran Bach Dang had turned to commenting on the economy. "We are in a bad situation," he said. "I have openly said we cannot but go up from this point, because we have reached the bottom. That is how bad it is."

Later I repeated this comment to a Vietnamese shop owner friend of mine. He laughed. "We all know what he says, he has said it a million times. So you know what the joke is now? We just say Tran Bach Dang is wrong. Underneath is a trapdoor, to the sewer."

18

A Viet Cong news cameraman whose name was frequently mentioned to me during 1988 was Pham Kac, who had been in action and won fame during the Battle of Saigon. On 5 May he had crossed and recrossed ground in Cholon that we too had covered. His film from that battle is among the most precious in the archives in Vietnam today, and is frequently used as flashbacks in locally produced modern films.

He was not the only cameraman, of course. In fact the film news coverage from the Viet Cong side, although totally different in its shooting and its intentions, was almost as big as the Western coverage. Not in quantity, but certainly in breadth.

After the interviews with the Vietnam News Agency journalists, with various photographers and other journalists and army artists, I was building up a huge file on how they operated and particularly on what dangers they faced. By the time I met Pham Kac I was in the strange position of being able to report back to the Vietnam Journalists' Association in Hanoi through Vietnam News Agency editor Do Hoi that I had a very good estimate of the number of journalists killed, something they had not yet been able to establish accurately. Combining our information we had soon found the estimates climbed from approximately forty to sixty. My private estimate was that the figure would eventually reach around one hundred.

This was the first aim in mind when I sat down to interview Pham Kac in what used to be the main TV station in Vietnam (TV Saigon) where he is now the Deputy Director of the renamed Ho Chi Minh TV station. The second was to continue building up a picture of the types of troops who had been in that part of Cholon during 5–9 May and particularly the Self-Defence Forces or local brigades.

I had been down several dead ends to this point, and expected to go down many more. Yet as the interviews went on, dead ends or not, I was slowly acquiring a picture of the men, their backgrounds, their fighting habits and even some personal traits of their leaders. They were composite pictures, in the main, but becoming much sharper. Surely *one* journalist had known who they were.

Strangely, the Pham Kac interview hardly helped at all. There was no doubt that what he reported, filmed and experienced, was accurate as he saw it. But he was operating at a very high level, keeping the big picture of the battles in his mind. There was almost no emphasis on the individuals in these coverages. The stories and pictures concentrated on the overall effort. Personal losses, both in print and on film, were represented as sacrifices for the national cause as they saw it.

Pham Kac had been deputy chief of the filming group that was to enter Saigon from the south. During one attack the chief of the film unit had been killed, so he was sent down as replacement chief. This was after the 31 January Tet attack that saw the Viet Cong occupy the US Embassy for some hours.

"The atmosphere was depressing," he said. A lot of journalists and film men had been killed, and when he went to head up the Liberation Film Unit — the name alone said it all: they had expected victory in early 1968 — there were five crews for him to manage.

"We stayed in the outer suburbs [during February, March and April] awaiting the Second Tet. The enemy had stepped up their attacks in the outer suburbs of Saigon, destroying many of our bases. We had orders from the military leaders not to hit back. We were to save our strength. We were to prepare for the Second Tet and we were to preserve secrecy."

Several regiments — hundreds and hundreds of men — were hidden under water coconut trees on a river not far from Saigon. He was to go in with the Leading Edge troops who were to be the most important troops in the Battle for Saigon. There were nine hundred of them. They were to meet at least three hundred others — mostly high school students — who were the underground forces in the 5th and 6th districts (inner suburbs of Saigon, using the French term *arrondissement*) and who had done their share of actions in the First Tet.

In the period between 1 February and 5 May Pham Kac and

these men had hidden during the day, and come out at night. "We went into villages and shared normal life with the people," he said.

The quantity of supplies they had would have frightened even the most optimistic South Vietnam and US forces leaders, had they known at the time. Food, drink, including huge supplies of beer, was trucked out to them from Saigon. The journalists had representatives buying film and other supplies for them. They were easily able to pay their way, so to speak, in these villages.

More importantly, into these villages and other staging posts came the Chinese weapons and ammunition. Tons of it. Automatic AK47 rifles, bazookas, rocket launchers. Ammunition, medical supplies, money. Pham Kac preferred not to comment on that. By 1988, Brother China had become Enemy China.

Today these "villages" are joined to the main city in the urban sprawl we are familiar with. Vietnam's population had doubled from thirty to sixty million plus since 1968, and Ho Chi Minh City is no different. The paddyfields they had to cross to get to Saigon's perimeter are now largely built over. That is how close all this action was.

I thought of what it would involve trying to hide nine hundred men on the edge of a similarly sized city in the US, say Phoenix. In what is today Scottsdale or the new areas beyond Phoenix's Camelback mountain there were nine hundred uniformed soldiers lying in wait to take charge of the city. Yet they were not harassed or detected.

Because of a defection by a Viet Cong colonel, the South Vietnam and US forces were aware a second Tet would come. But they did not know the day. The colonel had guessed around 8 May. The attack began on 5 May. Secret orders came: move on 4 May. Schoolgirls were to lead them in.

The leading troops and the film units were all in uniform, including the journalists. Every crew member carried ten rolls of film. It had been their habit to carry sufficient film for three or four months, sometimes six months.

It was not only the uniform which made Pham Kac a soldier before a journalist, but what he saw as his duty. "My main duties were to fight the enemies, not to shoot film, which came second."

He carried a windup Bell & Howell camera, stripped of even small metal items he thought unnecessary weight. That was across his right shoulder. "Across the front I carried the AK47.

On my left hip I had a K54 pistol. And across a bandolier I had three anti-tank grenades. One pushed a button before throwing these and a parachute would open above a tank. I used them quite often, but more often I directed others to use them."

"I was well known as a journalist then, so I was often called into small groups which had become fragmented through losses, and I gathered them together into new units."

He was in uniform, carrying a small arsenal, and adept in its use. It could be said that he made films as a sort of side occupation. One of these, pieced together later after the Battle for Saigon, was called *Fighting on Saigon Streets* and was released in 1988.

His exposed film he carried with him, never releasing it unless to store it in a US ammunition box, which, he said "sealed perfectly". These ammo boxes he dropped into streams. "In all those years I did not lose one metre of film!" he said proudly. The film was processed at the hideouts in Tay Ninh Province, which the Vietnam News Agency journalists had described in detail: huge underground complexes with central rooms as big as tennis courts.

He carried forty-seven kilograms at times, and never less than twenty-two kilograms. That included weapons, food water, medical supplies, and camera and film.

But not boots. "Never!" he said. "They could not have dried out. We waded through paddy fields, streams, mud. Only Ho Chi Minh sandals of rubber tyres were possible in these conditions."

On the evening of 4 May they began to move. When they reached a certain point on the outskirts of Saigon, several teenage girls met them. It was the girls' job to take hundreds of men safely through back streets as far into Saigon as possible. The girls did their job well. No one was caught. "They were very clever. Not once did we go on a main street."

Their targets were Americans and ARVN (South Vietnamese Army) forces. "We could never tell Westerners apart, American or Italian, for example. Your ambush was done by people who would naturally think you were Americans. Enemies."

We were targets, he said, just as he was. "As a cameraman the first person shot at was usually me, because they would see my camera lens." "I had a cameraman friend who was captured near Tay Ninh. He didn't dare tell the South Vietnamese forces he was a cameraman, so he said he was a soldier from Hanoi. As a soldier he would become a POW. But if he had said he was a cameraman he would have been considered a political cadre, and his penalty would have been far more serious."

He himself would have been classed as a spy or Intelligence person, Pham Kac claimed. He felt he and his teams therefore had doubly difficult and dangerous tasks.

Had Pham Kac been in the street when we came around the corner, he too would have opened fire at us, of that I was certain. He left me in no doubt either, with the declaration that on his side journalists were subservient to military leaders, and willingly followed orders.

Pham Kac saw everyone who opposed him simply as an enemy, as he had been taught. It was interesting to consider how he could fit this cramped thinking into running a TV station, especially now he was being ordered to be flexible and allow the views of other, non-party groups, or even individuals, to be aired. The Battle for Saigon failed. That is history. It would be seven years before Saigon was to fall, in 1975, to then mostly North Vietnamese troops. But in 1968, he and nearly all the attacking forces were South Vietnamese.

There were some very strange moments for them. "Once, our group went into a seven-storey building and took the bottom two floors. We wanted to make this a sort of headquarters. But in the morning we found the South Vietnam Army [ARVN] had taken the top two floors and were making it their headquarters!" They remained undiscovered and moved out under the cover of darkness the next night.

Both the Viet Cong and ARVN forces two or three times moved into rows of buildings to be used as "temporary headquarters", only to find they were facing each other across the street in the morning.

"The big difference was the ARVN could withdraw to safety. We had to stay and fight. When the ARVN withdrew the US Air Forces would hit us. In the Battle for Saigon we had very heavy casualties. Very heavy."

The interview was winding up. He could not help much with the ambush in Cholon, because he had passed through those streets just an hour before we had arrived there. He was at a loss firstly because he would never have considered it possible for us to penetrate so deeply. But he was certain that the low-level defence forces would have considered us enemy.

We left the TV station as we had come in, through a dowdy empty courtyard. Pham Kac had given me his card, on which the title "Eminent Artist" was noted. He was very busy, but few others were. He thought the TV station was doing a splendid job.

Ho Chi Minh City's TV station today is a shadow of its days as Saigon TV. There is some equipment, a few old-fashioned telephones, a certain amount of media atmosphere and a lot of paperwork. The station re-transmits Moscow news and talk shows, chess tournaments, games shows, and the Moscow version of soap operas, which are even worse than what we are used to in the West. The Vietnam news is good, considering the modest equipment they have.

Back at the hotel Cuu Long (Majestic) which had, like the Doc Lap (Caravelle) a TV set in the foyer, transmission had not begun for the day. Noon. It was Vietnamese soup time on the fifth floor of the Cuu Long.

A Taiwan-born Australian was there, and invited himself to lunch with me. We had met some days ago in the bar called the Venus Fly Trap, so named by some Australian telecommunications technicians who were installing new equipment on a subsidised basis from Australia.

He said he had offered the government 10,000 seventeen-inch screen TV sets, made in Taiwan, as the opener for a barter deal. They had not been interested, and he was downcast. Not that he was dependent upon TV barter. I was to meet him several times, ("call me Jimmy Park"), and he had lots more to offer. "We also can make this old-fashioned TV station like a real TV station," he said. He didn't know a thing about TV transmitting, knew nothing of how TV stations functioned, but was a perfect carpetbagger.

He had brought in a pirated Kung Fu master tape, broadcast quality, from Taipei. He had paid $200 to get this tape, and hoped to sell it to Ho Chi Minh TV for five or six times that price. "They are mad! They said they would be happy to have it as a gift. But they purchase nothing, they tell me. So all this Russian stuff you see? It must be Red propaganda. I try to help them. So now they'll fall for the Japanese tricks," he said.

The TV lit up at 4 p.m. Not the TV in my room, for that was merely for appearances; it had a permanent screen of snowstorms and blizzards whenever turned on. There was another prominently positioned set in the foyer. On this one, a domestic series from the USSR was showing. Was this the best that Pham Kac, with his revolutionary zeal, could do? It was after all, being transmitted from his office.

There was not a single other foreign correspondent in town to talk to. Even "call me Jimmy" had left for the afternoon flight. I settled for the TV.

It was Episode 34 of a Moscow soap opera, snatches of which I had already seen when passing through the foyer on other days. There had been a very impressive new bus in all these scenes. Shiny and smooth, this bus glided in and out of light traffic, taking people to work.

The soapie began with Scene One in the same new bus. The working wife and her just-married girlfriend were riding along. The wife was worried that her husband came home too late, and the girlfriend worried because she had discovered her husband drank.

We stayed in this bus for the whole thirty minutes of the episode, with flashbacks to a sanitised apartment where the two men, great buddies, were drinking and laughing, talking about plans for their next holiday.

I looked around the foyer. No Vietnamese were watching. Just a Russian who sat grimly through it all. The Cuu Long's manager spoke good English to me as she saw me looking around. "We don't like," she said. "They have no children anywhere. On bus or in the house. Wait for our show next." The Moscow bus pulled off into the distance, and the show ended. Tomorrow we would see what would happen to the marriages. Would the ladies ever get off the bus? Would the bus stay green? Did it have a black driver, as they do in London? A Pakistani with a Siberian accent? Who cared?

The Vietnamese show came on and there was suddenly an audience of twenty. A lovely girl, caked, however, with white makeup, got out of bed in a stylish apartment. She looked around in puzzlement. She went to a window of the apartment and looked down as a handsome young man, also caked with makeup, was about to get into a smallish but new-looking car. As she started to call out from her window, twenty voices around me also called out: "Don't go!" She looked back to camera, pained, turned again and all twenty in the foyer shouted as one: "Kam, don't go. Please don't leave me, Kam!"

They had seen the film ten or twelve times. They knew every

line. Every time they opened their mouths, these make-believe people wearing Bangkok fashions, they were distantly prompted by a massive unseen audience.

When it became boring, the Cuu Long employees would return to their work, only to magically re-appear when the better parts came up. The film showed people with TVs, cars and motorcycles, good homes, flowers in the living rooms, good furniture. Then there were boats leaving for distant lands — where as a matter of course their heroes were only boarding — then leaving again because of some drama at home.

Children flitted in and out of the scenes with no apparent motive, but those who turned their eyes to the cameras were cheered. In the end, the stars embraced and stayed together. Then there were more cheers.

Then followed the day-late news from Moscow. A man with a bow tie sat beside a globe of the world to indicate international news. There followed a number of hardly interesting news items concerning congresses and meetings and politicians meeting people, looking serious and smoking pipes. And then a cutaway to some military men, sitting bolt upright, wearing uniforms and medals, who appeared to pass final judgement. I could hear shuffles.

The Vietnamese audience had melted away like snow in the Sahara. I was the only one watching when a long interview began with a man who drove a snow plough (Scene: snow plough against background of snow), and as he finished the camera swung to another military man with medals and a peaked cap and he gave us the theory behind it all and presumably how nationally uplifting this was.

The Vietnamese were embarrassed by all this. No one understood the language, no one understood the subtle domestic policies behind the no-news news reports from Moscow. And most of them had no idea of or experience with snow, or sleds or bulldozers.

The Soviets in Vietnam I knew brought in pirated Western films from Bangkok.

At 6 p.m. there was a local news program, then an interview with a man who marketed Vietnamese perfume overseas and was earning himself a name and a large amount of money, as well as official praise. He was a man to be admired for his individual enterprise. The new policy of let the entrepreneur do his work and take his profits was well and truly launched.

Back at the TV station the winds of change would be very slow in coming. It was run by old soldiers who were untrained in what they were doing. Willing to change perhaps, but unable to. With nothing in their past that showed they possessed any sort of initiative, they now expect change to happen through some form of political osmosis.

What Pham Kac's TV station was broadcasting, no doubt on old vaguely phrased orders and under a dozen censors' eyes, was everything that was safe, dull, inexpressive, uncontentious and repetitious. The rest of the controlled television programs came free, as aid, beamed in from the people who gave them arms for the Communist cause. Along with the foreign ideology that won them a war, and failed them in peace.

When that irrelevant TV broadcast became just too depressing, I took a walk to the garden bar of the Rex — the Cuu Long is chaotic, on the waterfront, and any peaceful writing is impossible — and with pen and notebook started writing out what I had failed to get from the Pham Kac interview: a slightly sharper picture of the person or people I was seeking.

I called all possibilities the Man for simplicity. I had started out to find one, then a platoon or squad, but now anyone would do.

The Man had a fifty per cent chance of being alive after that day. He had a forty per cent chance of surviving the war, if he survived Tet II. In Cholon half of them would have been Chinese. Those Chinese might have been stripped of their wealth, if they were in commerce. In 1978, if they were soldiers they might have been senior-ranking by Liberation, and when Pol Pot started his undeclared war on the Vietnamese people inside Cambodia and raiding across the border into Vietnam in 1976, they may have been sent to that battleground. So far it seemed like a thousand-to-one chance find. I began to feel pessimism creeping in again.

19

Since arriving from Hanoi in mid-October there had been six official search meetings with military historians led by Major-General Tuot, and several Foreign Press Centre meetings. At a combined military/FPC meeting on 5 November we all agreed we seemed to be gradually moving closer to a result.

After the 5 November meeting I got frequent reports through the Foreign Office. Silence at that stage would have been the worst situation possible. I was quite prepared to hear that almost no one remained from the original ambush platoon; the Foreign Office had indicated this would be the case. We now knew of one possible member already, but he was far away, even the name of his village was unknown to them. I was asked if I could come back a little earlier than my planned return in March 1989. I said if they found any of the ambush members I would return as soon as I could.

I had first met General Tuot at the Round Table Conference in January 1988, when I had asked that the press be given the Viet Cong's version of the famous attack on the US Embassy. Tuot had been the historian called on to meet the visiting press.

Now I found myself working with him closely. He was the director of the History Division of South Vietnam, but more importantly for me he had decided to make it a personal quest to find the ambush squad. His interest became so strong that he was angered on more than one occasion when he was misinformed by his own people.

We had worked together all through November. But after extending my stay I had to return home as, once again, my money had run out. I had no idea how I was going to stay over in Bangkok on the way out. The realities of the cost of the search were pressing in on me.

I had calculated my finances to the last ten dollars. Then Minh Ha reminded me of the $5 departure fee. If I had to stay another day in Ho Chi Minh, I could not pay my way out. I had given away all my extra clothing, shoes, books and exchanged the few remaining rolls of film for meals.

Minh Ha caught the drift of the emergency. She, and every Vietnamese lived it day by day. So when I fronted the Air France counter to get one of the twelve seats left, with sixty people awaiting, she presented my case more forcefully than any lawyer could have done. That's how it is done at Ho Chi Minh airport, where order, queues or manners are unknown. From my last ten dollars I had set aside five for the airport tax. I set another five aside for a call to Bangkok.

Luck was with me. Keith Chapman had returned from Hanoi, to his office in the grounds of the Bangkok University. The call went like this:

"Keith. I'm flying in to Bangkok tomorrow."

"So, you'll need a place to stay."

"I'm sorry, yes, I'm broke again."

"I'll see you at the airport at five."

And then, three hours before leaving Ho Chi Minh City, an amazing message arrived from the military historians.

It said: *We have found a man. We will telex more.*

I stayed with Keith Chapman in Bangkok for those two days between the Air France flight and the departure of a Qantas flight. He paid for everything. One would have thought me a well-heeled tourist, for we dined at lovely little Thai restaurants, and stayed in his top-floor apartment in the heart of the city. I had no presents for anyone, I had no shaving gear, no extra shoes, no extra shirt. I paid my way in stories, and he was happy about that.

Yet I was truly tormented, and I didn't hesitate to show it. With Keith and other journalists in Bangkok I speculated on who the man was they were going to telex me about. Had the message been right? Where was the man found? When would the telex come? Every conversation seemed open-ended and inconclusive. Until I returned I would never know, so now every day spent away from Ho Chi Minh was a waste.

I was also out of money. My next trip would be on borrowed cash.

I found a $20 note tucked away in a side pocket which would pay for the airport tax at Bangkok, and leave me $3 for the ride home. Qantas charged me nothing for the trip to Australia. I had the $3 on arrival, only just enough for the family car's parking space. So I got home with twenty cents.

Anna looked older, as all four-year-olds do when one has been away for a long time. I vowed that next trip I would take them with me. Over the next days I delivered letters from Vietnam around town, had some Vietnamese soups with people who wanted to know all about Ho Chi Minh City or the possibilities of business.

I wanted to start writing, but I had given away my word processor in exchange for extended translation services over the last weeks. Back to my computer people I went, telling them my story. Could they let me have another one for just about cost? Ten minutes later I was driving away in my $2,000 van with a new word processor, my bank having given them a cheque for $1,430. I was not in Vietnam, yet my work was. Everything I did now was going to be precarious. It was an anxious time, waiting for that telex. I was now deeply in debt.

I got a telephone call, not a telex. I returned almost immediately in early December, determined to see this through. The morning of my arrival they discovered the man was a fake. He was from Cholon, certainly, and had been somewhere close in 1968. But he was demented and knew only sufficient about the ambush to get through the basic enquiries. This was proving a lesson for the historians, too. Rightly or wrongly, the fact that a foreigner was searching required them to bring a different kind of attention to the matter.

I had originally planned a wide search in Cholon from Road 46, hoping to find a former Communist Party leader. But most of them, being Chinese Communist and followers of Mao, had become boat people. Today in the US there are hundreds of "Vietnamese" who killed US and other Allied troops living as former refugees.

I returned to Australia to await news, which came almost immediately. By late December the trail had become hot again. They telexed me to return as soon as possible.

The telex that brought me back to Ho Chi Minh City on 30

December had said the military historians had found a man they thought would give me first-hand information on the ambush. From the moment I stepped off the plane, I knew something was wrong. Minh Ha was there with transport and she began immediately speaking in a mixture of French and English, a sure sign she was nervous or excited. Although I had been away for several weeks Minh Ha took up the conversation as though we'd been working together that morning.

"So, this man," she began, "this man is mysterious, I can tell you that. From the military historian I have as much as he can tell. The general himself has as much as he can get at this stage. And he tells me. And the poor man doing the running out to the village, well, he didn't have all the information himself so he is puzzled because we won't tell him exactly why we want to see this man. You and the general have agreed not to tell the whole story because you will not be able to prove his story, and so we go round and round."

I asked where the man was.

"He is still in his village. He is sick. But he is coming up tomorrow and we will all talk to him," she said.

But Minh Ha sounded doubtful. I asked her what her mother thought, which set her aback. "How did you know?" she asked. Her mother was politically mature and Minh Ha always discussed tough questions with her. Her late father had been an illustrious figure in the colonial days so politics was a way of life for them. "My mother is suspicious," she said.

Needless to say, the man did not appear the next day.

The inner city — still called Saigon — was oppressively hot, with 85 per cent humidity. There was little to do but await the next report from the courier who was shuttling between the sick man's village and Ho Chi Minh City.

Fortunately, I was spending New Year's Eve in Ho Chi Minh City with my wife, Alison, and four-year-old Anna, both in Vietnam for the first time. Alison was able to see the places I had referred to and the people I had worked with for the past thirteen months (for her sake at least I hoped it would not have to be another thirteen months).

On New Year Year's Day, 1989, I left the Hotel Cuu Long to buy some roses for Mister Ba, the Vietnamese-born Chinese-

Vietnamese father of Miss Linh, my Vietnamese language teacher in Perth.

Ba was a South Vietnamese agricultural engineer who chose dam sites, in order to build levies and other protections in the great Mekong River delta and tributary river systems in southern Vietnam. He had been selected to represent the government of South Vietnam in a new training course on modern techniques being held in Thailand in 1974.

The war raged on. Men of his skills and stature were being picked off by the Viet Cong as important targets, for these men represented a government and a system they wanted to bring down by any means. Many of his international colleagues advised him to stay a little longer in Thailand. He was learning, and his own contributions to them were very valuable. Stay while the war presented these dangers and uncertainties, for no work could be done if hostile forces would not allow the projects to proceed. Or worse, would kill the engineers involved.

Ba accepted an invitation to take up new citizenship in Australia. He could continue his work as an engineer and return to Vietnam when the time was right.

He took up the citizenship, and settled in Western Australia. Although a large state, one-third of the entire United States in area, it has only as much water as the tiny state of Louisiana. There were no jobs for him.

So he chose business. He was a migrant. Skilled yet alienated from his engineering skills, he did what the other skilled Greeks, Italians, Dutch, Germans, Czechs, Estonians and Yugoslavs had done. He adapted. He bought a restaurant, he imported, he battled, keeping an eye on Vietnam all the time. By the time the first Boat People had begun arriving on Australian shores he had reconciled himself to a permanent life in the West and given up all hopes of returning to the delta, where he was obviously needed, but not wanted.

I met him in mid-1988. He had been recommended to me as a man who would know where I could get Vietnamese language lessons. I found him in another building in the same street as his restaurant, working with his daughter Linh on a new company called Speedy Mail Services, which sent out accounts for large corporations. We struck up a deal on the language training. Linh's English was superior to his, he said. "So it should be. All that money I paid for her in the best schools!" But her Vietnamese was also excellent, he said.

After the shop closed at 6 p.m. every night we would do our lessons. In my old style of peripatetic learning — walking around pointing at objects, asking questions — we got through a lot in each two-hour session.

I was packing up on my final night, two days before another return to Vietnam, when Ba came in. Would I, he asked, go to a certain street stall in Hue Boulevard in Ho Chi Minh — he always called it Saigon — and ask about roses? He wanted to import roses from Vietnam. Roses from Dalat, the Highlands. Dalat, the hills retreat for the former king. The most fertile, cool area. He loved Dalat. Had I been to Dalat? "You must go to the highlands!" he said.

So some days later I presented myself at Stall 9G in Hue Boulevard, with Ba's card and instructions on exporting roses from Vietnam. There were no roses I could see in the whole street. Flowers by the thousand, but no roses.

It can be done, said the woman. They can be grown for you on order. Dalat is the best place. Have you been to the highlands? Have you been to Lamdong, Dac Lac, or Kontum provinces? They can grow them there. Roses. My husband was killed in the highlands, she said. She began to speak in a mixture of good French and very basic English.

I caught up with her in the conversation. Yes, I said. I had often been in the highlands. There was no need to say "during the war", for what else would I have been there for? I proudly said in Vietnamese: "I was in the Kontum Highlands in 1968. I was a journalist there."

The meeting turned a little sour. She turned over Ba's card a few times then looked at me. "So. You might have killed him yourself!" "It might have been you. You were there, dropping bombs. Shooting bullets. We were at home in our house. We grew roses, too. It was a very pretty cottage. A very big garden. We made it together." It was a sad, defensive moment for me. She had never said whose side her killed husband was on. Clearly he had been with the Viet Cong, or, the North Vietnamese forces.

I said: "No. I was a journalist. Observing."

That made no difference. She unleashed a torrent of stories about herself and her man, the cottage and the children they meant to have. Of the highlands gardens and their own, of their friends and neighbours, of the town it was. Of the obliterated ruins it became. She wished to be excused, but it was all my fault. She had at last met the man who had killed her husband.

It was a one-sided conversation, but I stayed because I felt in some odd way it was doing her good. She menaced me verbally, but wished me to stay. She mixed French and Vietnamese, no English now. She ended every statement with the wrong use of French: *"Ça va?"* She meant to say; *"Vous comprenez?"* I *comprenezed* only too well.

She held my hand while she told me I was her man's killer. She crushed my hand when she raised her voice and released the grip and stroked my fingers when she lowered her voice to speak of them still living in happiness in their cottage, on their little gardened land. The noise of motorcycles and human voices flowed into the little kiosk, but she didn't hear them. She had dropped Ba's card on the floor.

She spoke of flowers and streams. She twice opened her eyes widely in a glare and accused me: *"So, how did you kill him? They said killed in the highlands by foreigners. But no body for me to bury."* Then she let me off the hook again, as a judge would in excusing me for an accidental killing. I sat in a small cane chair which tightened around me as I sat. It was too low for comfort. Her eyes were a few centimetres above mine throughout, from her position on a high stool. She had a captive and sympathetic, if nervous, audience.

The quarter-hours spun by. I was almost immobile, she was in a state of agitation. As she spoke I was taken back to my early days in therapy. Talk it out, no matter if it seems incoherent. She talked and talked and talked.

I was the first Western soldier man white foreigner war person she had ever spoken to, she said. The journalist part had never registered with her. I tried hard, but I lost track sometimes. Even she had lost track. She would go from roses to bullets, from schooldays to red flags, from her daughter at school to secret meetings on Marxism and Socialism. From baking bread to unwanted guns and bullets hidden under her kitchen floor.

When she looked away while speaking, I glanced around. The insides of these stalls interested me, for I had only seen them from the outside. There were two sales counters to handle business from both the service road and the main boulevard. They were offset from centre, leaving a large space at one end which I thought would be a storeroom. Now, on the inside, I saw it was her home. Three metres wide between streets, and a metre-and-a-half deep.

There was a thick curtain now opened from the centre. Inside was a small bed, a small table that held a charcoal stove, above which were strung string-tied vegetables and herbs.There was a big piece of cardboard onto which several old photographs of a man and a girl were pinned. Under the bed was a trunk. On the bed was a small wash dish, and above it, strung on a string line, were panties and bras and bits and pieces.

She rose suddenly, breaking her grasp. Without seeming to look she picked up Ba's card again and began talking of export roses. Not the roses of her home, but export roses, for Mister Ba. She assumed, after a small smile of acknowledgment of our time together, a businesslike attitude. Yes, it could be arranged.

I broke free of the chair and stood just after she did.

"Please come back again. If you can ever see the highlands you won't be disappointed," she said.

I had seen the highlands. After returning from one mission from Kontum through or from Pleiku and Dalat, and too many hilltop camps to mention over a period of four weeks on various missions, I went to my hut in Da Nang and wrote a few words. Perhaps I wanted to ease my conscience from the horrors I had been witnessing.

In that hut in the region the flower woman had extolled to me, I wrote:

The Highlands are cold. Don't let anyone tell you they aren't. We were freezing.

The troops could hardly bend their fingers into the trigger guards. They were pretending they were sighting so they could rest their chins on the butt and close their eyes and dream about sunshine in the ballpark and a steak at the drive-in with the girl they didn't think they liked until now.

There were bodies all around. The North Vietnamese had been there before we came to bomb them from the air, mortar them from our hill opposite and then finally move in and blast them from the trenches with grenades. Fifty Vietnamese, stiff and ugly. Cold. Bits and pieces.

Fifteen of us, maybe, and losing one every quarter of an hour from the mortars and shells the North Vietnamese were sending in from their holes over there inside the Cambodian border. But it was the cold we worried about.

The helicopters were still coming in for the dead. Every thirty or forty minutes. The correspondents were going out, too. We were so cold we sat on the bodies to keep warm. When a fresh one was loaded we moved along and sat down again. No one spoke about it. It was too cold. Tropical cold. And the bodies were still warm in their sleeping bags of hessian and their long, wet zippers.

That is how it was in the highlands. Our reports said "Light contact with enemy in F Zone." They didn't say how cold it was.

20

The New Year's day meeting with the rose seller from Dalat unnerved me, reminding me sharply that I ought not take anything for granted. It was not an ordinary and impersonal assignment, like asking someone about the economy or reviewing an historic battle. If the flower lady lived now in a twilight world, teetering on the edge of reality, often preferring to pretend the war had never happened, there was every chance the man I was waiting to meet would be in the same condition.

To add to my concerns, a new factor had been added to the search. A film crew.

The night before our expected meeting with the man, Australian film writer Ken Kelso had arrived to join me. He was to witness the meeting promised in the telex to me to help him structure a screenplay on the search. The Australian Film Commission had decided my search could form the basis of a feature film that would also give a picture of New Vietnam.

Ken had met an Australian TV crew on the plane in from Bangkok and unwittingly told them of my expected meeting with the man who had killed four journalists twenty years before. That sounded to them a story at least as good as the one they would be sharing with most other world channels — the first troop withdrawals from Cambodia — so they targeted in, naturally.

That same evening I sat down with the crew over dinner at the Caravelle. It was an extraordinary coincidence that I should be talking with a crew from the same current affairs program on the same channel on which I had worked fifteen years earlier and on a story to which I would probably have been assigned myself.

I met with producer Stephen Rice and reporter Peter Wilkinson over dinner at the Caravelle, after we'd organised visas for them from the Cambodian consulate. They were to go into Cambodia and do their own stories as well as some specials with Queensland film man Evan Ham, whose inside contacts were very good.

The next morning Minh Ha called in to say the man would come the following day. A conference had been arranged for 11 a.m. We were now thirteen-and-a-half months into the search begun in the National Archives only three hundred metres from here at the Caravelle. I had always imagined it would finish in a room in Cholon itself, ten kilometres away. I occupied my waiting time by re-meeting old friends and writing stories about New Vietnam, but my heart wasn't in the writing.

There was some news. The first of the Vietnamese troops were withdrawing from Cambodia, the Thai foreign minister was about to visit Ho Chi Minh City, for the first time in nearly two decades, and there was sporadic foreign investment news. But nothing to take me from my immediate concern.

At the 11 a.m. meeting on 6 January I expected to find a new face in the group around the usual briefing table. And even after the meeting began I was hoping a man would soon be ushered in and introduced. No such luck.

Minh Ha, poker-faced, translated: "The man is not here today. His father is very ill and he will stay with him in the village." There were apologies. General Tuot was mildly angry, but not with me. Something had gone wrong, he said. The man was not all he said he had been. He could be brought in from the village, but he advised against it.

Slowly the story came out. It took a couple of days to emerge, but the main thrust of it was relayed to me at that meeting. The man claiming to have been in Cholon in or near the ambush site had not been acting in good faith. He had ulterior motives. The general apologised for the inconvenience, saying he too had been thoroughly inconvenienced. Would I prefer to remain here or return to Australia and await another call? I opted to stay.

By the next evening I knew sufficient to agree with his anger. The man had been an opportunist. He had somehow heard from Cholon friends that a foreigner wished to find someone from 5 May, 1968. Just giving the date told a lot of the story, for every adult would know it was Tet. If a foreigner was concerned there might have been a chance of big money or a passport out, so he had strung along the courier and improvised his story as he got more information. A fake. The second one in two months.

Minh Ha was despondent. General Tuot had only one final strand of inquiry to follow, and was no doubt beginning to think the search was now at its dismal end.

Between us, and General Than, and everyone else involved, there was a feeling we had circled the event, we had approached but been deflected, approached again and been misled, approached again and found a fake. We were so close that we knew a great deal more of events in those Tet days, yet our quarry still eluded us.

After the failed meeting, the television crew were still buoyant about the story, which was more than I could say for myself. We struck a deal. They were to return and do more stories in Ho Chi Minh City. I told them I was going to run out of money in another week and there was nothing left to finance filming of any meetings to come, so if they wanted me to stay another week I would need some help. They would need some help too, and so we agreed terms — no fee would be asked or offered for the interview, my 'fee' would be the original film and sound tapes from the meeting, should it eventuate, after their use on their programme, and Channel 9 would pay for the extra week's stay at the Caravelle.

The crew and the station honoured the agreement to the letter. I was glad they were on the scene — their assistance would turn out to be fundamental to my finishing the job I had set myself so long ago.

Soon after the television crew left for Cambodia, I heard that a third man who was supposed to be part of the squad, had been found, though his exact whereabouts were unknown. He was the other of the two possibilities raised by the historians after the first man turned out to be a phoney. The Foreign Office called to say that "some historians" were going to a certain village and rated their chances of finding the man as 50/50. They knew I was to leave in three or four days more, and were perplexed, so I gave them the good news I had arranged with the TV crew to stay on another week or more. This was the time they needed.

Long discussions ensued. Often we went to the Foreign Office, at other times talked in hotel lobbies. The historians were having the same sorts of problems I had experienced. In the suburbs many street names had been changed, houses removed, ricelands and even streets reclaimed to make way for housing. Often I had to seek out the oldest residents and get an oral history of the area before any information made sense. The historians were having the same trouble in the villages, many of which had changed their names, as well as street names, while others had amalgamated with bigger towns as populations grew.

Once having battled through this geographical landmine, we then had to deal with the changing names and numbers of military units. During the main Tet Offensive, for example, the losses were so high that of every hundred platoons which started fighting on 5 May only one or two were completely intact by 11 May. Between 5 and 11 May a man could easily have served in four or five different platoons, as they were destroyed when the remnants reformed into a new platoon.

When Minh Ha came to tell me that this third man had been found, her Foreign Office superior had relayed a message from the historians that there was a "seventy per cent chance" he was the man I wanted. I was totally in their hands this time, until he reached us, but the seventy per cent appraisal was encouraging. Again their enthusiasm for this pursuit, and their curiosity, surprised me. It had become a challenge to them and fortunately they had enough free time to pursue it.

Everyone by now knew the ambush had been reported by radio on the morning of 5 May, and although it was one of six jeeps ambushed, this was the only one where an "enemy" had dropped down (me feigning death) and escaped to the safety of the people. We knew from General Than the kind of men they were, the near-certainty they would have not known the difference between our jeep and a military jeep; we also knew that the circumstances were such that to see a jeep in that sector of Cholon which they held (for a kilometre-and-a-half around) would be immediately considered part of an enemy thrust into their rear defences. We knew that a man twice decorated as a Hero of Vietnam, Tang, had seen the jeep later, and known the platoon leader had been hit by a US Cobra helicopter rocket.

Most of the answers were with us. Perhaps that is why both the military historians and I were feeling frustrated at being so close. Yet our best efforts had turned up someone who was a fraud. But now we had another chance.

Into the middle of this stepped Mai Huong, the Hanoi interpreter who had done all the groundwork. She was taking a US crew down south for a CBS shoot and in those ten days from the fake report to the arrival of the man from the village given the high probability rating, she was able to stay only two days.

Mai was also frustrated. She might miss the showdown! She spoke at length with Minh Ha, who was to do the translations, but gave us both great encouragement in the thoroughness of the historians. Mai's contribution had already been considerable; it was she who had overheard Tang say, "I know that white jeep", a remark which helped give us a sharper focus for the search.

The Channel 9 team arrived back to learn that a new meeting with a better chance had been arranged. They went about the preliminary jobs, filming pre-interviews, street scenes and so on; then very kindly prepared a meeting place in the conference hall of the Majestic. I was grateful that they were able to look after such details, as I was too distracted and preoccupied with the forthcoming encounter to be of much help with such things.

On the day of the interview, a man arrived in Ho Chi Minh from a southern fishing village where he had been selling tobacco. All we heard was that he was surprised at the call.

21

I stood waiting at the far end of a big conference hall, facing the doorway. Behind me was a large colour photograph of Ho Chi Minh. There were two tables, pushed together, forming one long table. Eight chairs were equally placed around the long table.

A film crew unobtrusively went about its work. Lights, cameraman, sound man, a reporter sitting to my left, the producer to one side.

For all the formality, this was not like being in church, or a courtroom, or a business meeting. Nor was it like being with your own people after a family tragedy. It was more like being in a morgue. Everything brightly lit, but cold.

I felt very cold. Yet outside it was warm. A warm day in the tropics.

Among the many absences at that moment was the absence of hatred. The gun I once thought I would bring to such a meeting was not there. But nor was there any anger, just a feeling of alienation; I didn't know how to act because I didn't believe anything would happen. I hardly believed anyone would even turn up.

Now it was the third man's turn. But after two false alarms, two fakes, I was cautious. The second was a Chinese from Cholon who perhaps killed many Westerners and other so-called enemies; a man who was quite demented, and who they quietly turned away.

In his madness he had been clever. He knew the incident, as so many others did in Cholon on 5 May. He was Chinese and he heard that they sought a Chinese-looking man who lived there and who was part of the People's Defence Forces. These were civilians armed with lethal weapons to be used at any time they were called upon to kill or wound South Vietnamese Government officials or soldiers, and at any time any foreigner, for all foreigners were considered agents of the US government.

He was one of them, possibly with many kills on his record. But by 1989 he was an outcast, and out of touch with reality, mentally unhinged and desperate. When he began fighting for the cause he was an accepted Chinese-Vietnamese civilian supporter.

Now he was one of very few Chinese remaining, placed in a "new economic zone" and asked to do real work. No privilege, no access to the family business that had made life so easy for him before. Obviously, his various allegiances — to his business and the Vietnam Communist Party, and Mao Tse Tung and China (his nation, his own Chinese people had backed the Vietnamese with arms and materials) — had suddenly, in 1978, become useless to him.

Being a Chinese businessman in Cholon removed the first leg of his support. Being a Chinese member of the Vietnam Communist Party removed the second, because no Chinese would ever now make it through the ranks. Being a strong supporter of Mao ensured his final removal. By 1978 the Beijing regime had turned on Vietnam, for Beijing was propping up Pol Pot in Cambodia, and Pol Pot was by then halfway through killing approximately 250,000 Vietnamese. The Vietnamese saw any banner-waving Mao supporter understandably as a sort of fifth columnist.

I never did get to meet this second man. He was clearly there in Cholon, and knew how the ambush took place, although just as clearly, he had not taken part. They returned him to his new economic zone, sent him to till the soil with hands unused to that kind of work.

When they told me, all I had thought was: "Good riddance."

But now it was the third man's turn.

Odd thoughts came to me as I stood there. To distract myself I paced the room helping the crew prepare for the meeting. But still, as I robotically went about moving chairs, and checking power plugs, hundreds of pictures slid across my brain.

In half a minute I was back in the October 1965 days of the Indonesian civil war. The camera crew was making its adjustments in this Saigon hotel but I was in another place. No conscious effort could stop my mind turning over.

I am trying to get out of Jakarta while the communists are setting up ambushes along the roadside. There is only one road, blocked by about twenty thousand anti-Communist ten- to twenty-year-old students at the last major crossroads south of the city. I drive slowly five kilometres along the road out, often waiting fifteen to thirty seconds as people reluctantly clear the road for me. No other vehicles are on the road.

Approaching the five-kilometre crossroads I am stopped by a student who asks me who I am, where I am going, what my intentions are and am I a Communist? "My name's Kus," he says. I invite him into the car. I tell him I am a foreign journalist here in Jakarta to see the power of the student movement. He insists on putting a student flag on the car, and as we slowly drive through a mile of otherwise closed road the throng parts as we push through at little more than walking pace.

Kus finally jumps out and sits on the bonnet waving his flag as we part the waves of humanity. "A friend. An international friend!" Kus shouts as we drive slowly through. The car is slapped by hands and punched by knuckles as the students let off steam. Just before the crossroads, where I believe I will be free, he jumps off, waves to me and goes back to the crowd. At the crossroads I go to turn right to the Bogor and Bandung road but see bamboo barriers.

Where the student force ends, the Communist resistance begins. Instead of turning right and facing them, I continue slowly directly ahead. From my left there are tanks coming, but still at a distance of five hundred metres. To my right there are barriers, one hundred metres away. Behind me, to the north, twenty thousand students, keeping well clear of the crossroads. To the front of me a tiny dead-end road south, leading nowhere. There are six or seven houses on either side of this little road.

I drive south, halfway down this fifty metre road. There is dead quiet.

I turn the car around, leave the engine running, then walk to a house on my left. A simple four-roomed house with verandah. My car is then twenty-five metres south of the crossroads, the Communist barricades are to my left one hundred metres away. To my right the anti-Communist army tanks are approaching. They are heading straight for the Communist barricades.

The cannons aim directly at the barricades. I want to see the action so I bend low and run to the south-west corner house onto the verandah which has spaced bricks giving me peep holes. There are ten or twelve others here already. They have no interest in looking at the action. They are flat on their stomachs, with eyes closed. The only space for me is between an old man and a very young girl who had three live chickens tied by their legs. They are squawking loudly. To her left the old man says "Shushhh!" to the little girl.

I lie in the space between him and the little girl, whose tiny skirt is wet. Her small shoeless feet have toughened, leather-like soles. The old man has frightened her as much as the tanks had. She cries to me as I flatten beside her: "Ibu akan marah!" — "My mother will be angry if I lose these chickens."

The tanks rumble on until twenty-five metres before the cross-roads, then fire into the barricades. Twice. I think the building will come down on us. I have never heard a tank cannon fire.

Someone to the right of me sees the barricades blown away. He puts his head up and is about to shout some victorious message. The tank driver sees him, and turns the cannon on us. The tank cannon is aimed at us, but does not fire. Instead, a man climbs out of the tank and gets behind a machine gun.

The noise of the cannon fire sends the chickens squawking. They keep squawking when all else is silent. This makes the machine gunner even more suspicious. He turns the machine gun on us. To him it seems there are enemies hidden somewhere in our area. He swings the gun down and starts shooting into our verandah.

The little girl snuggles under my outstretched arm and then lies under me as the bullets rip through the airholes in the verandah, and bounce off the verandah front. Buried half under me, she hugs and hugs me, crying desperately. Like a child seeing, hearing her first thunderstorm and seeing lightning for the first time, and seeking shelter.

The firing stops. The gunner seems satisfied no enemies are there. The old man who had shusshed the girl starts to pray. The chickens are gone, but there is a thin string from their legs still dangling over the verandah, giving her a lead. As I speak comforting words to her she looks at me and realises I am a Westerner. I pick the string up from the verandah and tell her to go and search for the chickens.

Then I walk to the car slowly and even more slowly edge the car around the corner and drive through the broken barriers. I drive on to Bandung along deserted roads, lit only by the flames of burning houses.

Later, after covering the Bandung riots, I return to Jakarta where I find myself being questioned by some diplomats about what was happening. There, after I relate what I have seen, an elderly Indone-

sian man asks what is for him the only question — "What happened to the chickens?"

In the present, in the prosaic reality of the conference hall, that man's question hung in my brain. It took me a moment before I understood its significance. I knew all about the guns and the tanks and the rockets, but what I was hoping for, what I wanted from this coming encounter, was some human truth. I wanted to hear about things as they affected the human being, rather than the soldier or whatever.

I caught myself saying out aloud, to no one in particular, "what about the chickens?"

And then, there he was, one of a group of four who had entered the hall and were walking towards me with measured paces. By the time the man and the historians were seated the images of 1965 were gone. Forcing myself to look at him, I felt an ancient adrenalin rush, as if my body were saying, "You will have to deal with this man. There is no retreat".

He was introduced as Nguyen Van Cuong.

The others with him were the military historian General Tuot, a former Cu Chi tunnels hero, a Foreign Office official, Mang, and Minh Ha, my interpreter.

Minh Ha wore her reading glasses, and brought a thick diary padded by ten or fifteen loose pages of notes and sketches. As she sat down to my right the loose pages fell out and I saw fairly exact ballpoint sketches of a jeep, and the main Cholon street Minh Phung and several other smaller streets marked Road 46, Road 48, and so on. The words for rockets, platoon, and various arrows representing the advance that morning were overlaid on the sketches.

General Tuot smiled tightly to me and turned to Mang, who said: "We have found the man. We were seventy per cent sure. Now more than seventy per cent. Certain." We had agreed that the man I was looking for would have to provide certain details that I alone knew of the ambush. General Tuot, a man dedicated to research and verification, never did ask what those questions would be. He was by that time so involved in the search, as was the Prime Minister, Nguyen Van Linh, and the Tet Offensive Leader, General Than, that nothing short of certainty would be acceptable.

The historians had already been embarrassed by the cable to me in December saying they had found someone, who then turned out to be the first of the fakes. Channel 9's interviewer Peter Wilkinson had asked me how I felt as the group were about to be seated. "He might be another fake," I said.

The interview began but soon turned into tough going. Van Cuong had been told of the ambush and its implications only the day before, on 24 January. For twenty-one years he had never considered the ambush as anything but a memorable event at the start of the Tet Offensive, especially memorable for him, as it eventuated.

I began by asking if he remembered the morning of 5 May in Cholon. It was the easiest question to ask. He said he did, very clearly. He remembered the morning vividly.

From then on the story began to be told, uneasily, haltingly, but told nevertheless. There were many reasons why progress was slow. Cuong himself made it more difficult by attempting to be an all-round respondent; he wanted to get the story out, yet he wanted to get it out in a manner which he hoped would not present him in a poor light to a superior officer. Van Cuong had been assured there would be no blame attached to his actions of twenty years ago, but he wasn't quite sure about that.

He was sitting under television lights for the first time in his life, in a grand conference hall in a grand hotel, also for the first time in his life, with a national hero on one side of him and a high-ranking government official on the other side. He was surrounded by interpreters who obviously spoke both French and English as well as Vietnamese, translating everything he said to this former war correspondent sitting opposite him, and a crew of Westerners surrounding him.

We became mired in 1968-style heroic rhetoric several times, so I slowed down the questions and went back to the start of that day.

General Than, as the leader of the main attack forces in the Tet Offensive, and the man who ultimately got the radio report from Van Cuong's platoon, had prepared me for the villager-style soldier Van Cuong proved to be. Van Cuong was nervous, but outwardly composed. After five or six minutes he got the drift and the feeling of a more friendly atmosphere, so he began on a very natural, and surprising defence.

True, he was the platoon leader. But when our jeep had come around the corner in Road 46 he had been platoon leader for only one minute!

He recalled the morning of 5 May 1968:

> We were sixteen in the platoon. We had been together since 3 a.m., and came into the outskirts of the city near Cholon around 7 a.m. I was deputy commander of the platoon. The platoon commander was my closest friend. That's how I got to be his deputy.
>
> In all our fighting over nearly three years I had never given an order! Command came easy to him. And being his deputy was easy. We worked as a strong team because I knew his way of thinking. But I never read his orders or heard them over the radio. He would simply say: 'Get some men over there, and prepare such and such materials.'
>
> I also handled the bandages and medical supplies, and to get them I often had to go by myself in the night to appointed safe refuges in villages or other places near the city. I never had any bad wounds myself, even from your ambush in Cholon, but I bandaged hundreds of our fighters.

The morning of 5 May 1968, was the turning point of the Vietnam war. It was the Battle for Saigon where the desperation of the southern Viet Cong forces led them to fight so hard and so well that within weeks major military rethinking was in progress. And after then, civilians were in the streets in even heavier numbers than before, demanding a U.S. pullout. Yet the Battle for Saigon was unsuccessful. The city did not fall.

> We walked in across very dangerous territory. By the time we got to some Cholon factories around 7 a.m., the battle had started. Our job was to secure the rear areas, and move slowly towards Minh Phung road. As we were doing this there were enemy (US) helicopters in the air and we had to move very slowly, but we were well protected and moving towards Minh Phung (about one-and-a-half kilometres ahead) so we kept moving.

They were near what was called the Duck Feather Factory run by an Australian named Keith Hyland. (Hyland had made big money by exporting duck down for quality pillows and doonas. He was kidnapped, put in a trench, then suffered terribly before being ransomed for a reported one million dollars through the Bangkok agency of the Hanoi government.)

> About 8 a.m., an enemy helicopter (a US Cobra) saw us and started rocketing us. The commander, my best friend, was hit directly and killed. I was now the commander.
>
> [*The next thing I knew. . .*] your jeep came around the corner and we started firing on it. To us it was an enemy jeep with American enemy officers and our action was natural. It could have been leading some other enemy forces into our rear lines.
>
> I didn't see the first part of the ambush. It was carried out correctly in line with our normal procedures and the man who you say shot the two wounded men was carrying out normal procedures. We followed certain procedures to protect ourselves during ambushes.
>
> By the time I came out there I saw two killed instantly, two wounded. One wounded man was starting to crawl to the side of the road.

What he saw was two dead, one wounded man now with so many bullets in him I had reported him dead. In 1968, I believe Cuong saw a man who was dead, but sitting up in the jeep. He obviously thought the man sufficiently dead to take no action, although he carried his usual AK47 automatic rifle.

The wounded man he saw crawling was the driver, John Cantwell. I had reported him certainly dead, killed by the man who eventually chased me. This man — the man I had been looking for all those years — had to my mind killed John, who was already badly wounded from the opening rifle fire. I had been wrong.

A minute or two into the interview I turned to Peter Wilkinson as Van Cuong described all this, and said something like: "This is the right man. No one else could know these details." John, in one last desperate and courageous act, had apparently rolled over and begun to crawl to the north side of the road.

Van Cuong continued: "We were ordered to move to the Minh Phung road area. One wounded man was crawling to the edge of the road while we were moving forward. He was badly wounded and bleeding heavily."

I asked: "Then?"

Van Cuong did not answer.

This is what I think he did. He saw the jeep as he ran forward, with his rifle held forward. He saw the man and he shot him from close quarters. My supposition. It would explain why John's body was much further away than I expected when the *Time* photographer got in there several hours later.

I said to myself: "Well, damn you! An innocent unarmed man was trying to get out of this ambush and you had to finish him off."

Later I asked him what he did after he saw the man crawling away. In the interview he had deliberately avoided answering.

He said: "I had just lost my best friend, the commander."

"We then continued to our forward position. Enemy fire was very heavy. The enemy helicopters hit us very hard as we went to Minh Phung road. By the time we got to the end of the street we had lost six more dead."

That's all he would say.

I said: "Among General Than's records (at Tet headquarters) is a radio message something like: 'Four enemy dead, one dropped down then escaped to the people.' Who sent that message?"

Cuong replied: "The usual radio operator. I had nothing to do with radio."

I asked: "What happened to the man who came out after the ambush? A man with a semi-Chinese face, wearing full uniform, with a .45 automatic?"

"Possibly he did shoot them, but certainly not with a .45. He had a Chinese K54, slightly smaller than a .45. None of us had .45s. I myself had only an AK47. That man was killed by enemy rockets ahead of us."

He had run after me for almost seventy-five metres, firing. It was certainly true the Cobra helicopters were in action, right above us. In my flight I had drawn him into the open and brought about his death. In any event he was certainly dead from Cuong's account, along with five others, by the time they got to the street where I jumped into the relative safety of a small public three-wheeled vehicle and headed to town.

Cuong said: "When we had fought our way to Minh Phung road as ordered, only nine of the original sixteen platoon were alive."

I asked him how long it had taken him and how long he had stayed there. A Reuters employee had reported he went to the Minh Phung area at around 10 a.m. and said he had interviews with "black pyjama troops", meaning Viet Cong. (He had carried this story back, which Reuters had run in part and which a local Saigon newspaper, run entirely by Viet Cong Communists as it was later shown, had printed in its entirety. It was not favourable to the dead journalists and did not mention any witness to the event.)

Cuong replied: "Impossible. By that time we were far over the Minh Phung road and heading towards the Y Bridge. We spoke to no one. Not even the few civilians left in the streets. We secured Minh Phung then moved forward, on orders." Midway through, I started to lose the thread of the interview. Seeing me falter, Peter Wilkinson asked a question of Cuong: "How do you feel now, sitting opposite the man you tried to kill?"

Cuong froze. He had been guaranteed that there would be no retribution. Now he could see his earlier suspicions strengthened. I interrupted and said it was "an offensive question". It was not an offensive question, just one that would make no sense to a man blanketing his information with terms like "on orders we moved forward" and "our duties were . . ." and "we followed our normal protective procedures in ambushes".

If you were to ask the question of most Western soldiers, they too would repeat that they were on orders and so on, but then give you their private feelings also. It had taken me months to get Viet Cong soldiers to reveal even a little of their innermost thoughts during certain actions. Cuong was not about to do that now, in this inquiry, under strong lights, with superior officers alongside him. I was correct in thinking that he would not answer and possibly start on a long rhetorical response.

But Peter Wilkinson was right; he was asking a question to which I wanted the answer, but one we would not get just then.

Peter asked more questions. Van Cuong told him he was now a tobacco salesman. He had married after the war and had six children now. "Sadly, I have just divorced".

When he said "sadly", his face said "my world has fallen apart." We talked about that, later. At fifty-two he had nowhere to go for nine days out of ten. For nine days out of ten he did not see his children. For nine days out of ten he lived his thin-shirted, penniless existence, selling what he bought from others with a margin supposed to cope with his existence. No Fisher-Price toys in **his** bag when he returned to his six children.

The interview continued, but in essence it had ended for me. Both Minh Ha and I were relaxing; we had reached the end of the long search. I had hunted down the 'quarry' only to discover I was no hunter at all; there was no 'man' to kill, but there was much that was left unsaid. I found myself less concerned with Van Cuong's culpability or otherwise than with the fact that we were unable, in these circumstances, to open our hearts to each other.

I knew from previous experience that the atmosphere and protocol had to be right if you were expecting veterans to reveal their inner feelings. In this place, under these lights, and with so many other people, I knew it was all wrong. Far from wanting to harm this man, I found myself wanting to make it easier for him to tell his story.

As the interview began to wind down I recalled a session with two other veterans. One was a cyclo driver who had been a foot soldier in the South Vietnam Army, the other a former Viet Cong, now down on his luck. They shared a huge bowl of noodles and pork soup, they drank Saigon 33 beer and smoked their own brand of cigarettes, and they took great pains to listen to the other man's stories, then similarly expected no interruption while they had their turn. It was a form of mutual therapy. An evening of counselling each other.

This was eighteen years after their most serious fighting, thirteen years after the onset of poverty in a system that steadily peeled away their personal hopes. Something terrible had happened after victory. After the exhaustion of war, they were not equipped to handle the awful things that transpired.

Left only with rhetoric, or stories of their own honourable history, finally everyone came together in this shared poverty and in rare wonderful moments shared a meal and a drink and took themselves out of the present and into the past to help rid themselves of matters so deeply private and so deeply buried that even the daily struggles could not erase.

A year after my first glimpse of this I watched many of them stop returning GIs in the street and shake hands with them, and I saw many US veterans almost in tears as they awkwardly sat down on short wooden stools with former soldiers their own age drinking the offered coffee and nodding and smiling or speaking loudly and slowly simple English words they hoped the old soldiers would understand.

To the officials the veterans would say: "We are here to help rebuild." Others said: "It was about time we came back, this time as friends." Some more honestly said: "We're here to deal with our problems." To old soldiers they didn't have to say much at all. It was understood.

After the conference in the Cuu Long I planned a meeting with Van Cuong, to perhaps take place in 1990. I saw it in my mind as an evening at an outdoor noodle soup restaurant on the banks of the Saigon River. I would bring some toys for his children. Over a long evening we would unload a few matters over the table and fill in the story on the post-Tet years.

But then I will probably think of the dead men. The young journalists who deserved no such ignominious deaths, for just doing their work as they saw it and the best way they were able. And Michael who was killed while appealing to Cuong's point man to hold his fire, and to them all, really, to show we were all unarmed.

And I might remember when I wanted to kill the man who was himself dead within a minute or two of my escape, the man who was killed when he chased me.

I never had any doubts, nor do I today, despite the elaborate explanations of his background and his limited knowledge and the difficulties in the heat of war, that he knew exactly what he was doing. He died during a Cobra attack and I am comforted by that. He got exactly what he gave — no mercy. No thought for innocence, no thought for the truth of the matter. It was without any thought for innocence that he shot my friends, and would have shot me. And it was with plain murder in his mind that he chased me down the road to kill me.

Vietnam would not be more free if he had shot straight and maimed me then finished me off. He knew even then we were not armed. His intention was to kill a Westerner who had outwitted him. Our jeep was not followed by any other attacking vehicles. We were white, we were Westerners, and we had to be blown away with the smallest risk to themselves and the greatest number of heroic points accrued.

Van Cuong, it seemed to me, had no part in that. He would have had no idea of the ramifications of that ambush. He had orders to keep running. Whatever the man did out front on point duty would have been acceptable to him, just as the bits of his comrade's body on the road towards Minh Phung road would have been acceptable to him, as part of the war. Van Cuong remembered him, but not as someone special. He was no more than an afterthought. He was a man who had been dead twenty years less some minutes when I began my search for him.

I will sit down with him, Van Cuong, and tell him that man chased me down the corridors of my dreams for so many years. We will share our meal, and after two or three hours maybe he will want to tell me he did that final killing because he was just so damned angry . . . and like every soldier before him and after him who had ever seen his people killed, his heart was full of hatred. And maybe then after all these years, two men who had seen hell each in their own way, might be able to say they had begun to rid their devils.

EPILOGUE

Van Cuong and his village mate were the leaders of a consistently successful platoon given a variety of good and poor weapons, given a mixture of hard assignments, given a minimum of food and clothing and medical supplies and given a maximum of late-night lectures on the rightness of their war, the freeing of their nation, and the wickedness of their enemies. All through his formative years he fought that way. He was promised, along with everyone else fighting that war, a new nation and a new freedom, and a set of guarantees for his family to come; housing, food, regular work, schooling.

On the morning of 5 May 1968, he had gone into a special battle which was promised would be the battle to end them all. The final takeover of Saigon. It would be a present for the ailing Ho Chi Minh. (No one, even at very high echelons in the military, ever mentioned or had thought about it being a battle to win extra leverage at the negotiating table.)

The US Cobra helicopters, with their incredibly skilled pilots, had flown almost housetop level following street lines and blasted them as they moved forward into a city which, although ridden-through with their cells and sympathisers and turncoats, frankly did not welcome them, yet whose administration offered them nothing but a permanent role as peasants and servants. Nothing of the intangible freedoms the US and Allies had wished for them, which the South Vietnam Government would never have delivered. They took their cream from the US taxpayers' money and then ran and are now living in Orlando and Vancouver and Los Angeles.

The Cobra struck and his friend and leader disintegrated. Nothing was left big enough to hold. He was as mad as a disturbed hornet. The ambush began and he came out firing. His point man had followed the procedures of going in to clean us up, and had got carried away and instead of just admitting he had failed and let me go, he had run angrily and awkwardly after me firing. The Cobra, on another turn, had killed him in the narrow but open street. I had caused his death.

The others had waited for Van Cuong to lead out the hiding. They had been behind 44-gallon drums and timber stacks and other light-industrial debris, and Van Cuong had paused briefly when he saw a mortally wounded man attempting to crawl to some safety at the side of the road and he had shot him from close range with his AK47, then continued, on orders, toward Minh Phung street and in this remaining three or four hundred metres saw at least two or three others killed by the same Cobra helicopter.

Reforming at the crossroads known as Minh Phung Circle where several main roads converged, he took a head count and found only nine of his men were alive. He then headed, on the same orders, towards the Y Bridge, where they were ordered to go into deep hiding some distance away. No bandages were necessary; no new medical supplies were necessary. The men lost were all more than dead. They were in pieces. The ones remaining were completely intact.

Radio this and radio that. Hand-held Soviet instruments which spoke in code he had no practice in. Only minutes earlier they had reported a victorious message of four enemy killed, now they reported six heroically lost. Others from similarly broken platoons now joined them and they formed a new platoon given a temporary number and all this went back to General Than quietly making his way to the Y Bridge for the most devastating fight in the Battle of Saigon.

From the original sixteen, there were fifteen, then the ambush. From the fifteen there was the run to Minh Phung circle, then there were nine. From the nine they made their way over the next forty-eight hours towards the Y Bridge, then there were six or seven. Then there was the battle of the Y Bridge.

By the end of the war Van Cuong knew only three of the original sixteen to be alive. When he met me he could certainly account for only of those two, himself and one other, but he thought one other man, wounded, might still be alive. He doubted it. He said the man had probably died of natural causes. Van Cuong had no head for statistics. He would not have said to himself: "Of twenty-one in that ambush, five enemy and sixteen of us, only three survive today. That is an 85.7 per cent loss of life." He would not have said: "Of sixteen of us only two survive today. That is a 12.5 per cent survival rate."

He might nave said when Saigon fell on 29 April 1975: "Our big sacrifices were worth the freedom." He might just have not said that. He was courting his future wife and mother of his six children. He might have had wonderful things on his mind.

APPENDIX 1

"THE TWO TET OFFENSIVES"

In most Western eyes the 'Tet Offensive' was the battle the Communists launched on January 31, taking advantage of the Vietnamese Lunar New Year holiday on that day.

The January 31 offensive included attacks on installations all over southern Vietnam including Kontum, Nha Trang, Pleiku and Da Nang, whilst in Saigon the Viet Cong had targeted the radio station, Navy Headquarters, Independence Palace and the Joint General Staff Compound.

The ensuing battles were bloody, Allied casualties were high and the Viet Cong in particular took terrible losses. Despite those losses, and a general feeling held by some military men and journalists like Neil Davis that the US could have gone on to take advantage of that weakness, the Communists had won a huge psychological victory.

After Tet One Western opposition to the war further increased. The Vietnamese military historians interviewed in this book, took a different view of the Tets. They pointed out that Tet meant Spring, not just New Year's Day, and all their references are to First Tet and Second Tet.

The concentration of importance on the Second Tet (alternatively called the Battle for Saigon) they claimed was because the first battle was for a psychological victory whilst the second one was for the takeover of the capital.

This shift of importance in the Tets is just one of many aspects of the current review of the war by Western and Vietnamese historians. In simple terms, what the Vietnamese thought was important was not always what the West thought important. In this book I have used the Vietnamese emphasis on the Second Tet... after all, they were the ones who launched the attacks and they should know which one they considered more crucial.'

The following is the original story of the ambush filed world-wide by Associated Press, Saigon Bureau.

He Survived by Playing Dead

Newsman Tells How He Entered VC Deathtrap

Francis Palmos, 28, a freelance Australian journalist, was one of five newsmen riding in a small vehicle Sunday morning to cover the Viet Cong attack on Saigon. They were shot by the Viet Cong and only Mr Palmos survived, by playing dead. Here is his account:

By Frank Palmos

SAIGON, May 5 (AP) – We had been down the roadway that leads from Saigon to the Mekong Delta. There was nothing doing down there and we decided to drive back toward the city.

John Cantwell, a *"Time"* magazine staff member from Australia, was driving. Michael Birch of the Australian Associated Press was in the right front seat of the small, open, jeep-type vehicle. On the right in back was Ron Laramy, a Briton who worked for Reuters; in the centre was Bruce Pigott, an Australian and a staff member of Reuters. I was the last to get in and had to take the half-seat in the back, with my left leg hanging out over the side.

We had recrossed the bridge and were heading back to the city when we saw two gunship helicopters immediately above us and putting in rockets about 1,000 yards to the north. The rockets were exploding and sending up a column of smoke, so we decided to track it down. We plunged into a side street, heading into a very crowded and poor district.

Refugee Throng

Moving the other way was a strong current of refugees carrying babies and household goods, anything they could carry on their backs and in pushcarts.

We were the only people going in the other direction. I suppose we passed 2,000 people going south toward the road that we had come from. All the way along the road, people were saying, "Viet Cong, VC, VC, VC".

Suddenly the refugee stream started to thin out. I was sitting on the mudguard on the left, so I had a higher view and I said, perhaps from intuition: "The VC are up ahead. Stop! stop! stop!"

Bruce said: "Oh, go ahead anyway," but immediately after he said it, his face went pale. I knew him very well. Apparently he had seen something that I hadn't seen.

We drove into an open intersection with one little path about six feet wide leading off to the left. It was empty. The whole intersection was empty.

I shouted out to them: "Stop! stop!" because I was scared and I felt that there were VC there. Someone else, perhaps Bruce or Michael Birch, followed me in shouting stop.

Driver Swerves

Cantwell, the driver, swerved to the left and while he was trying to get into reverse, trying to back it around and get out of there, two Viet Cong opened fire. One on our left had a burp gun, the one on the right an AK–47. There were two other VC there in the background and the fifth, the commander as I learned later, was nearby.

It wasn't a real ambush. They were holding the perimeter of the VC area. The burp gun and the AK–47 pushed bullets for a full ten seconds through the jeep. I jumped to the left, staggered about ten yards pretending I was hit, then fell.

After the burst I looked under my shoulder and could only see two of the others. One, who I thought was Laramy, had his arms and head thrown back, his mouth open and he looked dead.

The second, wearing a pink shirt and who I believe was John Cantwell, was lying on his back to the left of the jeep, paralled to me but about six feet away.

The automatic fire stopped and the commander, wearing an unmatching camouflage "tiger" uniform and no hat, came forward with his left arm outstretched, holding a .45. It was then I noticed the other two holding automatic weapons had ordinary khaki drill uniforms and Ho Chi Minh sandals.

But the commander, who had ordered them to stop firing, had the uniform and boots. He was very solidly built, a very big man for a Vietnamese.

He began to walk toward the jeep. Everything was quiet for a few seconds. Then I heard Michael call out pleadingly: "Bao chi, bao chi," [Vietnamese for Newsmen].

The commander just looked at him, still pointing his gun and said derisively, "Bao chi". Immediately after he said it he pumped two .45 slugs into the jeep.

I don't know whether he fired at Birch or anyone. I was looking at his face and read on his face that everyone in the jeep was dead. I hoped they weren't dead, but from his face I could tell he thought they were dead.

I was lying there pretending I was dead. This fellow walked around the back of the jeep and the person lying on his back parallel with me was moving. I thought he had been wounded.

The man took very deliberate aim from about five feet away and he shot his Colt .45 automatic – I know the gun very well – three times.

The first one hit below the body, skipped over the body and missed my head by a fraction of an inch. I heard it zing. I could have been dead from the ricochet.

One of the next two bullets entered the body lying there. The body tightened up, then relaxed.

I waited until he had finished his clip and was starting to put the gun back in his belt.

Then I peeked under my left elbow and saw that the burp gunner had also lowered his sights.

What I didn't know was that both of them were really refilling their clips.

I had my left foot under my body, sort of in a starting position for running. I had about 100 feet to run and I ran a football dash, zigging and zagging.

The AK-47 and the burp gun opened up on me, but they were lousy shots. They hit poles and advertising signs in front of me. I can run the 100 yards in ten seconds, so I figured no Viet Cong was going to catch me.

I turned a slight corner and heard the automatics stop. Then I heard the commander coming after me. I knew it was him because he was the only one wearing boots and I could hear them slap, slap, slap on the road.

I caught up with the tail end of the refugee column, ripped my shirt off and splashed mud on myself.

I crouched over because I was a good foot taller than most of those people. I thought at the time that I would still be caught because the VC commander appeared, firing shots over the refugees' heads to get them to stop me.

But not one of those refugees helped the Viet Cong. Not only did they not give me up, but they didn't turn their heads. I reached some sort of a pushcart and hunched up behind it. There were many people without shirts in that poor area.

I walked for about 200 yards. The firing stopped, but I still had the feeling I was being chased. When I reached the end of the main steet, people were still giving me suspicious looks. I commandeered a little three-wheel pushcart and we drove about a mile. Then I saw an Australian soldier and I asked him to jump in with me and ride shotgun until we got to the American military police.

I was absolutely bloody shaken. I could hardly hold a a note-book. What I was still hoping was the others were playing dead.

APPENDIX 2

OFFICIAL STATEMENT

The Vietnam Government authorised this official statement of regrets issued on 1 February, 1988, after the January meeting between platoon commander Co Van Cuong and Frank Palmos in the Cuu Long Hotel in Ho Chi Minh City.

REGRETS

Vietnam has expressed "profound regret" to families and colleagues of four journalists killed in Cholon on May 5, 1968.

The chief of the Department of Defence's Military History Division (Southern Vietnam) General Nguyen Tuot, who worked with Frank Palmos for the second half of his fourteen-month search to find the ambush platoon, said the leader when finally located by historians had known nothing more than his report on the day, which was radioed in. It read: "four enemy killed, one dropped down (feigning death) then escaped to the safety of the people." General Huot said: "Our sympathy goes to all families with losses. Just as I am certain they would have sympathy for our own losses."

The director of the offical Vietnam News Agency, (VNA) Mr Do Hoi, said he was saddened by the news. "It was certainly a case of mistaken identity."

"During his research here Mr Palmos has traced many former NLF and Hanoi journalists who worked in the war, and has discovered far more information on the number of our journalists killed than we had ourselves. I have invited the Australian Journalists Association to visit us and help us complete the task, as a memorial to journalists on both sides."

The editor-in-chief of the country's most popular newspaper *Nhan Dan* Major-General Tran Cong Man, who is also vice-president of the Vietnam Journalists' Association said: "I can tell you for certain this was a tragic mistake. We were always doing our best to get to the facts of this story which frankly I thought was nearly impossible after twenty years."

The leader of the main military forces of the Tet Offensive and the "second Tet", called the Battle of Saigon, General Than, said the platoon members were "village boys who had probably never ridden in a jeep, who could not tell the difference between a diplomat's car and a private car (a West German diplomat was killed only minutes before the ambush of the press jeep), and certainly regarded you as US officers leading a convoy. How you got into our rear defences is one of the amazing stories of the war. They would not understand your Vietnamese if you called '*bao chi*' (press)."

The leader of the Viet Cong underground in Saigon in 1968, Mr Tran Bach Dang, said the ambush was "clearly a mistake by lower-ranking soldiers." In an interview in November, 1988, he recalled the day clearly.

"Sadly, it was only thirty minutes later I issued orders for our forces to be on the lookout for press, people carrying cameras, and so on.

"The international press was not to be harmed.

"That order stood from 5 May to the end of the war. We regarded the Western journalists as very important in our struggle because they were telling the truth of the war to the world outside."

APPENDIX 3

VERIFICATION

All of us — military historians, commanders and the soldiers involved in the fighting on the first day of the Battle for Saigon, civilians, interpreters, and myself — had had a great deal of trouble with verification.

At least twice we celebrated the end to the search prematurely. Once we found a jeep ambush with quite similar details, only to find the ambush took place five months earlier. Two of the captured men turned out to be catering assistants with the New Zealand forces and the other two were civilians, apparently still suffering a hangover. None of them realised how close they'd come to being killed. The Viet Cong set them loose, but kept the jeep. This story took four or five days to track down, then discard.

The second one was a jeep carrying four uniformed officers, all believed killed. We got this story from civilians who saw the men going into the ambush. It took another five or six days to track down and discard this ambush, which had taken place a year earlier. The officers had been captured and one was discovered to be a relative of a well-known US politician, so he was ransomed for medical supplies, and set free along with his friends who had been released in a prisoner exchange.

We had another bizarre, almost eerie false lead. When one of the fakes claiming they were in the ambush came to Ho Chi Minh City, the military discovered another ambush.

This was a military jeep, carrying four Western soldiers, followed by a white civilian car. The jeep was rocketed, two men killed instantly, two badly wounded. And from the white car two Westerners "and perhaps two Vietnamese" escaped.

We thrashed out that story, the man was thanked and he

returned to his village. What had made that one seem right apart from those coincidences, was the fact that at least one of the Westerners carried a camera.

As part of the verification agreement about midway through the search, General Tuot and I decided on an approach of keeping certain information back. It concerned things I had witnessed which only a man taking part in the ambush would remember. Van Cuong's description of the unfolding of the ambush gave me several verification points without him being prompted. None of the military historians had been given these details.

ACKNOWLEDGEMENTS

"Being a foreign correspondent in Asia means telling people unpalatable facts before they learn them for themselves.

—Dr Peter Russo, letter to Jakarta, 1961.

Ridding the Devils began as a work of journalistic investigation yet also evolved over those three years as a work of therapy. The people who helped me get through were those closest to me.

Pat Price saw me through the first crucial period of 1967–70, and shielded me from hostilities I thankfully knew little about.

Alison Puchy stayed by me through the second crucial period, albeit puzzled by my reticence to share the silences, and took over the household and children when I was away.

Ruth Perkins, as my counsellor, showed great skills, patience and wisdom in keeping me functioning by day while leading me out of my netherworld, in 1984–85.

Mai Huong worked with me from Day 1 of the search in Hanoi. As the search continued her interest grew, and her judgement and research capacities became invaluable to me. Her colleague in Ho Chi Minh/Saigon **Minh Ha** did magnificent work in the final stages. Foreign Press Centre director **Nguyen Cong Quang** and Foreign Office attache **Nguyen Quang Dy** gave unselfishly of their time and knowledge to ensure success, as did almost every member of the Hanoi Foreign Press Centre.

Vietnam's General Secretary **Nguyen Van Linh** and Foreign Minister **Nguyen Co Tach** not only ensured my freedom of travel and enquiry throughout all Vietnam but backed that initial help by ensuring my access to key officials in Hanoi.

Keith Chapman, as friend and adviser, in Bangkok and Vietnam, who, along with his wife Loraine, gave me material and intellectual support throughout the entire search. **Evan Ham**, Normella Pictures of Brisbane, almost single-handedly managed my first weeks in Vietnam, and with his wife Robin, provided vital communications help. Without Keith and Evan the search would have taken much longer.

Ken Kelso, Fremantle-based screenwriter, for his guidance on my writing and whose vision and friendship I value. **Alison Delaney** started me writing about Vietnam after a twenty-year break, **Keith Saggers** bullied me into continuing it. **Michael Baker** originated the idea of a documentary film which **Ross McDonald** ensured would proceed by providing finance. **Bettina Moss** in New York, **Suzy Baldwin, Judith Curr, Jillian Coutts Skinner** and **Richard Deutch** in Sydney contributed heavily and convinced me to continue.

Chris Lewis and **Jim Ward** of Ward–Holt, and their staff, for their time and use of office facilities. **John Browne** of Get The Picture did all my photographic reproduction work on Vietnam.

Angelo Loukakis, who may have not offered Transworld's Bantam imprint had he known the mitotic nature of the work, or that he would be editing an author who for months could not face reading what he had written.

VIETNAM: At least one hundred and forty other men and women, many mentioned and given credit already in these chapters, helped in this search or in enabling capacities, from **Viet**, my cyclodriver in Ho Chi Minh and **Swan My**, my cyclodriver and co-owner of my bicycle in Hanoi, through to **General Tuot** and his assistants in Ho Chi Minh's Military History Division.